# THE GIRL WHO PLAYED WITH THE OUIJA BOARD

WILLIAM MALMBORG

DARKER DREAMS MEDIA

Publishers Note: This is a work of fiction. Names, characters, places, and incidents either are the product of the author's imagination or are used fictitiously. Any resemblance to actual persons, living or dead, events, or locales is entirely coincidental.

ISBN: 978-0-9962831-9-9

# THE GIRL WHO PLAYED WITH THE OUIJA BOARD

# PART ONE

# ONE

*"Oh my God!"*

*"That's not funny!"*

*"Penny?"*

*"Penny!"*

*"Is she okay?"*

*"Penny, come on."*

*"Guys, I think she's—"*

*"Penny!"*

*"Jesus Christ."*

*"Don't touch her!"*

*"Call 911."*

*"Fuck that, call a priest!"*

*"Shit! My phone's dead."*

*"Are you getting this?"*

*"I'm getting this."*

*"She stopped."*

*"Penny!"*

*"She's waking up."*

*"She okay?"*

"Penny?"

A dozen eyes were staring at her, her own eyes blinking several times as the darkness cleared.

"You okay?" Olivia asked, her face and eyes the closest and most concerned.

Penny stared at her cousin for a moment, trying to grasp what was going on.

"Here," someone—Martin—said, handing her a cup.

"What's that?" Olivia asked.

"Coke."

"Coke?"

"Yeah. Has sugar."

"That's for diabetes, you retard."

"So? It might help."

"How?"

Confused, Penny took the cup, her fingers barely able to grip it, and sipped.

It tasted great.

And it did seem to help, her focus returning. Or her mind was simply clearing with the passage of time. Whichever it was, her thoughts were coming back. With them came questions.

"What happened?" she asked, her voice weak.

"You don't know?" Olivia asked.

"No."

"It was creepy as fuck!" a voice said.

"Ned!" Martin snapped.

"It was!" the voice insisted.

"Yeah," someone else agreed.

"Like *The Exorcist* or something."

"Did you see the other side?"

"Seriously!"

"Guys, chill!" Martin snapped.

"And give us some fucking room," Olivia added.

A few mumbles followed as the group started to disperse.

"You okay?" Martin asked.

"I don't know," Penny admitted. Her thoughts were clearing, but she felt really weak. Almost to the point where she simply wanted to crawl into bed and go to sleep. "I think so." She took another sip of the Coke. "What—" Her eyes caught sight of the coffee table and the Ouija board that was sitting atop it, memories returning.

Olivia followed her gaze and said, "Is it coming back?"

Penny nodded, a memory of adding her fingers to the planchette unfolding. After that, everything was blank.

"We asked if any spirit beings were present and if they would speak to us," Olivia said.

"And then?" Penny asked, concern building.

"And then you started mumbling something and went berserk, arms flailing to the point where you knocked over the candles and then your head was jerking, mouth spitting. It was really creepy."

"Shit," Penny said. She had no memory of that.

"Yeah," Olivia agreed.

"It was like you were possessed," Martin said.

Olivia turned and glared at him.

"What?" Martin demanded.

"That's not helpful."

"But it's true."

Penny felt chilled at the thought.

"Don't listen to him," Olivia said.

"Yeah, you really shouldn't," Martin agreed.

Penny put a hand to her head.

"Okay?" Olivia asked.

"I need to lie down."

"Want me to take you home?" Olivia offered.

"No, no, your mom will freak," Penny said. "I just need like thirty minutes."

"My sister's room," Martin said. "It's just down the hall." He offered an arm.

Olivia offered hers as well.

She took both.

They helped her up, her body wobbling to the point where she would not have been able to walk unaided.

"YOU SURE YOU'RE OKAY?" Olivia asked once they were in the bedroom.

"I think so," Penny said, her body atop the pink bedspread, right hand on her forehead. "I just need to close my eyes for a while."

Olivia nodded and then looked around the room.

Penny followed her gaze, realizing that her cousin was reluctant to leave her alone.

Out in the main room, music began to play once more.

"Guess they called it quits with the Ouija board," Olivia said, letting out a hesitant chuckle.

"Sounds like it," Penny said.

"I'm going to kill Martin for bringing it out."

"Nah, don't. Not his fault."

"I told him not to."

"It's his house."

"Still."

"Olivia," Penny said, a hand reaching out to touch her hand. "Let it go."

Olivia looked down at Penny and smiled. "You sure you're okay?"

"Yes," Penny lied and then winced.

"What?"

"My hand." She eased it away from Olivia's grip and looked at it. "It stings."

"You flailed around quite a bit, hitting things," Olivia noted.

"It feels like a burn."

"Maybe from when you hit the candles."

"Did I hit the flame?"

"Don't know. Your arms were going everywhere and hitting everything." She gave a helpless shrug. "It all happened so fast, and once the candles were hit, everyone kind of focused on them, worried that they would start a fire."

Penny gently rubbed at the sting, the flesh below her knuckles blistered.

"And you totally burned Leanne," Olivia added, another slight chuckle echoing.

"I did?"

"Yeah. Splattered her with candle wax."

"Is she okay?"

"Oh yeah. It was just her chest, arm, and a bit of her cheek."

"Oh jeez."

A knock echoed and then the door opened.

Martin walked in.

"What?" Olivia asked.

"Just checking. You okay?"

"I'm fine," Penny said.

Martin nodded.

Olivia turned and looked at him, and then motioned for him to go.

He turned and left.

"Can I get you anything?" Olivia asked.

"No, I'm fine. Just going to rest for a bit." She rubbed at

her head. "I'm exhausted."

"All that flailing about probably burned more calories than going to the gym," Olivia said.

Penny chuckled. "Let's market it as the Ouija Board Possession Workout."

Olivia laughed and then said, "Let me know if you need anything, or if you want to head home. I can always tell my mom that Liz got the stomach flu or something."

"I'm okay," Penny said.

Olivia continued to hesitate.

"Seriously, I'm fine," Penny said. "Go have fun."

Olivia nodded and stepped out, pulling the door shut as she left.

Penny closed her eyes, the exhaustion overwhelming.

SOMETHING WAS COMING for her in the dark, something that she couldn't get away from. No matter how fast she ran, or where, it was always right behind her, the distance closing with each passing second, its talons reaching for her, trying to take hold, Penny knowing that once it got a grip, there would be no escape.

PENNY OPENED HER EYES, confusion dominating her mind as the unfamiliar dark bedroom came into focus.

And then she heard an odd squeaking sound.

She looked toward the far wall.

The squeaking continued.

Confusion appeared but then was quickly replaced with understanding.

*No way!*

A grin spread across her face.

First Olivia had lied to her mom about where they were spending the night, and now she was having sex with a boyfriend that her mom didn't even know about.

She shook her head.

Everything she had known about her cousin was wrong, the image she had always carried of the uptight Bible-thumping Catholic girl so far off that it was almost comical.

Her aunt, on the other hand ...

*Yikes.*

It was hard to believe her mom and aunt had been cut from the same cloth. It didn't seem possible.

*Mom.*

A hollow feeling hit, one that caused her lower lip to quiver.

Tears followed.

She reached for her phone, a sudden need to see a picture dominating her thoughts.

Her hand struck something.

Glass shattered.

*Oh fuck!*

The squeaking in the other room stopped.

"YOU OKAY?" Olivia asked while standing in the bright doorway, the shirt she had thrown on looking like the one Martin had been wearing earlier in the evening.

"Yeah, I'm fine," Penny said. "Just knocked over a glass."

"You sure?"

"Uh-huh. It's nothing." She looked on the nightstand for her phone, but it wasn't there. "Do you know where my phone is?"

"Oh, I put it in your coat pocket." She stepped into the

room and went to a chair where the coat was, hand quickly pulling out the phone. "Ta-da."

"Thanks," Penny said, taking it.

Olivia hesitated.

Penny eyed her and then said, "Really, I'm fine."

Olivia nodded and stepped back into the hallway, the sounds of her steps followed by the echo of a door closing.

Penny sighed and unlocked her phone and then thumbed open a picture of her mom.

Sadness returned, as did the tears.

# TWO

"I can't believe I have to wear this," Penny said while standing in front of the tall mirror in the bedroom she shared with Olivia.

"Ah, it's not so bad," Olivia said.

"Not so bad? These outfits are a fetish." She spread her hands out. "If I posted a picture of myself in this on Instagram, thousands of guys would spend hours jerking off to it."

"That's probably why we have to wear them," Olivia said. "All the school officials are perverts who walk around with huge boners all day."

Penny laughed and then said, "I almost feel like I should have my hair in pigtails."

"It would complete the look."

"You know what," Penny said, pulling a hair tie from her wrist. "I'm so doing it!"

"Me too!" Olivia announced.

Penny grinned while securing the hair on the right side of her head and then shifted to the left, her fingers freezing when she saw the scar and realized it would be completely visible.

"No good?" Olivia asked as Penny undid the pigtail on the right.

"Nah, not for the first day," Penny said, fingers running through her hair, scar once again hidden.

"Nicky! Girls!" Aunt Susan called. "We need to go."

"Coming!" Olivia shouted, her own fingers removing her pigtails.

Penny took one last look at herself in the mirror and then turned to head out, one hand grabbing her backpack while the other pocketed her phone.

"OLIVIA SAID boners while they were getting dressed," Nicky said as he followed the two into the kitchen.

"I did not!" Olivia scoffed.

"Did too!" Nicky insisted. "And they were talking about sex stuff."

"Penny?" Aunt Susan asked.

"We weren't talking about sex," Penny said, confusion spreading across her face.

"She's lying!" Nicky insisted.

Aunt Susan looked from Nicky to Penny and then said, "We need to go."

Olivia gave a brief glare at her little brother and then grinned at Penny, who grinned back.

"JESUS!" Penny said as the school came into view, a giant stone tower with a huge cross atop it dominating the landscape.

"Penny!" Aunt Susan snapped.

"Sorry."

"We've talked about this."

"I know. I'm sorry. I'm trying."

Aunt Susan didn't reply to that and instead reminded them that she was going to be visiting their grandfather today and then taking Nicky to Scouts that evening, so they would be on their own for dinner.

Olivia nodded and then opened her door.

Penny did the same on her side.

"Ready for this?" Olivia asked.

Penny eyed the front door, where tons of students in white shirts and plaid skirts or pressed pants were entering, and said, "No."

Olivia laughed. "Come on, it won't be so bad. You already know all the cool kids."

"Yeah, and they know me as the heathen girl who freaked out while using a Ouija board."

"Which is why you'll be the big hit here...if you don't get struck by lightning while touching the front door."

"Maybe you should stand away from me when I try to enter."

"Fuck that. If you're struck, I'm struck."

PENNY MADE it through the doorway without being struck by lightning and then made it to her first class without issue, the rooms looking fairly similar to the rooms of her old school out in California, the only exception being all the religious stuff that lined the walls. And the uniforms.

No one paid much attention to her as everyone filtered in, which was most likely due to this being everyone's first day. That was a plus. Had she been forced to switch schools mid-year, she would have had a "new girl" stigma attached to her, but since it was the beginning of the year, it would take some time for everyone to realize this was her first time in this particular school.

"Penny?" a voice asked.

Penny looked up from her schedule and saw Martin looking down at her. "Hey!"

Next to him was another familiar face from the party, though the name escaped her.

"These seats taken?" Martin asked, motioning to the ones to her left.

"Nope," Penny said.

"Great." He took the seat next to her while the familiar-faced guy secured the one behind him. "You remember Joey?"

"I do," Penny said, the name now clicking. They had talked a bit at the party. She gave him a "Hey."

"Hey," he replied back with a nervous grin, eyes quickly going down to his schedule.

"So, you any good at math?" Martin asked.

"Not at all," Penny replied.

"Well sh—" An authoritative-looking figure entered the room. "Shish kebab."

Penny snorted and then looked around in horror.

No one had noticed.

And then a bell buzzed, several students hurrying to grabs seats.

"Okay, everyone, simmer down," the authoritative-looking figure said.

Penny had been expecting a nun, but this was just a middle-aged man whose aftershave dominated the room.

"My name is Mr. Foster," the teacher continued. "I'm going to take roll, during which I want each of you to—" He stopped as a student hurried into the room, her tiny voice apologizing profusely about having gotten turned around.

Everyone watched as the young lady found a seat and collapsed into it.

"She was probably in the bathroom puking," Martin whispered.

Penny gave him a puzzled look and then quickly turned her attention back to Mr. Foster, who was saying that when he called out their names he wanted them to stand and give a brief introduction to the class.

*Oh God,* Penny said to herself, panic beginning.

She hated drawing attention to herself. Especially in a classroom setting. Just raising her hand with an answer was often too much for her. Standing up and introducing herself...that was even worse.

Adding to the horror, her last name started with a *W* and thus would be one of the final names called. If she made a fool of herself, everyone would remember it because they would be relieved about having already gone and not be worried about making a fool of themselves.

One by one, students stood as their names were called, some speaking right away, some composing themselves first. Some spoke loud enough for everyone to hear; others needed to be encouraged to speak up.

Martin was bold. Joey was shy.

Any moment now...

Anxiety grew.

And grew.

And grew.

The girl next to her stood, smoothed out her skirt, and talked about a mission trip she had gone on that summer.

Penny knew she was next, though she wasn't sure how. It was simply known.

On and on the girl went, Mr. Foster nodding in the way people do when they're too polite to cut someone off in mid-sentence but at the same time want to keep things moving.

*Maybe she'll run out the clock.*

Just as the thought arrived, the girl ended her introduction about spreading God's message and sat back down.

Nothing followed for several seconds, almost as if Mr. Foster was making sure that she truly was finished.

When he finally did speak, it was Penny's name that left his lips.

Heart racing, Penny tried to stand, but the room spun.

*No!*

She grabbed the desk to steady herself, her eyes attempting to blink away the nightmare that was unfolding. It didn't work.

Darkness slithered through the doorway and spun into the air, her name echoing as something called to her.

Faces changed, their round shapes elongating into wretched monstrosities.

And then hands were grabbing her, ripping at her clothes, trying to disrobe her.

*No! No! No!*

"Penny!" a voice said. "Penny!"

She blinked.

Martin was kneeling over her, along with Joey and Mr. Foster. Behind them, dozens of startled faces stared.

"You okay?" one of them asked.

"I-I- " she mumbled, nothing making sense.

"Stood up too fast?" another suggested.

"Y-yes," Penny mumbled.

"This has happened to her before," Martin advised.

"Honey, do you need to see the nurse?" Mr. Foster asked.

Penny shook her head.

"I think she's okay," Martin said. He turned to look at her. "Right?"

She nodded and then asked, "Bathroom?"

Mr. Foster seemed puzzled for a second and then understanding arrived. "Yes, of course. Um...Cheryl, can you escort her to the ladies' room?"

Penny didn't hear the reply, but it must have been a yes because the next thing she knew, Cheryl was walking down the quiet hallway with her toward the bathrooms.

Neither spoke, Cheryl seeming somewhat wary of her.

Penny stepped into the bathroom.

Cheryl waited outside.

It was a nice bathroom, one that looked far cleaner than any of the bathrooms she would have found in her old school. Whether this was due to students being more respectful or the staff being more thorough, she didn't know. And it didn't really matter.

She had made a fool of herself.

Again.

Only this time was worse.

Not in the physical impact, since she was already able to walk around, but in the audience that had witnessed it.

This would stick.

Cheryl was probably already texting everyone she knew about it.

Facebook probably had a page dedicated to it.

A hashtag would be going viral on Twitter.

And on Instagram...

Something would happen.

Something always did.

*Why?*

*I don't know!*

She looked at herself in the mirror, questions flying all over the place.

And then a shadow grew behind her.

*No!*

Cheryl appeared.

"You okay?" she asked.

Penny blinked.

"Yes," she said and forced a smile.

*Am I? Really?*

The answer she gave herself differed from the one she gave Cheryl.

It also brought about a question, one that gave her a chill.

Was this linked to her having played with the Ouija board?

A week ago, she would have laughed at such a suggestion, but now, after what had happened that night...

She shivered.

# THREE

Olivia greeted Martin with a kiss, one that grew in intensity once they were in his car, tongues circling each other while Martin palmed her right breast, fingers attempting to tease her nipple to attention through her blouse and bra.

He failed.

Olivia had better luck with him, her hand toying with his manhood through his pants, the two layers of fabric failing to mask the bulge that quickly appeared.

*Thunk! Thunk!*

Olivia pulled away as Joey opened the rear passenger door of the car, a comment about how foggy the windows were getting leaving his lips.

No fog was present.

Penny opened the other door, silently slipping into the rear passenger seat.

For a moment, all was silent.

"What's wrong?" Olivia asked.

Penny looked at her and shook her head.

Olivia frowned but decided to let it go for the moment.

"So..." Martin said.

"So..." Olivia replied.

"Want to chill at my place for a while?"

"Your parents home?"

"Not until six. My mom's showing a house this afternoon."

"Cool with me then." She turned toward Penny. "That cool?"

"Sure," Penny mumbled.

Olivia felt her frown returning. Something was really bothering Penny.

"Hey now, don't I get a say?" Joey asked.

"Nope," Martin said while starting his car.

Olivia chuckled.

MARTIN'S HOUSE wasn't very far. In fact, they could have probably walked to it in the same amount of time it took to drive, given how long it took to get out of the crowded school parking lot, but being able to drive to school was a status symbol, one that had to be maintained at all costs.

"Okay, what happened?" Olivia asked after pulling Penny aside while the guys headed down into the basement lair.

"It's nothing," Penny said.

"It's obviously something," Olivia said.

Penny hesitated.

"Was it another student?" she pressed. "Did someone say something?"

"Yeah, but that's only part of it."

"Okay..." Olivia said and waited.

"I had another moment," she said. "During a class."

"A moment?"

"Like the other night with the Ouija board."

"Oh fuck."

"Yeah."

"Right in the middle of class?"

"Yeah."

"Jeez. I'm sorry." She shook her head. "I can't even imagine."

"And then someone muttered 'demon girl' at me during lunch."

"Do you know who?" Olivia asked, anger appearing.

"No. I just heard it. And then some giggles from the table."

"Guy or girl?"

"Girl."

Olivia considered that, but of course had no idea who it could be, and since they didn't share the same lunch period, she couldn't even have Penny point out the table to her.

"Some first day, huh?" Penny muttered.

"Don't worry," Olivia said, putting her arms out for a hug. "It'll get better."

"Maybe," Penny said.

"And if it doesn't, I'll just have to cunt-kick some bitches."

This brought about a grin. "Thanks."

"No problem. Oh, by the way." She looked around and then in a somewhat hushed voice said, "I have it on good authority that Joey totally has the hots for you."

"What?" Penny gasped. "Really?"

"Yep. He apparently told Martin that you're totally babelicious."

"Babelicious?" Penny questioned.

"They're guys," Olivia said, which she felt summed up the word choice. "So, anyway, don't be surprised if he acts all fidgety for a bit once we're down there. And if he asks for a moment alone with you, it's most likely because he has finally worked up the courage to ask you out."

"Great, now I'm going to be all fidgety too waiting for him to get over his fidgetiness and pop the question."

"See, this is why you two will be perfect together." She took her hand. "Come on."

"Wait, wait," Penny said, resisting the pull. "Does he know about..." She motioned to her head and then her torso.

"Of course. Everyone does. Not the grisly details or anything, but about the accident and stuff."

"Hmm."

"It was in the news," Olivia added.

"All the way out here?"

"Well no, not so much out here. But it's all online. You can Google it."

Penny considered that and then nodded.

Olivia waited.

"Have they asked you about it?" Penny asked.

"A bit," she admitted.

"And?"

"And what?"

"What kind of questions?"

Olivia shrugged. "Just typical questions."

Penny frowned while gently touching the area of her head where the scar was.

Olivia had seen her do this many times and wondered if it was a conscious act or something her hand just did—like twisting a strand of hair.

Footsteps echoed on the stairway, Martin quickly appearing.

"You two get lost?" he asked.

"We're coming," Olivia said, taking Penny's hand.

Penny didn't resist.

MARTIN WAS OBVIOUSLY eager to get upstairs and finish what they had started in the car, but Olivia didn't want to simply deposit Penny with Joey and head up—not after the horrible first day the poor girl had had. So instead, they all chilled on the old ratty sofa and chairs, drinking sodas and talking about random topics that sprang up. Some were about school and their new classes, others about various shows they were watching or games they were playing. It was very relaxed, though several times during the discussions, Olivia felt Martin's fingers creeping up into her more sensitive regions, the position they were in on the sofa allowing for stealthy sneak attacks that the other two could not see—sneak attacks that were more annoying than pleasurable, given his lack of understanding in how things worked down there.

God bless him though for trying.

Such attempts meant he had listened to some of the things she had pointed out during their more intimate moments together that summer, and though he still had a long way to go based on what he was doing now, his current actions did alert her to the fact that he had the basic idea of what he should be doing when trying to tease her.

In the end, it was Penny that gave Martin what he wanted—indirectly.

She mentioned that she had some stupid first-day homework assignments that she wanted to get a jump on and suggested that maybe Joey would like to walk her home.

"Oh...um...yeah, sure... I'd love to."

Penny smiled, Joey smiled, and then Martin and Olivia

both smiled, all knowing but not voicing the real reason behind Penny's suggestion.

"DO you think he'll pop the question?" Martin asked once Penny and Joey had stepped out the front door and started down the sidewalk.

Olivia watched them through the window for several seconds before turning and saying, "He better. She needs something like this in her life right now."

Martin seemed unsure what to say in reply to that.

"Speaking of needs..." Olivia said and took his hand to lead him from the window and over to the nice family couch where she sat down and spread her legs. "You have some work to do after all that fumbling about down there."

"Me?" he questioned, mounting a fake protest. "What about what you started in the car?"

"As soon as you finish with me, I'll finish with you...if we have time once you're done."

Martin needed no further encouragement and quickly got down onto his knees so that he could get his lips and tongue where they needed to be, Olivia leaning back while he did this, her mind knowing things stood at about fifty-fifty on whether she would actually be taking him in her mouth this afternoon.

# FOUR

They walked for quite some time without really speaking, the silence getting to the point where Penny started to wonder if Olivia had misled her about the interest Joey held.

*Or been misled herself?*

Maybe it had been a simple misunderstanding.

After all, guys talked about girls all the time, and just because he had said she was hot—or whatever that word was he had used—it didn't necessarily mean he was interested.

When he finally did speak, it wasn't the question she had been anticipating.

"Do you miss your old school?" he asked.

"My old school?" She considered the question and then shrugged. "I don't know. I guess. As much as you can miss a place you never really wanted to be at. I was comfortable there. Knew the ups and downs. Now..." She shrugged again "It's like I'm starting all over."

"Technically you are."

"True."

Silence.

"Was it a lot different?" he asked.

"Not really. Well, I don't know. Hard to say after one day. The biggest difference so far is having to wear a uniform. I feel ridiculous. Oh, and all the religious stuff. But other than that, it just seems like a typical high school with teachers and teenagers."

"My parents think public schools are full of drugs and sex. Temptation around every corner, blowjobs in the bathrooms, and occult rituals in the basement."

"It's actually blowjobs in the basement and occult rituals in the bathrooms."

Joey laughed.

"Seriously though, they really think that?" she asked.

"Well, maybe not to that extreme, but yeah. They feel public school has led the country on a sinful path of moral decline, one that will soon lead to the total collapse of our society."

"Sounds like my aunt," Penny said.

"I've heard she's pretty extreme," he noted.

"Let's put it this way. She totally lost her shit when I was unpacking my stuff and pulled out one of my old Harry Potter books."

"That might not actually be considered extreme in this area. Lots of us had to read Harry Potter in secret."

"Really?" she asked, her disbelief hard to mask.

"Yeah. I read the first one at the library one summer. The public one. I actually still remember how nervous I was when I started reading it. It was like...I don't know...finding a dirty magazine or something, only worse because I started to fear for my soul. I eventually brought it up during confession."

"Wow."

"It all seems kind of silly now, but back then, I got so worried about having read it that I could almost feel the heat as Satan's minions stoked the fires of hell in anticipation of my arrival."

"Jesus Christ."

Nothing followed for several seconds, the only sound that of their shoes clapping on the sidewalk.

"My aunt wants me to go to confession," Penny said, breaking the silence. "I keep trying to tell her I'm not Catholic, but she doesn't want to hear it. Says I was baptized a Catholic when I was little, and since I've never been excommunicated, I'm still Catholic...a very, *very* lapsed one, but still."

"Do you think you'll do it?" he asked.

"I don't know. Maybe. Olivia thinks I should. Just to keep the peace."

"Hmm."

"You don't think so?" she asked, sensing something in his tone.

"I think you should only do it if you personally feel the need."

Penny thought about that, nodded, and then said, "Anyway, enough about me. Tell me about you."

"Me?" he asked. "Um...what do you want to know?"

"I don't know. Anything."

He hesitated and then let out a stunted chuckle. "You've totally caught me off guard. I'm drawing a blank."

"Okay then. Um...let's see." She considered some questions and then asked, "What's your favorite band?"

"What's yours?" he countered.

"Oh, no you don't," she said.

"Honestly, I don't have one. I just scan until I find something I like and then listen to it."

Penny stared at him for a moment, trying to figure out if this was true or if he was just trying to be vague so she didn't think his actual favorite was ridiculous. In the end, she decided it was true.

"Favorite show?"

"That's currently on, or favorite show of all time?"

"Um...of all time."

"*Breaking Bad*."

"Harry Potter is forbidden, but you can watch *Breaking Bad*?"

"They've eased up a bit now that I'm almost eighteen. I'm even allowed to stay up till nine now."

She laughed and then asked, "Current favorite?"

"*Stranger Things*."

"Mine too!"

"Really?"

"Totally. I can't wait for season four."

"Me either."

"Maybe we can watch it together when it finally comes out."

He didn't reply to that, which was a bit awkward.

She waited several seconds and then, in an attempt to break the awkwardness, asked, "So, who do you think the American is at the end of season three?"

"I'm really hoping it's Hopper, but..."

"Me too. My mom and I were bawling our eyes out at the end."

*Mom.*

*She will never get to see the final season.*

Sadness hit.

She tried pushing it away, but as always it was pretty stubborn.

Joey started to say something but then stopped.

"What?" she asked.

"Nah, nothing."

"What?" she pressed.

"I was going to ask something, but I think it's too..." His voice faded.

"Too what?" And then, when he didn't reply, she added, "Please. I don't want to be that girl that everyone is overly careful around. I'm not a piece of glass that will shatter."

His hesitation continued.

"I can hear the eggshells crunching," she said.

"What?"

"You're walking on eggshells."

He still seemed puzzled.

"Never mind. Ask your question. I promise, whatever it is, it's okay."

"I was going to ask...your mom and your aunt, they were sisters, right?"

"Yeah."

"So, what happened?"

"What do you mean?"

"Between them. Olivia says they were like complete opposites and barely ever spoke, and that you two were pretty much strangers until this summer."

"That's true. And honestly, I'm not really sure. I know it happened during college. They both went to the same university. They were actually roommates for a while. And then something happened. Something so bad that my mom would never talk about it with me."

"Wow," Joey said.

"You know what the ironic thing is? Apparently, my aunt was the rebellious one at that point and my mom the good Catholic girl."

"And whatever happened between them changed that?"

"Not sure exactly. We never talked about it. Apparently, I was baptized though, so I guess she was still with the church after I was born. And I do vaguely remember some church stuff around the holidays when I was little. I think I was an angel in a nativity play or something. But after that..." She held up her hands.

Silence settled once again.

"So there you have it," she said. "*The Life of Penny.*"

"Ha," he replied. "That was simply *The Prequel of Penny.*"

She grinned while his face went red.

"That sounded really stupid, didn't it?" he said.

"Most of what we say does."

"True."

Another block came and went, Joey slowing as they arrived at a quiet intersection.

"What is it?" Penny asked.

Joey looked to the left and then the right, and then left again. "Do you know where we are?" he asked.

"No. I was following you."

"Uh-oh."

"Are we lost?" she asked.

"No, not quite," he said while scanning the area. "Just turned around a bit."

Penny waited.

And waited.

And waited.

"Okay, we're lost," Joey admitted, pulling out his phone. "What's your address?"

"Um..." she started and then shook her head. "I have no idea."

Joey scanned the area once again and mumbled something about how he was pretty sure they always dropped Olivia off somewhere around here.

"You don't drive her all the way home?" Penny asked.

"Oh, no, she won't allow it. Not with how insane her mother would be if she found out about her dating Martin."

"Ohhhh."

That made sense.

Olivia had gone to quite the extreme to keep the relationship secret, the fake Facebook profile for a friend named Liz who she was always hanging out with a testament to that.

"And it didn't even occur to me that you wouldn't be familiar with the area yet," Joey added.

IT TOOK several texts and then a call to finally get Olivia to answer her phone, a breathless question of "What's wrong?" leaving her lips.

"We're lost," Penny said.

"Lost?" Olivia asked. "How?"

"Well, I don't know the address, and apparently Joey has never actually been to the house."

"Oh. Shit. I didn't even think of that."

"It's okay. I didn't either. All I really need is the address. If you text it to me, I'll map it."

"Okay, will do." A pause. "Everything else okay?"

"Oh yeah. We're good. Just lost."

"Okay. I'll get that to you in just a few seconds."

"Thanks." Then to Joey, "She's sending it."

"Excellent."

"I feel so bad about interrupting them."

"I wouldn't worry too much about it. Those two are like rabbits."

"Really?"

"Yeah, and when his house isn't an option, they go to one of the empty houses his mother is trying to sell."

"No!" she said, disbelief heavy.

"God's honest truth," he said, holding up his right hand.

Penny didn't even know what to say to that.

"In fact, if all goes well, we're going to have an epic Halloween party at an old place in the middle of the woods."

"Oh my God! That sounds awesome."

"Yeah. Fingers crossed she doesn't sell the place before then."

"How long has it gone unsold?"

"Like almost two years."

"That's a long time. And no one lives there?"

"No. It's totally empty. I guess like two really old spinster sisters used to live there or something, but then one of them died or something and the other ended up in an assisted living place."

Her phone buzzed, the address appearing on the screen.

"I wonder why no one wants it?" she questioned while clicking the address and then the directions icon.

"Something about knob wiring and bad pipes." He waved his hand. "How far off track are we?"

"Actually, it's only three streets over..." She looked up and then twisted to the left. "Thataway."

"Oh, that's not too bad."

"Not bad at all. Now the question is, are you going to walk me all the way home, or is that a no-no?"

"I suppose that's up to you," he said.

"Hmm, do you have a car?"

"I do," he confirmed, an unspoken "why do you ask?" hovering within the reply.

"Then I think it would be best for you to know what the house looks like so that you can pick me up on Friday," she said, heart racing.

"Pick you up?" he asked.

"To take me out. You were planning to ask, right?"

"Wh—yes! But..."

"But...?"

"Sorry. No but. I just wasn't expecting you to ask me. That's all. Caught me off guard."

"I suppose I can be a tad bit forward sometimes."

"And I can be a tad bit hesitant and overthink things, so..."

"Well then, I suppose I'll just have to take charge." With that, she took hold of his hand and started toward the house, a pleasant warmth spreading through her body.

# FIVE

"So..." Olivia pressed once she was back home.

"So?" Penny asked while looking at her iPad, even though she was pretty sure she knew what Olivia wanted to know.

"Did he ask you out?"

"Nope."

"What?" Olivia demanded, fingers halting with her blouse only halfway undone.

"I beat him to the punch."

Olivia frowned for a second and then laughed. "You asked him?"

"Yep." Penny grinned. "We're going out on Friday."

"Nice!" Olivia finished unbuttoning her blouse and shrugged it off, her favorite hoodie quickly replacing it. "Where're you going?"

"Not sure yet," she admitted. "He just texted me asking what kind of food I like, and I was looking to see what was around here. I'm guessing sushi might be out of the question."

"Gag!" Olivia grimaced. "I still don't understand how you can eat that."

"Sushi's great!"

"You know that people get worms in their eyeballs from it."

"Yeah, and every single teenager did the Tide pod challenge. Come on! You know things like that are really rare despite what the media might make you think."

"Okay, point taken. Though I hate to break it to you, but I don't think you're going to find a sushi place around here."

"Phooey."

"But we do have excellent BBQ."

This time it was Penny who made the gagging noises.

Olivia laughed.

"Wait a second," Penny said. "You have a Thai place on Main Street."

"Eh...you might want to stick to something a bit more basic for a first date."

"Why?"

"Joey has stomach issues."

"Really?"

"Big time. IBS or something."

"Really? That sucks."

"Yeah."

"Hmm. What do you think, then? Ah, here's a Red Lobster. That's pretty basic, right?"

"Yeah, though that one might not be such a good idea either..."

"Why?"

"His ex works there."

"*Whoa*. Crossing that one off the list."

Olivia laughed while pulling her skirt off.

"Was it amicable?" Penny asked.

"Not at all." She grabbed a pair of pajama pants.

"Great. This is just what I need."

"Come to think about it, I wonder if she was the one at lunch today that called you demon girl."

"What? But we weren't even going out yet."

"Yeah, but she's a bitch anyway. Plus, you and Joey did talk quite a bit at the party, which might have pissed her off."

"She was at the party?"

"Yeah. She's the one you burned when you knocked over the candle."

"Oh great." A few seconds later. "Why would Martin invite her if they were through?"

"Because Martin's a bit of a pushover. Plus, they share the same friends. Lastly, and most importantly, she totally would have ratted him out if he told her she couldn't come."

"Jesus."

"Yeah. I'll never forgive myself for setting them up."

"*What?*"

"Lapse of judgment." She gave a dismissive wave. "What should we do for dinner?"

"Whoa. Wait. One last question. How long did they go out for, and when did they break up?"

"That's two questions."

Penny crossed her arms and stared.

"Okay, let's see. They got together last year for the homecoming dance, and they broke up about a week before Martin's party."

"*A week before?*" Penny questioned, shocked.

"Yep."

"The party was last Friday!"

"So?"

"So they've only been broken up for two weeks!"

"Just about."

"That's not enough time for him to get over her."

"Sure it is, especially since he dumped her."

Penny rolled her eyes.

"Trust me, that relationship was over months ago. He just didn't have the nerve to end it."

"Because of her craziness?"

Olivia made a *so-so* gesture.

Penny couldn't believe it. "So, I'm like a rebound girl, then."

"What? No! You asked him. If anything, it's like you rescued him from the post-breakup despair."

Penny shook her head. Now she understood why he had been so hesitant. He wasn't looking to date anyone, and her forwardness had caught him off guard in a way that she hadn't even contemplated.

"I should call him," she said.

"Why?"

"I don't think he's ready for a new relationship."

"No, no, you can't do that to him."

"Do what? Let him know it's okay for us to just be friends if he isn't ready."

"That's not how he'll see it."

Penny didn't reply.

"In fact, it'll be like taking in a stray from a shelter, making them feel all nice and loved, and then bringing them back the next day."

"That's a bit extreme, wouldn't you say?"

"And it's a kill shelter."

"Okay, okay, I get it. I won't call him. But still, you should have told me about all this."

"Honestly, it didn't even occur to me until just now."

Penny was about to call bullshit on that but then realized that she actually believed her. Something like this totally fit with Olivia's personality.

"OH MY GOD!" Penny snapped.

"What?" Olivia asked, startled.

The two were in the family room, the TV on, waiting for the pizza to finish.

Rather than reply, Penny simply held out her iPad.

Olivia took it, looked at it for a second, and then touched the screen.

Voices erupted, some frightened, others simply surprised, Penny's name echoing several times.

Olivia touched the screen halfway through, killing the video.

"Did you know someone filmed it?" Penny asked.

"No," Olivia said, voice soft. "If I had, I would have..." She didn't finish.

*What? Smash their phone?* Penny silently wondered. *Yeah, right.*

In the kitchen, the timer on the oven dinged.

Neither moved.

Several seconds came and went.

"I better pull that out," Olivia said, handing back the iPad.

Penny looked at the screen.

Olivia had paused it at a point where Penny's right arm was bent inward as if trying to grab her own chest, all while her face was contorted in such a way as to look like she was crazed.

*Demon girl.*

Was this what she had looked like in class today?

Had the classroom incident caused the commentary at

lunch, or had this video already made the rounds by then?

No answers arrived.

One thing she did know, based on all the tags she found in the original post: tons of people had seen in. Many had also shared it, which was how she ended up seeing it since she had not been tagged in the original post but in one of the comments on one of the shares.

Olivia came back into the family room, a statement on how the pizza needed to cool off leaving her lips.

"It was posted on Sunday," Penny muttered.

"By who?"

Penny backed out of the full-screen video and then looked at the post that had been shared, her finger clicking the text to get to the original post.

"Jocelyn Warrington," Penny said and then looked up at Olivia.

"Who?"

Penny repeated the name.

"I have no idea who that is."

"You're friends with her," Penny noted.

"I am?"

"So is Martin and Joey." A few other mutual friends were listed as well, all being people she had met at the party and friend requested prior to the incident.

"Let me ask Martin," Olivia said, pulling out her phone.

Several seconds came and went.

"Where the hell is he?" Olivia muttered.

"Maybe he's having dinner or something," Penny said.

"Yeah, maybe—okay, he just read it."

They waited.

"He's typing," Olivia announced.

More seconds passed.

"Come on," Olivia urged.

More seconds.

Penny glanced toward her iPad while waiting. Several more comments had already appeared. The video was going viral.

"'She's a friend of Leanne,'" Olivia read from her phone.

"Leanne?"

"Joey's ex."

"Great."

"Let me see it again," Olivia said.

Penny handed over the iPad.

Olivia watched the video, this time until the end. "It's not a very good video. If you didn't know it was you, it would be hard to tell."

"My name is said several times," Penny noted.

"Just your first name and they didn't tag you or anything, so..." Her voice trailed off.

Penny gave a weak smile.

People would know. Even those that hadn't been at the party. The comments in the lunchroom were just the beginning. This was going to get bad.

# SIX

No one said anything about the video during the days that followed, yet Penny felt as if everyone had watched it as she walked through the hallways and sat in her classes. She could see it in their eyes when they looked at her. It was surreal. And humiliating. Like she was the butt of an unspoken, collective joke—one that she couldn't even skirmish against given everyone's uncanny discretion.

"Honestly, I don't think anyone is really saying anything," Olivia said one night while they lay awake in her bedroom. "Everyone's too focused on their own shit."

"Maybe," Penny replied, even though she knew this wasn't the case.

People were talking. She read the comments. Most were simply tags of people's names so they could see the video, but others were actual statements on what had unfolded. One of the most popular was one that said it looked like she was being ass-fucked by Satan, a carefully selected screenshot of her face having been posted to emphasize the comment. In it, her mouth was half open while her eyes were rolled back.

Others voiced concern about her being possessed, stating theories that she had opened the door with the Ouija board. Some agreed, while others thought such things were nonsense.

Penny wanted to be in the latter category but worried about the former, given what had happened during her first class the other day. Something had been in the room with her. Something had been calling her name.

"Oh hey," Olivia said across the darkness. "I meant to ask, do you want any condoms for tomorrow night?"

"What?" Penny replied, startled.

"You know, just in case."

"We're not going to have sex."

"You sure?"

"Yes."

"Still, better to have them and not need them than not have them and need them."

"Isn't that what people say about guns?" Penny asked.

"Guns, condoms, pads...it's pretty universal."

Penny didn't reply.

"So..." Olivia pressed.

"Olivia," Penny said, voice firm. "We're just going to be having dinner."

"Okay, but if you want some, just let me know."

Penny shook her head, which Olivia obviously couldn't see.

And then a thought arrived.

"Wait," Penny said. "You don't think he's expecting us to...do you?"

"I don't know. Joey's hard to read."

Penny didn't reply to that.

"I do know one thing," Olivia added.

"What?"

"He wouldn't say no."

"But I will."

Olivia chuckled.

THE TWO ENDED up going to Chili's for their first date, Joey voicing surprise at it being her favorite place once they were seated.

"It actually isn't, but you all don't have sushi around here, so..." She spread her hands in an *oh well* gesture, one that she hoped would cover her embarrassment.

"One of the biggest downsides of living in flyover country," he said.

"You like sushi?" she asked, surprised.

"Love it. And you can actually get some good stuff out here if you're willing to go all the way into the city. The drive sucks and parking is a nightmare, but it's worth it. They also have a tea room out there that I really like."

"Tea room?"

"Yeah. Like one you'd find in England. You order a pot of tea and then they have tiny finger foods, and you just sit and relax, drinking your tea and eating the little sandwiches."

"Huh, sounds interesting."

"We'll have to go there sometime."

"Sushi place first though."

"For sure."

She grinned.

A waiter came by and took their drink orders.

An odd silence followed in his wake.

"So..." Penny said after several seconds.

"So..." Joey replied.

Nothing followed, the silence returning.

"You look nice," Penny said.

"Oh," Joey said, awkwardly glancing down at himself. "Thanks."

"I'm sorry I didn't pick a nicer place."

"What, no. This is fine. They have good burgers here."

She forced a smile.

He had worn a suit, which meant he had been expecting something fancy, while she had on simple slacks and a comfy sweater. He had also brought her flowers, which she wanted to bring back to the house and put into a vase but couldn't because it would ruin the fiction Olivia had created for them, the two supposedly heading to Liz's house for an evening of pizza and movies.

The drinks arrived.

"Are you two ready to order?" the waiter inquired.

"Not yet," Penny said.

The waiter left with a promise to return shortly.

Penny didn't look at the menu.

Instead, she said, "If you want, we could go somewhere else. I really don't mind."

"No, no, we're already here and have our drinks."

"But you were obviously expecting something more," she said, motioning to his clothes.

"What, this?" he said. "I simply came straight from a business meeting."

She grinned.

"In fact, I can take off the tie if it makes you feel better."

"No, don't. It looks nice."

It really did.

No one had ever worn a suit to pick her up before—unless one counted the homecoming dance she had gone to last year. Such attire was required at the dance though, so she didn't. Wearing one for a simple date. It completely caught her off guard. Turned her on too, though she wasn't sure why.

THE FOOD WASN'T BAD, but that didn't alleviate the disappointment Penny felt with herself at having picked it. Adding to the disappointment, Joey apparently liked the Thai place that Olivia had steered her away from.

"They have a panang curry that is to die for," he said, a gleam in his eye. "And their tea is amazing. I think I had four glasses last time I was there."

Penny smiled to mask her frustration.

*I'll never listen to Olivia again.*

"But enough about all the places we could have gone. This isn't a one-time thing. We'll have plenty of time to try all sorts of fun stuff."

"I know. I'm sorry."

"Speaking of fun stuff, have you visited the Galleria yet?"

"I guess not since I don't even know what it is." In her mind she pictured an art studio.

"I'm just joking. The Galleria is the local mall. For some reason all the cool kids have started hanging out there."

"Really? Why?"

"I don't know. Maybe it's a throwback to the '80s. That's all the rage these days."

"Guess I'm not one of the cool kids," she said, pretending to pout.

"Me either."

Nothing followed for a few seconds, the two returning to their meals.

"What did the cool kids do out in LA?" he asked.

"Not sure. I'm not from LA."

"What? I thought you were."

"Nope. San Francisco."

"Huh. For some reason I thought it was LA."

"You're not alone. Quite a few have mentioned it. I think when everyone hears California they automatically think LA. And when they hear it is actually San Francisco, they think, *meh, same thing*, even though it's over five hours away."

"Five hours?"

"On a good day."

"Wow."

"Yeah."

"Well then, what did all the cool kids do in San Francisco?"

She shrugged. "Don't know. I think some would sometimes stand around outside of the *Full House* house."

He grinned. "Seriously, what did you and your friends do for fun?"

"Mostly we would just hang out and play D&D."

"Really? How does your aunt feel about that?"

"Actually, I don't know. It hasn't come up." She thought for a second. "What would your parents think?"

"Not sure. They probably wouldn't like it. And the school might get involved."

"What do you mean?"

"I'm pretty sure playing such games goes against their code of conduct, which means..." He made a *smack* sound.

"Really? Even if you play it outside of school?"

"Yep."

"That's ridiculous."

"Most of our rules are."

The conversation would have continued, but the waiter came by to ask if they would like dessert, which prompted

Joey to ask her if she wanted to go to an ice cream place that was up the road a bit and then walk along the river.

"Sure," she said.

"Great."

Ten minutes later, they were at the ice cream place, which was actually a frozen custard stand, waiting in a line that stretched around the block.

"Is it always this busy?" she asked.

"On weekends it usually is, especially now since this is one of the last nights it's going to be open."

"Really? Why?"

"It's only open during the summer."

"Ohhhh." She had momentarily forgotten about the changing seasons. "When do you usually get snow?"

"Hmm, good question. It can vary. Sometimes it will fall as early as Halloween, but usually the first actual snowstorm will be in November."

"I'm kind of excited."

"Will this be your first time seeing snow?"

"Ha! No. We used to go skiing in the mountains every December."

"Oh, cool. Was it like a school thing or just you and your friends?"

"No, my mom's company hosted it. Kind of a year-end celebration for all the employees and their families."

"Ah," he said, hesitation following.

Penny waited, sensing a question brewing.

It didn't happen.

Instead, the line moved enough for them to see the giant wall menu, which prompted Joey to start asking what types of flavors she liked. Suggestions followed. It was charming how enthusiastic he was about the various custard concoctions that could be created.

# SEVEN

"It's all she thinks about," Olivia said.

"Really?" Martin asked.

"Yeah. I keep telling her no one is paying any attention to it, but she doesn't believe me. And she keeps reading all the comments."

"She shouldn't do that. People are dicks."

"Exactly, though I guess that's easier said than done. I'd probably look at the comments too if that were me."

"Yeah, me too."

A few seconds came and went.

"You really haven't heard anything?" Olivia asked.

"No. Nothing. The only thing anyone has been talking about is her mom."

"Her mom?" Olivia said, concern brewing.

"You know how guys are," he replied, caution now present in his voice.

"What are they saying?"

"They're just curious. It's not every day you get to meet the daughter of a porn star."

"For the love of God!" Olivia snapped.

"Whoa, whoa!" He held up his hands. "I'm just telling you what they were talking about."

"Well, I hope you told them to knock it off."

"I did, though it is hard to—" He froze.

"What?" Olivia asked.

He shushed her and cocked his head to the left.

Olivia waited.

Several seconds came and went.

"Shit," he said, voice hushed. "Someone's here."

"Are you sure— " she started and then heard the back door opening. "Oh my God, is she showing the house?"

"She wasn't supposed to," he whispered, panic evident.

"What do we do?" she asked.

He looked around.

They were on the second floor, in one of the back bedrooms—chosen because of the carpet, which helped add a layer of cushioning that the other rooms of the house did not provide when they spread their blanket.

"What do we do?" she repeated.

"Hide," he said, grabbing the blanket and nodding toward the closet.

Downstairs, a muffled voice was explaining something.

Olivia couldn't tell if it was Martin's mom or someone else with the agency. Not that it really mattered. If caught, they were fucked.

Martin carefully made his way to the closet.

Olivia followed, struggling to get her top back on.

Once she was inside, Martin pulled the door closed, engulfing them in darkness.

Neither spoke.

Heart racing, Olivia waited, her hands clasped against her chest.

If the closet door were opened, they would be caught. It

was that simple. And why wouldn't the closet be opened? Buying a house was a big deal, which meant they would be checking everything out.

Unless they didn't like the house from the start.

Could that happen?

Could they take one look at the first few rooms on the ground floor and decide the place wasn't for them?

*Please! Please! Please!*

Seconds turned to minutes, the sound of muffled voices going from one room to the next on the ground floor.

It didn't seem like they were leaving after just a few rooms.

On cue, the sound of the stairs creaking echoed.

*No! No! No!*

She could already hear the screams as her mother went berserk.

"No bathroom up here?" a voice asked after several seconds.

"Just the one downstairs," another replied.

*Was that Martin's mom?*

Olivia had met her a few times but couldn't match the voice she had heard during those encounters with the one she heard now.

A discussion followed, the lack of a second bathroom a big deal it seemed—one that was a lifesaver for them because it ended the showing.

"Close call," Martin said once they were alone again, voice heavy with relief.

Olivia didn't reply, unless one counted the glare she gave him.

"Oh, come on, you can't blame me for this," he said.

She continued to glare.

"Fine," he said. "Be like that."

"Be like what?" she demanded.

"Pissed off and going silent."

"You're supposed to know your mom's schedule," she said, arms crossed.

"That wasn't my mom," he advised.

"Then what were they doing here?"

"Other people at the agency can show these houses. It was probably a last-minute thing."

"If I had known that could happen—"

"Oh, come on," he said. "You've always known this could happen."

Once again, she didn't reply, only this time it was because he was right. She had known. But given how often they had done this without incident, the possibility had seemed so remote that it had gotten pushed way back into the darkest corner of her mind.

She sighed and then nodded.

"We cool?" he asked.

She nodded again and then said, "We're cool."

He put his arms out and then wrapped them around her when she stepped into them.

"ARE they really talking about her mom working in porn?" Olivia asked ten minutes later, the two now sitting in his car after having gone out through the back door and crossed through several yards to where it was parked on the street.

"Yeah," he said.

"And they've seen her videos?"

He nodded.

"How did they even find them?"

"You can find anything online."

"Yeah, but how do they know it's her? The most recent would be like what, five years old?"

He shrugged.

"Have you watched them?" she asked.

"Bits and pieces," he admitted after a few seconds.

"Why?"

"I was curious."

"*Curious?*"

"To see what she was like."

"That's sick."

"It's not sick."

"It is!"

He shook his head. "You don't get it."

"Get what? That you got your rocks off watching my dead aunt fucking some guys on camera?"

"It wasn't like that. Ned sent me the link to one of them from his phone and I watched it. That's it."

"When was this?"

"I don't know, like two days ago."

"And he's spreading it all around the school?"

"I wouldn't say he's spreading it."

"How would you say it, then?"

"I don't know," he said with a shrug.

She stared at him for several seconds and then simply shook her head.

"You know, having people see and talk about the old videos might not be such a big deal."

"*Not a big deal?*"

"She's grown up with it."

"Are you for real?"

"Seriously! Do you really think this is the first time her classmates and friends have seen the videos?" he asked.

Olivia started to reply but then stopped.

"This is something she has lived with her entire life," he said. "And it's not like it has been a secret. Her mom won awards. Hell, Penny was even interviewed for a documentary."

"She was?" Olivia asked, caught off guard.

"Yeah," he said with a grin.

"Why?"

"They wanted to know what life was like once the cameras were off. Homelife stuff. I don't know." He shrugged. "Sort of like an episode of *Cribs*, only for porn stars."

Olivia didn't even know what to say to that.

"So yeah," Martin continued. "I think it's safe to say that she's probably used to people knowing what it is her mom did for a living."

"You still don't need to be watching that shit," Olivia said.

"I'm really not."

"No, you've just seen the videos and then sought out documentaries about her."

"Like I said, I was—"

"Curious, I know."

"What about you?"

"Me?"

"You're not curious about them?"

"What? No!"

"Not even a little?"

"She's my aunt!"

"I meant the documentaries."

"Liar."

He grinned. "Seriously though, I think maybe you're trying too hard to shield her."

"She's just been through so much though. I feel horrible

for her."

"Been through and survived it."

"True. Though I still want to cunt-kick that bitch for posting the video."

Martin laughed.

Following that, they went in search of food.

# EIGHT

"Joey says this is where all the cool kids hang," Penny noted as they stepped out of the car.

"It is and that's why we're here," Olivia replied.

"As if!"

The entrance they had parked near was next to The Cheesecake Factory, the sight of which caused Penny's mouth to water.

Olivia seemed to have the same thought because she said, "I think we should totally sweet-talk the boys into buying us lunch before we leave."

"Agreed." Then, "Wait! Are they meeting us here?"

"Mayyyyybeeee..."

Penny let out a playful sigh.

She had no idea what they were doing, Olivia having simply whisked her away from the book she was reading with a statement on how they were going to the mall.

And it seemed the secrecy was going to continue as Olivia took a moment to look at the large map and then started leading the way to the left, her eyes on the lookout for something as she scanned all the storefronts, a "ta-da!"

eventually leaving her lips as they came to a halt somewhere on the second floor in the far west wing.

Puzzled, Penny looked up at the gaming store and said, "Okay, I'm confused."

Olivia grinned. "Come on."

Penny followed.

The store was bigger than it looked and a bit disorienting, given the maze of shelves. Board games seemed to be the product of choice, though there was also a small area of overpriced jigsaw puzzles and some weird fidget items and Funko toys.

"Okay, what in the world are we doing here?" Penny finally asked as they rounded a corner, surprise arriving as Joey and Martin appeared.

"Finally," Martin said. "What took you so long?"

"Driving, parking, walking," Olivia said, an implied *duh* punctuating the statement.

"Hey, you," Joey said to Penny, a box in his hands.

"Hey," Penny replied, smiling.

The box he held was a Dungeons and Dragons starter kit.

"You guys are buying D&D stuff?" Penny asked and then looked at Olivia for clarification.

"Trying to, but we have no idea what we need and are totally lost," Martin said.

"You said you used to have a group," Joey added. "We figured we could totally start one up out here."

"They actually wanted to surprise you, but..." Olivia simply spread her hands.

"Yeah, epic fail," Martin said.

Penny chuckled and said, "Okay, first, we don't need any of this stuff. I already have the books and tons of character sheets tucked away in one of my boxes. The only thing you each should have is a figure piece that represents your character, though you don't even really need that. We always used them in my group to help visualize each other. I could also use more monster pieces and dungeon items."

Everyone stared at her for several seconds.

"Have any of you ever played at all?" she asked.

Two *nos* and a *nope* echoed.

"Hmm, okay, we should then probably go sit down so that I can explain it a bit," she suggested. "Maybe over at The Cheesecake Factory."

"I vote yes," Olivia said.

Martin and Joey exchanged glances, Martin eventually saying, "I think we were just shanghaied into buying them lunch."

"I think so," Joey said.

"SO, THERE'S NOT A GAME BOARD?" Joey asked.

"Well there can be, but you don't have to have one," Penny said, concerned that after nearly fifteen minutes of explaining, they still didn't really grasp how one played D&D.

"But if you don't have one, how do you know where you're going and what's in front of you?" Olivia asked.

"When you roll for discovery, you then learn what is around you," Penny said. "And then you can react to it."

"By rolling again?"

"Yep."

"And *you* know ahead of time what is there," Martin noted, nodding toward her.

"Yep. Well, whoever the DM is for that game. It's all planned out ahead of time."

"Okay, I think I'm starting to get the idea."

"You two?" Penny asked, looking at Joey and Olivia.

"A little, but I'm going to have to play a round to fully grasp it," Joey said.

"Same," Olivia said.

"How much time do you need to plan a game?" Martin asked.

"Actually, we could do one tonight if we have a place to play," Penny said. "I'll just have to tweak a few things with one of my old campaigns."

"Your basement?" Olivia asked Martin.

"Sure," he said.

"Your parents won't care?" Penny asked.

"Nah. As long as we're not drinking, doing drugs, or having sex, it's all good." He turned to Olivia while saying this.

Olivia shook her head.

"What time?" Joey asked, obviously trying to shift the topic a bit.

"Seven?" Martin asked and looked around.

No one objected.

Shortly after that, their food arrived, and then following that they headed back to the game store so that Olivia, Martin, and Joey could pick out figures to use as representation while playing.

"WHOA, HOLD UP FOR A SECOND," Olivia said.

"What?" Penny asked.

The two had been heading toward the entrance they had arrived in, ready to head back home so they could get ready for that evening.

Olivia didn't reply right away, her eyes simply focused to the left.

Penny followed her gaze, a small coffee area coming into view.

A group of girls with tall cups were gathered, several of their faces familiar looking. Laughter echoed.

Olivia started walking.

"Oh, Olivia, no," Penny said.

"I just want to say hi," Olivia replied.

Penny took her arm. "Please don't. Let's just go."

Olivia hesitated.

Penny started to turn, sensing that Olivia would follow.

"Oh hey, it's Satan's bitch!" a shrill voice announced.

More laughter.

Penny's heart began to pump faster.

She took a deep breath.

"That's it," Olivia whispered.

"No," Penny cautioned. "Let's just go."

Olivia wasn't having any of it and started toward the girls.

Penny followed, the strong scent of scorched coffee and overused perfume hitting her senses.

"Oh, Olivia," one of the girls said. "I didn't recognize you without Martin's cock in your face."

"Remember what happened last time a cock was in your face?" Olivia asked.

The girl's face went pale.

"It was a pity too. That was a nice dress. Did you ever get the stains out?"

"At least she doesn't take it up the ass like Penny's mom," one of the other girls said.

"Victoria," Olivia scoffed. "I didn't take you for a porn freak. Are you studying up in hopes that someone might ask you out one day?"

"No!" Victoria spat.

The screech of milk being steamed filled the air.

Penny twitched.

Darkness began to slither in.

*No! No! No!*

"*I bet your mom is sucking cocks in hell,*" a voice said.

"*Next time we have the Ouija board we can ask her,*" another echoed.

The room shifted.

Penny grabbed Olivia's arm.

"*Penny!*" a voice hissed.

She twisted toward it, her eyes going wide as something dark emerged from behind the counter of the coffee stand. It was coming for her.

"No!" she cried, putting her hands up.

It was no use, the darkness quickly enveloping her.

# NINE

A high-pitched wailing sound pulled her from the darkness, her mind a confused mess as she looked up at a young man who was hovering over her, his lips giving voice to words that she couldn't understand.

Something on her arm tightened.

*Shackles.*

She was chained to the wall.

*No.*

"Penny," the voice said as she yanked at the restraints. "You're okay. We're almost there."

*Where?* she tried to ask, but couldn't quite force out the word.

A radio squawked.

The young man read off some numbers and then leaned in to loosen the cuff from her arm, the sound of peeling Velcro echoing.

A question about her mom entered her mind but then faded without being asked as a memory of the mall appeared.

Laughter and then someone shouting her name.

Shrieks may have followed, though she couldn't be certain.

And then the horrible place where the demon lived, her body chained up against a stone wall ready to be used in every way imaginable.

*Had that been real?*

*It seemed real.*

*But could it really be?*

CONTROLLED CHAOS. It was the only way to describe the emergency room.

Amid that chaos decisions were made, one of which eventually concerned her and the need to take blood and do a CT scan.

After that, she was left in a hallway for quite some time, nurses and doctors passing by her as if she did not exist, her need to pee growing stronger and stronger until she had to cry out for help.

*Satan's bitch.*

The comment stuck in her mind while she sat on the toilet, imagery of the creature she had seen after the darkness had engulfed her returning.

If there was a hell and demons lurked within it, that had certainly been one of them.

*Why me?*

Had she accidentally summoned it?

With the Ouija board during the party?

Or did it go further back?

*The accident?*

A knock echoed on the door followed by a question on if she was okay.

Not long after that, they brought her to a hospital room,

a statement on how the doctor would be in shortly being made.

"SHORTLY" ended up being nearly an hour later, at which point the doctor came in as if he were on a moving conveyer belt that looped around the room, his feet unable to step off.

She had a concussion from hitting her head when she fell and they would be keeping her overnight.

That was the big reveal.

Penny tried to get more from him, a question on why she had fallen in the first place leaving her lips, but all she got was a shrug and a comment on how these things can happen when someone gets worked up or overexcited.

*Worked up?*

*Overexcited?*

Her bullshit meter was buzzing, but she decided not to press the issue given her prior experience in a hospital. Being sixteen, some would treat her like an adult, others like a kid. When it was the latter, no amount of pressing would bring about a change.

"I WAS STARTING to think I was at the wrong hospital," Olivia said once she came into the room. "No one seemed to know where you were or what was going on."

"Sounds about right," Penny said.

"Have they told you anything?" Olivia asked.

"Apparently, I hit my head."

"That's it?"

"Yep," Penny confirmed. "Oh, and I have to stay here overnight."

"Really? Why?"

"Because I hit my head. They want to run more tests tomorrow to make sure everything is okay."

"I guess that makes sense. You did whack it pretty good on the edge of the table."

"So they've said. I don't remember it at all."

"Nothing?"

*Just the demon...* she said to herself. "Was it like the other night?"

Olivia made a *so-so* gesture. "You started mumbling something and twitching a bit, but I don't think anyone really noticed that because a second later you fell and cracked your head on that table."

Penny reached up and fingered the bandage that covered the lump protruding from her forehead.

"And then all hell broke loose," Olivia added.

"What do you mean?" Penny asked.

"I think someone thought there was a shooting or something...I don't know. It was crazy. One minute you had hit your head and the next people were running and screaming. It took forever for them to realize you had simply slipped."

"I didn't slip."

"I know, but better they think that than people talking about—"

Olivia stopped as the door opened, a nurse guiding Olivia's mother and brother into the room, the two having obviously been at a Scouts meeting, given Nicky's uniform.

Questions followed, Penny stating several times that she was okay and that everything was fine.

*It isn't though...*

Something more was going on than met the eye.

Something horrible.

Something she couldn't even begin to understand.

. . .

JOEY CALLED HER THAT NIGHT, their conversation short-lived given that her phone was almost dead and she didn't have her charger. Nothing serious was discussed, the conversation very superficial. Once it was over, she simply stared at the wall, her previous moments of channel surfing having already alerted her to the fact that there was nothing on that she would want to watch—not even as background noise.

A SCREAM FOLLOWED her into the waking world, along with a smell that could only be sulfur. Panic arrived. She had no idea where she was or what was happening.

The door opened, flames silhouetting a figure that strolled in.

Eyes wide, Penny let out a shriek.

"IT WAS JUST A NIGHTMARE," the nurse said, trying to calm her.

"*No,*" Penny insisted. "It was real."

"Shhh, it's okay," the nurse cooed, rubbing her shoulder. "Let me bring you something that will help you sleep."

"No! It'll get me if I sleep," Penny warned.

A smile was the only response, one that looked cruel in the semi-darkness that defined the room.

*Is she one of them?*

*A servant of darkness?*

The ridiculousness of the thought should have brought about her own smile, but instead it did just the opposite.

If the demon was real and was able to reach into this world, then maybe it had touched others as well.

Others that it would use to get to her.

*No.*

*She's right. It was just a dream.*

*It isn't real.*

*But what if it is?*

Could her mother have been wrong all these years?

Was the church right?

Was there really a battle between heaven and hell being waged? Did angels and demons lurk among the human population, working unseen in hopes of helping their side gain victory?

A few months earlier, such thoughts would have made her laugh, but now they were far from amusing.

The nurse did something with her IV.

"Wait, stop," Penny voiced, her consciousness fading to the point where she didn't even hear a reply.

NO DEMON WAS WAITING for her this time around, and the next thing she knew, it was morning and she was being wheeled through the hallways so that more tests could be run, a promise of being able to eat breakfast once they were done being made.

Following breakfast, which was actually pretty good, the doctor returned, feet still seemingly planted on an unseen conveyor belt

She was going to be fine, the "bump on her head"—his words—nothing to worry about any longer. Another day of rest and she would be "right as rain"—his words again.

"So I can go home?" she asked.

"Yep," he confirmed. "As soon as your mother arrives and all the paperwork is signed."

The use of the word "mother" pretty much summed up

his level of interest in her situation. She considered saying something about it but then let it slide.

Several more hours came and went before her aunt did arrive to bring her home, at which point another hour was needed for the paperwork to be signed and processed, Penny growing more and more impatient with the entire process.

# TEN

"This is totally bogus," Olivia said while getting dressed for school. "I should get to stay home too so that I can keep an eye on you and make sure nothing happens."

"I suggested it, but for some reason your mom doesn't seem to think I'd get the rest I need if you did," Penny said, grinning.

Olivia shook her head.

"Honestly though, I'd rather go to school."

"Why?"

"To help keep the rumor mill from churning."

"Pssh," Olivia voiced, waving a hand. "That's gonna churn whether or not you're there."

"But it will be even worse now."

"Eh, fuck 'em."

"Olivia!" Aunt Susan snapped from the hallway.

Penny's eyes went wide as Olivia turned to face her mother, who was stepping into the room.

"Phone," Aunt Susan said, hand out.

"Mom, come on."

"You know the rules."

"I need my phone."

"Give it to me."

"No."

"We're not leaving until you hand it over, and if we're late, I won't call the school to excuse you."

Panic set in, Olivia looking from her mother to Penny and then back. "What about the swear jar? Can't we start doing that again?"

"That didn't work," Aunt Susan said.

"Please. I can't go without my phone for a week."

"I could make it two weeks," she warned.

"What about no TV or no soda or something?" Olivia begged.

"You really want it to be two weeks, don't you?" Aunt Susan said.

"Please!"

"Fine. I'll give you a choice like they do at school. You either go two weeks without a phone or you can be paddled."

"What!" Olivia cried.

Penny's mouth fell open.

"That is the choice they give you, isn't it?" She looked at Penny while asking this.

Penny nodded. "Either a detention or being paddled." It was something she had learned on her first day, something that she was still surprised about, given that such actions would never have been allowed at her previous school.

"We don't even have a paddle," Olivia said, crossing her arms.

"Actually, we do," Aunt Susan said. "It's in a box in the cellar with your grandfather's things."

Olivia didn't reply to that.

"So, which will be it?" she asked, crossing her arms. "No phone for two weeks or fourteen swats with the paddle?"

"Fourteen?"

"One for each day."

Olivia once again looked from her mom to Penny and then back to her mom, her face a mixture of frustration, anger, and panic.

"You better make a decision or else we're going to be late and then you'll have to make the same decision with your—"

"Fine!" she shouted. "Paddle me!"

Aunt Susan seemed startled by the choice.

Penny, however, wasn't surprised.

"You'd rather have me blister your butt than go two weeks without your phone?" Aunt Susan questioned.

"Yes."

"I don't even know what to say to that," she said, shaking her head.

"You're going to spank Olivia?" Nicky said from the doorway, a hint of excitement present in his tiny voice.

"Go get yourself ready," Aunt Susan said, voice soft yet stern.

Nicky hurried down the hallway.

Aunt Susan turned back and looked at Olivia, who stared back at her.

"So, do you want me to bend over now, or are we going to do this after school?" Olivia asked.

Aunt Susan shook her head and walked out of the room.

"Do you think she's really going to do it?" Penny asked, voice barely above a whisper.

"I don't know," Olivia replied.

"Has she ever spanked you before?"

"When I was little, yeah, but that was like ten years ago.

And never with a freaking paddle. I didn't even know we had one."

"What about at school? Have you ever been paddled there?"

"No. I don't even think I know anyone who has. Everyone always takes the detention."

"Wow."

Nothing else was said, mostly because Olivia had to get moving or else she would be late.

Penny watched her go and then listened as the three left the house, an odd silence arriving.

Had Aunt Susan been bluffing about the paddling?

Had she given Olivia the choice thinking there was no way she would choose being paddled?

If so, she obviously didn't know how important that phone was to Olivia. The device was a part of her. Taking it away would be like removing one of her limbs.

*Will she actually do it?*

*Will she paddle her sixteen-year-old daughter?*

*What about me?*

*Would she punish me like that?*

Penny thought about this for quite some time, but then realized she would have probably simply given up her phone.

*Or would I?*

No phone meant no texting, which meant she would have no way to talk with Joey while Aunt Susan was home.

A few weeks ago she wouldn't have thought that a big deal, but now that the two were texting every night, it might be tougher than she realized.

And if Aunt Susan somehow managed to unlock the phone...

For Penny that wouldn't be too bad, given how tame the conversations were, but with Olivia...

Not only did she and Martin fuck like rabbits, they also were constantly sending each other dirty pictures.

But still, two weeks without that versus being paddled...

And fourteen hits?

Olivia might not have known anyone who had been paddled before, but Penny did. Most of the videos her mom's company had produced were standard porn movies that either featured men with women or women with women, but one arm of the company did produce kinky videos, many of which featured spankings and other S&M storylines. One of the ladies who was always being spanked in the videos had been a frequent guest in their house, Penny's mom often joking about how she needed to pull out extra cushions for Kimberly whenever she visited.

PENNY HAD NEVER HAD her aunt's house to herself before, and now that she did, she didn't know what to do with the solitude. It was odd. Back in San Francisco she had grown accustomed to being on her own for long chunks of time, her mom's career often seeing her on sets well into the evening hours during the week and sometimes on the weekends. Here that wasn't the case. Even when her aunt was at work, church group, or services, Olivia was here. Nicky too if he wasn't at Scouts, Bible Club, or some playdate that Aunt Susan had arranged for him. And if Olivia wasn't home, it was because she and Penny were both out, chilling with the fabricated Liz.

In the end, she simply made a fresh pot of coffee and brought a mug of it with her into the family room where she curled up on the sofa to read. It was the only thing she could think of doing that she couldn't do when others were home since her aunt or Nicky were usually watching something.

A TEXT from Joey asking how she was doing arrived around 10:45.

The conversation that followed was brief, given that he was between classes. She let him know she was good and was looking forward to heading back to school on Wednesday so she could see him. He replied with a similar statement. They then agreed to talk more later once he was at lunch. Several heart and kiss emoji faces followed.

After that, Penny abandoned her spot on the sofa and went in search of a snack and then, once that was devoured, started back upstairs to get out her D&D books so she could decide upon a campaign for that weekend.

Her phone buzzed while she was doing this.

Olivia.

*Hey, can you hide the paddle?* it read.

*Are you serious?* Penny asked back.

*Yes!*

*I don't even know where it is.*

*It's in the boxes in the far corner, near Grandpa's old room.*

*Okay.*

THE BASEMENT of the house was mostly unfinished and had become a maze of discarded furniture, boxes, and a really creepy collection of headless mannequins that had been used for sewing dresses—something that she knew her grandmother had done for many years, thanks to statements that had been made at the funeral she and her mother attended six years earlier.

It had been during that funeral when she had first met her aunt, Olivia, and Nicky, Olivia having treated her with a cautious curiosity, one that was almost amusing to think about now, given how much she had changed since that first visit.

No drama had unfolded during the funeral, but afterward there had been a heated discussion between her mother and aunt. The actual words of the discussion had not made it through the closed door, but the anger within them had. Olivia had told her it was because her mother was a sinner and brought shame to the family. In reality, it had been about a safety deposit box, one that her mom had wanted to open but couldn't because her aunt had the key. No other details had followed, her mom refusing to go any further.

*Maybe I'll find the key while looking for the paddle,* she joked to herself while searching for the area that had her grandfather's things.

Nothing seemed to be labeled, which was a problem, especially since she couldn't text her aunt to ask where it was located. All she could do was peer into boxes and see if the contents resembled something that belonged to the grandfather she had never gotten to know, one who now was in the dementia ward of an old folks home.

# ELEVEN

"She's going to paddle you?" Joey said, shock on his face.

"Yeah," Olivia confirmed.

"That's hot," Martin voiced.

"Shut up!" Olivia snapped.

"What? You liked it that time I spanked you."

Olivia gave him a look that wiped the grin from his idiotic face.

Joey looked between them and after several seconds said, "So...you're having Penny hide the paddle?"

"If she can find it," Olivia said. "It's kind of a mess down there."

"Won't your mom just use something else then? Or simply decide to take the phone away instead?"

Olivia stared at him for several seconds and then said, "Fuck."

"Excuse me," a voice called across the room, tone authoritative.

*Oh shit.*

Olivia turned and saw Mr. Abbot standing by his desk.

He called her up to it, jotted down her offense on a pink slip, and told her to head to the office.

PENNY NEVER DID FIND the paddle, but she did uncover a box that had her mother's name on it, one that seemed to contain things from her childhood. Another box contained photo albums and trophies. A third clothing. In the fourth she found a stack of journals and cards.

Journals in one hand and a photo album in another, she made her way over to an old torn sofa that had a small table and rug in front of it—evidence that someone, likely Olivia, had tried to create a hangout spot at one point but then abandoned it.

HEART RACING, Olivia stood before the desk of the assistant principal, who was looking over her file, the silence while he did this stretching out to the point of becoming nearly unbearable.

"I'm happy to say, it appears you've never once been sent down to my office, which means you don't seem to be a troublesome student," he said, closing her file.

Olivia didn't know how to reply to this, so she simply stayed silent.

"And it appears your use of the word 'fuck' was not directed at anyone in particular," he added.

"No, sir," she said. "It just slipped out."

"Slipped out because you frequently use such language off campus?" he asked, voice changing a bit.

"Um..." she started, ready to say no but then changing her mind. "Sometimes."

"I see."

He tapped his fingers across the surface of his desk.

"You're aware of our discipline policy?" he asked.

"Yes, sir," she confirmed. "I have a choice between detention or a spanking."

He nodded and then waited.

She couldn't believe this was happening. Twice in one day. What were the chances? It seemed too perfect, like something was pulling strings to put her into this predicament.

*Penny's demon?* she wondered and then quickly dismissed it as nonsense.

Then again...

"Well?" he asked.

"How many spankings?" she asked.

"For the word 'fuck'," he said. "Five. Ten if you had directed it toward a teacher."

"How many detentions?" she asked.

"Cussing earns a Saturday detention. Seven forty-five to noon. You would be cleaning the bathrooms."

"Seriously?"

"Yes."

She grimaced.

*Fuck it.* "I'll go with the spanking."

He raised an eyebrow, obviously surprised, and then said, "Very well. I need to have you sign this acknowledging your choice." He pushed a form toward her, along with a pen. "While you do that, I'll go get a female staff member."

"Why?" she asked, signing her name.

"Policy," he said. "We need a member of the same sex in here when your butt is bared."

"It's on my bare butt?" she asked, startled.

"Yes."

"I have to remove my underwear?"

"You will have it pulled down, yes."

She hesitated.

"It's right there on the form," he noted.

She looked at it and suddenly saw the words "Bare Bottom Paddling."

Panic set in.

"Would you like to change your mind and do the detention?" he asked.

*Scrubbing shit-stained toilets?*

Five hits with the paddle would be far quicker and less disgusting.

But painful.

And they would see her semi-naked.

*Just my butt.*

Well...

If she was bent over, they would see a bit more.

*Fuck it. Fuck it. Fuck it.*

"I'll still do the spanking," she said.

PENNY HAD NEVER REALIZED how much alike her mother and aunt had looked while growing up. If she hadn't known better, she would have thought they were twins while looking at the photos. It was surreal.

Fortunately, this similarity had not carried over into adulthood. At least not middle-aged adulthood. If it had, living with her aunt now after the accident would have been too much for her to bear.

The photos also highlighted how inseparable the two had been while growing up, something Penny had known prior to looking through the album, given things that had been said over the years. Her mother had never outright talked about her childhood or her relationship with her sister, but from time to time things would slip out.

And then they had gone to college, her mother first, followed by her aunt the following year.

What had happened?

Why had they grown to hate each other?

It couldn't have simply been because her mother had starred in some amateur porn videos and gotten kicked out of school. There had to be more to it.

OLIVIA BEGAN to tremble as she leaned over the desk, her hands having lowered her panties to her thighs before stretching forward to place her palms on the wooden surface.

"Can you fix her skirt, please?" the assistant principal said.

"Yes," the young secretary replied, her hands suddenly lifting up Olivia's skirt and tucking the end into her waistband.

Air touched her nether regions, her flesh prickling with humiliation.

It was like being at the doctor's office for an exam, only worse.

*Crack!*

She screamed at the sudden impact, her mind completely unprepared for how hard the strike was going to be.

Tears exploded.

A second strike hit, her hands quickly reaching back to block the third, pleas mixing in with her sobs.

"Move your hands," his voice said.

"No, no, please," Olivia begged, snot and tears ruining the words.

"We will start over if you don't move them and keep them on the desk."

"Please!"

"I will not ask you again."

Olivia moved her hands back onto the desk, palms flat, and then shifted her head so that she could press her right cheek into the wood, tears still flowing.

*Crack!*

A shriek echoed, this strike being even worse than the first two.

*Crack!*

Another shriek.

"One more."

She braced herself, hands squeezing into fists, head shifting so that her forehead was now against the wood rather than her cheek.

The final blow had more force behind it and was obviously meant to leave her thinking about this for a long time, her body collapsing down into a quivering mess against the desk.

The two stared at her for a few seconds.

"Should I get the nurse?" the young lady asked.

"Olivia, do you need to see the nurse?" he asked.

Words were too much at the moment, so she simply shook her head.

ORGANIZING the journals was easy since her mother had dated every entry. On some, she had even noted the time period inside the cover, likely to help catalog the journal after it had been filled.

The college years were easy to find.

She didn't even have to do any arithmetic to figure out the correct years since her mother had written the word "college" in big bold letters and then decorated it with squiggles, balloons, and happy faces to further enhance it, her excitement impossible to ignore.

Sadness arrived.

Similar pieces of artwork had been used for posters for her birthdays and other fun celebrations, her mom always going all out with both homemade and store-bought decorations.

*Heart-shaped meatloaf on Valentine's Day painted red with ketchup.*

A smile joined the sadness.

Amusement too as her thoughts shifted to the green-themed St. Patrick's Day dinner that had been made last March, one that they couldn't eat because everything ended up looking moldy. It wasn't, of course, but they still couldn't do it and had gone out for sushi instead.

*Why couldn't it have been Olivia and Nicky coming to live with my mom rather than me living with Aunt Susan?*

As soon as the thought was voiced, she chastised herself for it. Wishing her mother was still alive was fine, but doing it while wishing someone else's mother had died just wasn't right.

AS THE PAIN of the paddling faded into a dull ache, the humiliation of it grew. And it wasn't just because the two had seen her bare butt and the shaven area between her legs. (God, had they noticed?) It was the shrieks she had made, ones that were still echoing within her mind.

Everyone in the office had heard her. Of this there was no doubt.

Adding insult to injury, none of them would even look at her as she left the office to head back to class, her tear-streaked face something they obviously didn't want to see, as they all turned away as if completely unaware of what had unfolded beyond the closed door.

Seeing this somehow made it all worse.

She had no idea why, it just did.

Overwhelmed, she hurried to the nearest bathroom, fresh tears arriving as she faced the mirror.

"You okay?" someone asked.

Startled, she twisted to the right and, to her horror, saw a male student standing a few feet away. She then knocked her bag to the floor as she tried to grab it.

"Whoa, easy. It's okay."

She didn't reply to that, just leaned against the sink, sobs starting once again.

"How about I keep an eye out so no one comes in," he said. "That way you can take all the time you need."

She nodded.

He stepped out.

# TWELVE

Penny heard the garage door opening up above and pulled out her phone to check the time, her mind certain that she had not spent the entire day reading through the journals. Her certainty was correct. It was only one o'clock.

Upstairs, the door between the garage and mudroom opened.

The sound of heels on linoleum echoed, followed by hardwood as her aunt entered the kitchen and then the hallway toward the stairs.

"Penny?" her aunt called, the sound of her name just barely reaching her down in the cellar.

Penny closed the journal and headed for the stairs, emerging into the kitchen just as her aunt came back down.

"Oh, there you are," her aunt said.

She had taken off her heels and slipped on some indoor shoes to protect the soles of her stockings.

"I thought you'd be upstairs resting," she added.

"I came down to the couch," Penny said. "Feels weird being in bed during the day."

Aunt Susan nodded and then motioned toward her hand. "What's that?"

"Oh, it's one of my mom's old journals. I was looking through it."

"Ah, quite a few of those. Your mother always was quite the writer."

"She was?"

"Oh yeah. Stories, screenplays, novels—she never went anywhere without a pen and paper."

Penny stared for a second, surprised.

"She used to get us in so much trouble," she added with what could only be described as an amused sadness.

"What do you mean?"

"Well, we all loved her stories, but they really weren't the proper thing for young ladies to be reading—or writing for that matter. Anytime any of us was caught with one of her lurid tales, the story would be confiscated and our butts would be blistered. No choice between a detention or paddling back then if it was at school, and if it was one of our mothers..." She shuddered. "Still, we didn't stop. They were just too good. And being forbidden made them seem even better."

"She never told me about that," Penny said.

"No?"

Penny shook her head.

"Hmm."

"Do you have any of her stories?"

"I don't really know," she said, shaking her head. "There might still be a few tucked away in some of the boxes, but most are probably long gone. Stuff was harder to save back then. We had floppy disks toward the end of high school, and I know she started backing stuff up on them, but I have no idea what she did with them. Or if we could even open them now." She frowned. "I can't even remember the last time I saw a disk drive on a computer or laptop."

Penny wasn't sure what to say to that.

"You know, I always wished she had stuck with the writing. She had such a talent for it and the stories she came up with, I couldn't even begin to understand where it all came from. She could have been so successful."

Penny bristled. "She was successful."

"Oh, honey, I just meant in the writing field. As a novelist or screenwriter. Something more..."

"What?" Penny urged. "Respectable? Something that could be bragged about to your church friends rather than hidden away."

Her aunt didn't reply.

"You know, she won awards. People knew who she was and respected what she had accomplished. We had a good life. A happy life." Her lower lip began to quiver. "And yet she couldn't share that with any of you."

"Is that what you think? That she wasn't welcome here?"

"That seemed pretty clear when we came out for the funeral."

"I think your interpretation of things might have been a bit skewed."

"Nothing was skewed. Olivia flat out told me that my mom was a sinner and was going to hell. Why would she say that if you all didn't put that into her head?"

"Olivia used to say everyone was going to hell when she was ten. She told me I was going to hell after she found out I had fibbed about McDonald's being closed. Her brother, grandmother, teachers, friends, the weatherman, all going to hell for one reason or another. It was a phase. Nothing more."

Penny wanted to counter that, wanted to say something that would prove her mother had been disowned and not welcome here, but realized she didn't really have any evidence of it.

*What about the shouting match after the funeral?*

*And the safety deposit box?*

"What happened during college?" she asked instead.

"What do you mean?"

"Between you two? The falling-out?"

Several seconds came and went.

Penny waited.

"We—" her aunt started but then stopped as her phone came to life. "Nicky's school," she muttered and then answered it, her face frowning as something was conveyed to her. "Possessed by a demon?" She glanced at Penny. "No, I...video?" She shook her head. "No...okay...yeah, I'll be right there."

She tucked the phone away.

"What happened?" Penny asked, even though she was pretty sure she knew exactly what it was.

Her aunt stared at her for a few seconds and then said, "Nothing. Just some kids scaring Nicky. I shouldn't be long."

Penny didn't press the issue. Instead, she waited until her aunt left and then pulled out her phone and texted Olivia.

I THINK *your mom is about to find out about the party.*

Olivia stared at the text, the statement the last thing she

had expected after feeling the buzz in the folds of her skirt where she always kept her phone tucked during class.

*How?* she quickly typed and then shifted her attention back to the front of the room where Sister Mary Ann was trying to generate enthusiasm about their upcoming reading assignment.

She was failing.

A buzz hit her leg.

She waited until there was a blind spot between her and Sister Mary Ann and then looked at the phone.

*She got a call from the school about kids telling Nicky that I was possessed by a demon. They said something about a video.*

A sinking feeling hit her gut.

If her mom found out about the party...

A new text arrived, this one causing the phone to buzz while it was touching her desk, the unmuffled rattle against the wood clearly audible.

*Shit,* she thought while tucking the phone back into the folds of her skirt.

Sister Mary Ann turned and studied the room.

*Stop staring at me!* Olivia silently hissed toward a fellow student who sat next to her, his name slipping her mind.

"David?" Sister Mary Ann asked.

"Yes, Sister?" he asked, turning back to look at the front.

"Is one of the young ladies next to you proving to be a distraction?"

"No, Sister."

"You're sure?"

"Yes, Sister."

Sister Mary Ann waited a few seconds and then went back to talking about Hawthorne and how she would expect them all to find examples of how society today still bore similarities to the time period reflected in the novel.

Another buzz, this one thankfully muffled.

Olivia resisted looking at it, aware that Sister Mary Ann was on full alert now. Fortunately, only fifteen minutes remained in class, at which point she would be able to call Penny and find out what exactly was going on.

PENNY PACED while waiting for a reply, and then nearly jumped when her phone rang, given that she had been expecting a text.

"Hey," she answered.

"What happened?" Olivia demanded.

"I don't know. Your mom came home early for some reason, and then she got a call from Nicky's school. She didn't say much, just that some kids were telling Nicky that I was possessed by a demon."

"Shit."

"Yeah."

"Did she actually say anything about the party?

"No, but if she sees the video she'll know."

"Not necessarily." Hope was present.

"Huh?"

"The video just shows you freaking out."

"Yeah."

"Unless they were there, one wouldn't know where the video was or that we were at a party. I don't even think I'm in the video, and she won't know any of the others in it."

"Okay."

"So, if she asks, we simply tell her it was something that happened back in California. Maybe with your old D&D group."

Penny didn't reply to that.

"Penny?"

"I don't know."

"It's perfect."

"But—"

"Trust me. It'll work and it will save our asses. Hey, I gotta run. I don't want to be late."

The phone disconnected before she could reply.

# THIRTEEN

"It fucking hurt," Olivia said in reply to Martin's question about her spanking. "It was like he was trying to hit a home run with my ass."

"And now you get to go home and get another one," Martin noted.

"Yeah, we'll see," she said.

"If I were you, I'd just give up my phone," Joey said from the back seat.

"Me too," Martin added.

"For two weeks!" Olivia questioned, voice raised. "No way."

"Buy a burner phone to use in the meantime. We can swing by a store right now."

"A burner phone," she said. "What're you, a drug dealer now?"

"Oh yeah, I'm totally cooking meth. Got a lab beneath the chapel in the old catacombs."

Olivia chuckled and then said, "It's not being without the phone that is the problem, though that would totally suck. It's all the pictures and texts."

"So, just lock it."

"Yeah, and she'll just bring it to Verizon to have it unlocked."

"She wouldn't do that."

"Have you met my mom?" she asked, sarcasm heavy.

"Actually, no, I haven't," he replied without sarcasm.

"Okay, good point. Anyway, she would totally do this and since she pays the bill, I doubt they would even hesitate, and the next thing you know..."

"More home runs with your fine ass."

"Shut up."

"Are you gonna paddle me if I don't?"

Olivia shook her head and turned toward the window.

"Olivia, I'm just teasing you."

"Yeah, well, don't, okay? You have no idea how humiliating this is."

"Okay. You're right. I'm sorry."

She didn't reply.

They came to a stop at her drop-off point.

"You sure you don't want to come back to my place for a bit? Kind of wind down before you go back to face things?" he asked.

She didn't. Even without the threat of another spanking looming, she wouldn't have wanted to. Not that day. Not after what had happened. She simply wanted to be alone.

*And yet I won't be.*

Not with Penny living in her room.

Even if Penny left the room, it wouldn't feel like she really was having any down time because in the back of her mind she would be conscious of the fact that Penny was waiting to be allowed back in.

*Penny has it even worse.*

The poor girl went from having a mansion at her

disposal to being a guest in a cramped bedroom. Talk about a mindfuck.

Then again, she did have a nice big inheritance coming her way in two years, plus whatever the sale of the house brought, plus the money from the studio her mom started, so…

She opened the door.

"Hey," Martin said, leaning over.

She turned away, startling him, then felt guilty about it since he really hadn't done anything and leaned toward him. The kiss was brief.

"Let me know what happens," he said.

"I will—if I have a phone."

"If not, I'm sure Penny will let you use hers."

"Yeah, for sure."

With that, she stepped out of the car and started walking home.

"SHE BELIEVED ME," Penny said.

"You're sure?" Olivia asked.

"Yeah."

"What did she say after?"

"Just made me promise to never play with a Ouija board ever again."

"That's it?"

"That's it."

Olivia seemed disappointed.

"I feel bad about lying," Penny added a few seconds later.

"Why?"

"I don't know. It just doesn't feel right."

"Lesser of two evils."

"What was the worse evil?"

"Her finding out about the party and grounding us for the next thirty years."

"Oh." That wasn't really an evil, but Penny let it slide. "By the way, Nicky's terrified of me now."

"Ha, that's awesome."

"Not really. He's genuinely afraid that I'm possessed by a demon. It's sad."

"He'll get over it."

Penny didn't reply.

Olivia didn't seem to have anything else to say either.

Not that it would have mattered, since her mom called her downstairs a few seconds later.

"Shit," Olivia muttered.

"Careful," Penny warned. "Don't want another fourteen added in."

Olivia gave her a look.

"Sorry," Penny said.

"Just wait until you take the Lord's name in vain again. She's setting a precedent here, one that she'll have to follow now when you slip up."

"Fuck that. I'll just give up my phone."

"And miss out on talking with Joey for two weeks?"

"Just one week since I won't argue. And since he didn't even call me at lunch like he said he would, I don't think I'd be missing anything."

"Oh yeah, he wanted me to tell you. His phone died."

"It did?"

"Yeah. He forgot to charge it and was watching something stupid that someone showed him right before lunch and boom, dead."

"Olivia!" her mom called again.

"Coming!" Olivia said and quickly left the room.

Penny watched her go, a question on if her aunt was really going to spank her passing through her mind.

*At sixteen...*

It seemed too ridiculous to even comprehend, but then again, the entire world seemed like it had been turned upside down these days.

HER MOM DIDN'T SPANK her...at first.

She made as if she was going to, having Olivia go so far as to lean over the arm of the sofa and lifting her skirt while brandishing the paddle, but then never actually swung it.

"This will be the only warning you get," she said, Olivia now sitting on the arm of the chair rather than leaning over it. "From this point forward, I'm using the paddle anytime you step out of line. Understand?"

"What about Nicky and Penny?" Olivia asked.

"What about them?"

"Are they going to be paddled too if they get in trouble, or is it just me you plan on abusing?" She crossed her arms.

"You chose this over giving up your phone for a week."

"*Two weeks* and only because you gave me a stupid choice."

"You know what, I've changed my mind. Lean over the arm again."

"Wait, no!"

"Lean over."

"Please. I'm sorry."

"Lean over."

"This isn't fair."

"Fair! I was being lenient and you pushed it. You always push it. And I'm tired of it. Lean over or else I'll take away the phone once I'm finished paddling you."

"Fine!" Olivia shouted and spun around, hands yanking down her panties while leaning over the arm again.

"I didn't say to pull those down—" her mom started and stopped.

Olivia waited.

"What are these marks?" she asked.

"Apparently, today is my day for being paddled," Olivia said.

"At school?"

"Well it wasn't here!" she snapped. "Yet!"

Her mother didn't reply to that, and for a second Olivia started to think she was going to backtrack once again and have her get up, and then *whack*, the paddle cracked against her ass with about the same force the assistant principal had used that morning, a horrible cry of pain and surprise leaving her lips.

PENNY ACTUALLY HEARD the impact of the paddle against flesh.

A shriek followed.

Both were horrific, though it was the sound of the impact that really left an impression upon her mind.

Several more followed, Penny eventually putting her hands over her ears to block out the sounds, a question on if the neighbors could hear this entering into her thoughts.

*If so, will they call the police?*

*If they did, would the police do anything?*

A few years earlier, a sixteen-year-old daughter being punished like this would probably have sparked social outrage, but now it would likely do just the opposite, given the crazy mindset that had swept the nation.

Just the fact that more and more states were allowing

the return of corporal punishment was a sign of this, and Facebook itself was full of memes that said things about how kids today needed to hear the crack of a belt on their butt more often.

Penny remembered having a discussion about this with her mom and Kimberly, the spanking enthusiast who took part in many of the kinky films. Both disagreed with this attitude, Kimberly's opinion on the matter being a surprise until she explained that spanking between adults as a form of kink was one thing, but as a punishment for children, or even wives, which some groups now advocated, it was another. Studies had proven it left psychological scars upon younger kids, and with older kids and young adults, it just sparked rage rather than regret. Fear as well, which wasn't something one should ever live with given the damage it caused to the mind and body.

# FOURTEEN

Olivia said maybe five words during the time period between the spanking and leaving for school the next day, and two of those words were a form of *ouch* when she forgot about easing herself down while sitting.

Aunt Susan was quiet as well, though she did try to explain why the paddling had unfolded in a mini-meeting with Nicky and Penny shortly after the event itself.

Nicky seemed to accept what was said during this, but Penny felt the entire explanation was more of an attempt by her aunt to justify to herself why she had done it, almost as if she were trying to smother regret that was bubbling up.

By eight the next morning, Penny was once again alone in the house.

As before, she wasn't sure how to spend her time.

Had the boxes in the cellar been forbidden to her, she would have ventured back down, but her aunt had been so unfazed by her having explored them and the cellar that it now didn't seem like a good use of her time while alone.

Plus, there really wasn't anything all that enlightening within the journals she had read, and while all the pictures and knickknacks from her mother's childhood were interesting, they weren't anything to get excited about.

Her aunt's bedroom, on the other hand...

It was around nine thirty when she headed down the hallway toward the room, an odd curiosity to see the paddle guiding her steps.

No lock barred her way, her hand able to open the door without a problem.

The bedroom was typical, just like the rest of the house.

Penny had been in it before, so she knew what to expect when stepping through the doorway. Bed, dressers, nightstand, TV stand, makeup stand, closet, and a bathroom.

The paddle was on the nightstand.

It wasn't as big as she had been expecting, her mind having envisioned one of those large cricket-like paddles that were featured in movies with scenes displaying sorority and fraternity initiations. Instead, it was like an over-sized hairbrush with no bristles. Holes had also been drilled into it.

She lifted it, surprised by the weight.

It was heavier than it looked.

*Crack!*

*Shriek!*

She shuddered at the memory, her mind unable to even comprehend what that must have felt like. And then to have thirteen more right behind it.

A realization arrived.

The paddle had been in their grandfather's things, which meant it had likely been used on her mother while growing up.

Anger blossomed.

She hadn't liked her grandfather when she met him at the funeral, and now she thought even less of the old man.

How could someone do that to their daughter? To their daughters? To children in general? To anyone?

Disgusted, she dropped the paddle back onto the nightstand, her fingers releasing it sooner than she should have, a heavy thud filling the room.

A buzzing sound appeared.

It was coming from within the nightstand.

She opened the drawer, a surprised laugh escaping her lips as her eyes settled on the vibrator that had sprung to life.

It wasn't the only device.

Her aunt had a whole assortment of pleasurable toys in the drawer, some battery operated, some not, all within easy reach once she was in bed.

And here Penny had always pictured her simply reading once the door was closed, since she always had her Kindle in hand while saying goodnight.

*Her Kindle...*

It too was within easy reach of the bed, sharing the surface of the nightstand with the paddle.

Curiosity piqued, Penny picked up the device and hit the power button.

The screen loaded to a book that was at the 27-percent-complete mark.

Penny scanned the passage but didn't find anything interesting, so she hit the menu button.

Bingo.

Several lurid book cover icons displaying scantily clad women and men in suits appeared.

*Playtime with Daddy* was her current read, while *The Billionaire's Daughter* and *Forever Young* were on deck.

Amused, Penny returned the Kindle to its spot on the nightstand and then started to close the drawer, deciding to simply let the vibrator vibrate itself out so she didn't have to touch it.

Guilt followed.

This was her aunt's private area. She shouldn't have been snooping.

Pity came next as she contemplated how lonely her aunt was, imagery of her coming up here every night and bringing herself to orgasm with one of her various devices while reading smut filling her mind's eye.

OLIVIA COULD NOT SIT on the hard wooden desk chairs.

It didn't matter how carefully she planted herself, or how much cushioning her school sweater gave once it was balled up into a makeshift pillow, after a few minutes the pressure would become too much and she would find herself squirming about, trying to find a new position.

The squirms didn't go unnoticed, a few of the teachers asking her if she needed to use the washroom. Humiliation always followed the question, though she wasn't sure why.

For lunch, Martin took her to Taco Bell—another perk of being able to drive to school.

She ate enough for three people while in his front seat, the car cushions a nice reprieve from the wooden desk chairs.

"Was it really bad?" Martin asked afterward, his words like a cautious probe.

She nodded and burst into tears, catching him off guard, her body slamming into his as she sought the comfort of his arms and chest.

He held her for several minutes, her sobs soaking through his shirt.

"I don't want to go back to class," she said.

"We have to," he said.

"No."

"If we don't, we'll get in trouble."

"I don't care."

He didn't reply, his arms around her.

"Can we go to one of your mom's houses?" she asked.

Again, he stayed silent.

"Please?" she begged. "I can't go back to class or go home right now."

Still nothing.

"I just need you."

"Okay," he finally said.

"Thank you," she sobbed.

*THOU SHALT not suffer a witch to live.*

The comment was waiting in her Facebook inbox, the profile itself simply saying Facebook User, which she suspected meant it had been deleted after the message was sent. The fact that there was no picture added weight to her theory. She also couldn't click on the profile to view it.

*Or I've been blocked.*

A similar message was waiting in her regular Gmail inbox, several screenshots of her during the freak-out moment imbedded within the body of the email.

It had been sent by someone using a Hotmail account with the name Cain927.

Startled, she deleted the message, concern about how they had gotten her email address dominating her thoughts for several minutes until she realized it was visible on her Facebook profile.

All of the About Me stuff was.

It even listed her school and phone number.

*Fuck! Fuck! Fuck!* she thought while she went about resetting everything to "friends only."

Why it hadn't been at that setting to begin with she didn't know. Normally she was good about things like that, especially given what her mom did for a living, but somehow with Facebook it had slipped her mind.

Or had it?

Given all the recent news about the site and issues they had with privacy, maybe they had switched it themselves. Or it had defaulted to that when she made the update about her new school.

Whichever the case, it was now fixed.

MARTIN TOOK them to the old house on Elm that his mom couldn't sell, a sudden talkative streak unfolding as he drove.

He was nervous.

She was too.

Neither had ever skipped school before, and now that they had crossed over the time frame when they were required to be back at class, it was starting to sink in.

*He's doing this for me,* she noted. *He would do anything for me.*

The thought soothed her, and for the first time since the paddling, she started to feel at ease.

"WHAT IS IT?" Olivia asked as Martin pulled his hand away from the key holder that dangled from the back-door handle.

"I don't know, something gooey," he said, looking at his hand.

"Gooey?" she asked.

"Yeah." He rubbed his fingers against the door with a grimace and then went back to punching in the code for the key holder.

A few seconds later, they were stepping inside, a familiar emptiness greeting them.

"What is that?" Olivia asked, wrinkling her nose.

"I don't know," Martin said, his feet slowly taking him toward the kitchen.

Olivia followed, the smell getting stronger and more pungent.

Nothing seemed amiss in the kitchen.

"I wonder if the sewer backed up," Martin said, looking at the cellar door, which was standing open.

"How?" Olivia questioned. "No one's using it."

"I don't know," he admitted. "Unless..."

"Unless what?" she asked.

"Nothing. I just remembered a story I heard about a brothel in New York that got busted because they backed up the sewer system with condoms that were being flushed."

Olivia rolled her eyes and said, "If that's the case, then I'm going to say your mom has started renting this place to couples in need because there is no fucking way we have flushed that many rubbers."

He chuckled and then hit the switch on the wall for the cellar.

"What're you doing?"

"I'm going to check it out, just to see what happened."

"And then what, call your mom to tell her, 'hey, we

skipped school to hang out in the house on Elm and it looks like the sewer backed up'?"

"No way, I'll cut out letters from a newspaper and send a note."

Olivia shook her head, a buzz from her phone echoing as she did.

Martin headed down the steps.

A shriek echoed.

"What is—" she started as Martin raced back up the steps and then pushed by her, heading for the kitchen sink.

The sounds of him vomiting followed.

Olivia covered her ears while swallowing back a tickle, the sound nearly triggering her own purge.

And then Martin had his phone out, his fingers barely able to hold it as he dialed a number and then put it to his ear.

Olivia lowered her hands.

He was shouting into the phone, his voice hysterical.

Olivia turned toward the cellar door, a question on what he had seen getting the better of her.

She took a step and then another.

Martin didn't seem to notice, his voice still trying to convey what he had seen.

She started down the steps.

# FIFTEEN

Olivia couldn't focus on the questions that were being asked. Not at first. But then, once they brought her to the police station, her mind cleared enough for her to realize they were in trouble, and not simply because they had skipped school. That was the least of their worries.

"Shouldn't I have a lawyer?" she asked.

"Why would you need a lawyer?" the detective questioned.

"Um...because"—she motioned to her surroundings—"I'm in an interrogation room."

"We're just having a conversation, and this is the best place for it. Too many distractions out there." He waved his hands toward the door that opened into the hallway.

"So I can get up and leave if I want?" she asked.

"Not until your mother gets here."

Olivia thought about that for several seconds, her mind playing over the various crime shows she had watched during the last several years. *Making a Murderer* was the most significant of them, the scenes with Brendan being interrogated at the forefront of her mind. "But I can leave this room if I want?"

"Don't you want to help us figure out who murdered your friend?"

"She wasn't my friend," Olivia said and then instantly regretted it because it sounded cold.

"Oh."

"I mean, we didn't hang out together or anything. I didn't really know her all that well."

"I see..."

She waited.

"What about your boyfriend? Did he know her well and hang out?"

"What?" she asked.

"Seems odd that she would be found inside an empty house that he frequently brought you to, doesn't it? I mean, with one needing a code to get inside and all. A code that he knew."

"Martin wasn't cheating on me," she said.

"You sure about that?"

"Yes."

*Am I?*

*Why would he cheat?*

*Why wouldn't he cheat?*

"Was Jocelyn involved in the occult?"

Olivia blinked, thrown off by the change in direction. "The occult?"

"You know, witchcraft, satanic worship, trying to summon spirits from beyond the grave."

"No way."

"What about you?"

"Are you for real?"

He waited.

"No, I'm not into witchcraft or satanic worship."

"What about Martin?"

"No!"

"You sure?"

Olivia crossed her arms and glared.

"What about Dungeons and Dragons?" he asked.

"Dungeons and Dragons?" she questioned, a chill developing.

"We found character sheets in his backpack."

"You looked through his backpack?"

"We did."

"Why?"

"The same reason we wanted to look through yours. You two broke into a house where a teenager had been killed in a ritualistic way."

"We didn't break in," Olivia snapped.

"Did you have permission to be in there?"

Olivia didn't reply.

"Why did you refuse to let us look in your backpack?"

"Because."

"Because why?"

"Just because."

"You have something in there you don't want us to see?"

"No."

"Then why?"

She didn't reply.

"If you have nothing to hide, then you should let us look inside."

"You know, it was the Nazis who first coined that type of logic."

"What?" the detective said.

"During the 1930s. The Nazis started to listen in on everyone's conversations and read mail and when questioned about it they said, 'If you have nothing to hide, then you have nothing to fear.'" She grinned, satisfaction present. "I watch a lot of documentaries on Netflix."

The detective stared at her for several seconds and then said, "You think this is a game?"

"No."

"Then why are you jerking me around?"

"I'm not—"

A knock echoed on the door.

The detective turned as a uniformed young woman poked her head in and said, "Her mother is here."

Olivia stood.

"You wait here," the detective said, tone snappish.

"I don't think so," Olivia said and walked to the door.

PENNY'S EYES shifted from the TV screen to her phone, which had the latest reply from Joey, who had been texting her nonstop since the news broke about a body being found in the cellar of the house on Elm.

*I still haven't heard anything from Martin,* his text announced.

*Same with Olivia,* she replied. Then, when nothing followed, *Are you sure they went to that house?*

*All's I know is they didn't come back to school after lunch.*

A dot bubble appeared.

Penny waited.

*And his car was gone once school ended,* he added.

*This is crazy,* she replied. It was all she could think to say.

*Yeah.*

Nothing else followed.

On-screen, a reporter from St. Louis was saying they had unconfirmed reports that the murder had a ritualistic nature to it and that police were looking into whether the victim had been part of a group that practiced witchcraft.

*They can't be serious,* Penny said to herself and then thought about texting Joey to see if he was seeing what she was seeing.

The garage door started to open.

Penny went over to the window and saw her aunt's car pulling into the driveway.

Olivia was in the front passenger seat.

*Olivia just came home,* she typed and hit Send.

OLIVIA STORMED INTO THE HOUSE, her steps forceful enough to rattle items in the kitchen as she cut through it to the stairway, a call from her mother for her to wait going unheeded as she headed upstairs.

Penny followed her.

"Go away," Olivia said, face in her pillow.

Penny didn't, a question on what happened leaving her lips.

Olivia didn't reply, her face still pressed into the pillow.

Several seconds came and went.

Penny left the room.

Hearing that, Olivia removed her face from the pillow and pressed herself up into a sitting position.

The bedroom door opened.

"Penny, I want to be—" *alone!*

It was her mother.

"What?" she asked, rubbing at her eyes.

Her mother hesitated.

Olivia waited several seconds before asking, "What?" a second time.

"How long?" she asked.

"How long what?"

"You and this guy you were with. How long have you two been together?"

"None of your business."

"It is my business, and if you ever want to see him again, you'll tell me."

"Two years."

Her mother blinked. "Why didn't you ever tell me?"

"Because I knew you'd freak out and make me stop seeing him."

"Why would you think that?"

"Because you freak out about everything!"

Her mother didn't reply to that. Instead, she said, "The police said he had condoms on him. Have you two..."

"Mom!" she cried, face going red.

"I take it that is a yes."

Olivia couldn't reply. Not to that. It was just too much.

"Honey, I'm not upset..." She paused. "Okay. I am upset. But not for the reasons you think. You're almost an adult now, and though you might not believe it, I was your age once too and understand the urges and curiosity that come with it."

"Mom, please. I don't want to talk about this."

"And when I saw you had shaven yourself yesterday, I started to put things together—"

"Mom!"

"Okay, okay," she said, holding up a hand. "I know. I guess I'm just trying to say, I'm not going to stop you from seeing him, and though I hate the thought of you two having sex, it would seem ridiculous for me to try and put an end to it."

"Really?" Olivia questioned, surprised.

"Really," her mother said. "I just...I know this makes me a bad mother and an even worse Catholic, but I'm glad you two are using protection and I hope you keep on doing so."

"We will."

"Is Penny seeing someone too?" she asked.

Olivia nodded.

"Are they active?"

"No," Olivia said with a slight chuckle. "Who would have thought she would make a better Catholic?"

Her mother didn't reply to that.

"Mom!" Nicky called. "What's for dinner?"

"How does pizza sound?" her mother asked Olivia.

"Okay," Olivia said.

"I'll go place an order." She turned to leave the room.

"Mom?" Olivia voiced.

"Yes?"

"Thanks."

Her mother nodded and then left the room.

# SIXTEEN

The news eventually released the name of the victim found in the house on Elm, but by then everyone already knew it was Jocelyn, given how fast things traveled through the social media feeds. Word had also spread about Olivia and Martin having found the body, though that wasn't part of any official release from the authorities. In fact, they hadn't said anything about who had discovered it. They also weren't saying anything about the nature of the slaying, though word on that was spreading faster than anything.

*Satanist.*

Olivia wouldn't talk about it, but Joey did confirm that Martin had said the body had been in the center of a large pentagram, one that may have been drawn in blood.

Penny shuddered at the description yet also thought it unlikely that a group of Satanists were active in the area. It seemed too Hollywood.

"I'd agree," Joey said as they took their seats in the bleachers of the gymnasium, "except it does seem pretty crazy that she would be displayed like that."

"I think that's why she was displayed like that," Penny

replied. "So that the police would get all caught up in searching for a satanic cult."

Joey gave that some thought but didn't say anything else, his focus shifting as the school principal called for everyone's attention.

What followed was a long-winded and seemingly pointless talk about what had happened to Jocelyn, and how if anyone had any information on the incident they needed to let a member of the staff know so the police could come interview them. Lastly, he suggested everyone say a prayer for Jocelyn's family and for the police as they sought to apprehend the godless individuals who had carried out this atrocity.

"Want to go to the chapel?" Joey asked as they stood up to filter out of the gymnasium.

"What?" Penny asked. "We have to go back to class."

"Not if we're upset. We can spend time in there for 'reflection and prayer.'"

"Really?"

"Yeah."

"You sure?"

"Totally. You just have to let your teacher know so you don't get marked absent. They'll give you a pass."

"Are you going to do that?"

"I will if you will."

"What do I tell Sister Hinkbe?"

"Just that you're upset and feel like you need to spend some time in the chapel."

"That's it?"

"That's it."

"What if she says no?"

"She won't—unless you start doing it every day. Or if you have a test."

"Wow. Okay. Do we have to do anything once we're there?"

"No, we just have to stay quiet and make it look like we're reflecting."

"Okay, I'm going to do it."

"Great. I'll meet you by the door."

"Okay."

The two split as they headed back to their respective classes, Penny's being on the ground floor while Joey had to head up to the far east wing that was near the library.

Not long after that, Penny was heading to the chapel, the note having been easy to secure. No questions had been asked. Sister Hinkbe had simply written out the note and told her that she hoped she got some peace.

Joey was waiting for her at the chapel doors.

Seeing him brought relief.

She had never done this before and wouldn't have wanted to go in by herself.

"Mission accomplished," he said.

"That was way too easy," she noted.

"Like taking a sick day for the soul."

She grinned.

"Shall we?" He motioned toward the door.

She nodded.

They headed in, Joey leading them to a spot halfway into the chapel that sat near an odd alcove that had a sad-looking female statue in it surrounded by candles.

Other statues were present as well throughout the chapel, the expressions somewhat eerie. The worst though was the giant crucifix on the wall in front of them, the tortured Jesus looking down at everyone. Had she been a kid, it would have given her nightmares. Even at sixteen, she didn't want to look at it.

Joey caught her gaze and said, "The sculptor got it wrong."

"What?"

"Jesus wouldn't have been wearing a loincloth while being crucified by the Romans. He would have been naked."

Penny gave him a look.

"It's true. But I guess they didn't want us all to be distracted by Jesus dick while listening to scripture."

Penny shook her head, trying not to laugh.

"Plus who wants to be responsible for figuring out the dimensions of that sort of thing? Too big and everyone would have perverse thoughts. Too small and Jesus might look down and say, 'hey now!'"

Penny snorted, which caused some heads to turn.

"Stop!" she playfully hissed. "You're going to get us in trouble."

Steps echoed.

Someone was approaching.

*Oh great.*

Penny risked a glance back and saw a fellow student heading their way, the clip-clap of her Mary Janes getting closer and closer.

Relief followed as she gave a brief nod toward Penny and Joey and then turned to face the alcove, fingers carefully extracting a taper and using it to light one of the unlit candles.

After that, she stood for a while staring at the statue before giving a bit of a curtsy and then heading back to wherever she had chosen to sit.

"What are those candles for?" Penny asked, eyes starting to water from the scent of the one that had just been lit.

"What?" He looked over toward the alcove. "Oh, those are prayer candles."

"Prayer candles?"

"Yeah, you light one before offering up a prayer for someone."

"Are they always that strong?"

"People donate the candles, so sometimes they get scented ones mixed in." He saw her rubbing at her eyes. "Do you want to move?"

"No, no, it's fine." She didn't want to call any more attention to themselves than they already had. "Kind of nice, actually. I like cinnamon."

"Me too, though that one is really strong." He rubbed his own eyes. "Reminds me of those Atomic Fireball candies that we would shove into our mouths as kids."

"I remember those. I'd always have to spit mine into a cup of water for a while to let my mouth rest. Way too intense."

Joey chuckled.

Penny blinked and titled her head for a moment, looking up at the crucifix.

"What is it?" Joey asked.

"Nothing, I just thought—" She stopped as the smoke from the candles started to thicken and billow into the chapel.

And then Jesus turned toward her, eyes glaring, her name echoing from somewhere.

His loincloth was gone, an erection pointing her way, fluid oozing.

*No! No! No!*

She turned to Joey for help, but he was no longer there, his body having been replaced by something horrible, something wicked.

It grabbed her, hands like iron manacles on her wrists.

Something else grabbed her ankles, spreading them as she was thrust back against the hard wooden pew.

And then Jesus was coming toward her, erection growing until it was the size of a tree limb, fluids oozing out and trailing behind him as he approached.

"*PENNY, STOP!*" a voice cried, a hand struggling with her wrists. "*Stop!*"

Gasps echoed all around, one being from a nun who suddenly was standing over her, a hand going to her mouth.

"Stop!"

The hand pulled, and to her horror, she felt her own fingers slipping out from inside herself.

"What is going on here?" the nun demanded, hands reaching down for Penny's blouse, which she now realized had been ripped open, her breasts fully exposed.

And then she saw the eyes staring at her from the pews ahead, most belonging to students, but some were also adults who had come to the chapel, all of them shocked.

Joey was the one holding her wrist.

She fought against it, a ragged, "Let me go," leaving her lips.

He did.

She closed her blouse but couldn't secure it, the buttons having been ripped free.

"This is a church!" the nun snapped. "How dare you profane—"

"Sister, this isn't what it looked like," Joey protested.

"Up, both of you!" the nun snapped.

Penny struggled to her feet, one hand grabbing the pew for balance while the other held her blouse shut.

A second later she was on the ground, her legs unable to support her body.

"Young lady, I will drag you to the office if I have to," the nun said.

Penny got up once again, her legs better this time.

Unfortunately, both her hands were needed while doing this, which allowed her blouse to fall open, her breasts once again visible for all to see.

The nun grabbed her left wrist and Joey's right wrist and started marching them toward the doors, Penny's right hand unable to get both ends of her swaying blouse so that she could close it.

Shocked faces greeted her as they left the chapel and emerged into the hallway, the nun finally stopping when she saw Penny's breasts were once again exposed.

"Fix yourself," the nun demanded.

Penny did, tears streaming down her face, all while Joey continued to protest.

THE WORD "EXPULSION" came up while Penny was in the office but then was somehow dismissed after her aunt arrived, Penny being forced to sit out in the waiting area, a school sweater having been given to her to cover herself while her aunt and the school officials discussed things.

This lasted for over an hour, Penny forced to endure the stares and quick *look-aways* from everyone who was in the office. It was humiliating.

*Going back to class will be worse.*

*Simply walking the halls will be like enduring the walk of atonement in* Game of Thrones.

She almost wished she would be expelled.

That way she would never have to endure showing her face within the school again.

It didn't happen.

She was not expelled.

She also did not have to go back to class, not that day at least, her aunt simply telling her to gather her things and that they were going home once she emerged from the office.

NOTHING WAS SAID as they drove home, but then, once they were in the house, her aunt halted her from going up to her room to change.

"I want to talk to you," her aunt said, motioning her into the family room.

Penny hesitated, a desire to rid herself of the torn blouse and the shame that it now carried almost making her defy the instructions. Plus, there was her underwear, which were still damp from her activities, a faint smell present. She desperately wanted out of them.

She did as instructed.

"Tell me what happened," her aunt said once they were seated.

"Didn't they tell you— " she started.

Her aunt waved that away. "I know what they say happened, but I want to know what really happened, because despite what they might think, I know for a fact that you wouldn't just expose yourself like that in church and start masturbating."

Penny felt heat racing into her cheeks.

How could she ever go back there?

She couldn't.

She wouldn't.

"Penny," her aunt said.

Penny looked up.

"Tell me what happened," her aunt instructed. "Did you see something?"

Penny stared at her for several seconds, a question on how her aunt knew that she saw something going unvoiced.

Her aunt must have sensed the question though because she said, "Your mother used to have visions. Disturbing ones. And then started acting weird. After we played with a Ouija board."

"What?"

"She never told you?"

"No."

"It happened while we were in college. I don't even remember where we got the board or why we decided to try it, but we did." She paused. "That video of you that scared Nicky...it was almost identical to what happened to your mother when we played. Not long after that, she started doing odd things. And then obscene things." She paused again. "I'm guessing you've seen the movie *The Exorcist*?"

Penny nodded.

"Well, your mother once did the same with a crucifix. I woke up in our dorm room to see her in bed with it. She also once put rosary beads up inside herself and left them there all day long, finally pulling them out when we went to bed."

"Did you tell anyone?" Penny asked.

"Not at first. I wanted to, but your mother warned me that she would sacrifice me to Satan if I did. Afterward she was so tearful and apologetic. It was like she was two people in one. A split personality thing. And then one night..." She stopped, shaking her head, a hand wiping at her eyes. "Well, it got to the point where she started having me tie her to the bed so that she didn't do anything to me while we slept."

Penny couldn't believe it and simply stared at her aunt.

Her aunt wiped at her eyes again.

"What happened?" Penny asked. "To make you start tying her to the bed?"

Her aunt shook her head. "It's too—" She shook her head again.

"Please," Penny urged. "I need to know."

"I woke up one night with your mother on top of me. She was naked and straddling my chest. And then she scooted up and made me—" The sobs hit full force now, and she covered her face.

Penny didn't need her aunt to give voice to what had happened. It was pretty clear. Horrible too. She couldn't even comprehend the trauma of it, the total mindfuck that her aunt had experienced.

"I'm so sorry," Penny said, reaching out a hand.

Her aunt pulled away from her touch, and then apologized and let her take her hand.

"Is this why you two stopped speaking with each other?" Penny asked.

Her aunt nodded, mascara running down her face from the tears. "We both knew it wasn't her fault, that it wasn't *her* during that moment, but even so, it was impossible to get over." She wiped her eyes again. "And now I fear the same thing is happening to you."

Penny wanted to protest that theory but couldn't. Not after what had happened in the chapel.

"You've let something in," her aunt continued.

Again, Penny wanted to deny this, but she couldn't figure out how. Instead, she asked, "What do we do?"

"For starters, I think we should move you into the room in the basement. Just as a precaution."

"What? No," Penny said without even thinking. The

room down there was dark, damp, and frightening.

"Honey, I think it is for the best."

Penny didn't reply.

"Look what happened in the chapel." She waited a few seconds and then added, "What if something worse happened with Olivia or Nicky? What if you got on top of them like your mother did with—"

"Okay," Penny said, not wanting to visualize that. "You're right. I'll move into the basement room."

"Thank you."

"What else do we need to do?"

"I think I know someone who can talk with you. He's a priest, though he isn't with the local church. He has some experience with this type of thing."

"You mean do like an exorcism?"

"No, nothing that extreme. *Yet.* I think just having a talk with him would be good." She considered something. "If I contacted him today, he could probably be here by tomorrow."

"Okay."

"How do you feel about staying home the rest of the week?"

"Yes," she said, relief present. "After today, I don't think I could face anyone there, and now with what you've told me..." She didn't really need to finish.

"It's settled then," her aunt said. "We'll get you situated in the basement room and tomorrow, if he is willing, which I'm sure he will be, Father Collins will come speak with you."

"Okay."

"Now, why don't you go up and change and then meet me downstairs, so we can get the room straightened up a bit."

# SEVENTEEN

Penny heard the knock on the door and said, "It's open."

Olivia walked in. "You okay?"

"No," Penny said, wiping at her face. She hadn't been crying, not since earlier that afternoon, but she could still feel the streaks from where the tears had been. "You heard what happened?"

Olivia nodded.

"I'll never be able to go back."

"Yes you will. A couple days, everyone will have something else to fixate on."

"Bullshit."

"You'll see."

"I ripped my shirt open and started fingering myself in church," Penny said. "I can't even imagine what someone would have to do for everyone to shift their focus." She shook her head.

Olivia started to say something, but then stopped, and then started again, and then stopped again.

"What?" Penny asked.

"Nothing, it's just...well, I didn't know you were..." She made an obscene gesture with her hands near her groin.

"Masturbating in church," Penny said.

"Yeah."

"You said you knew what had happened?"

"I thought I did, but that's not what people are saying."

"What do you mean?"

"It's actually not as bad as you think."

Penny stared, waiting.

"Everyone says you two were having sex," Olivia said.

"What!"

"Yep. Right in front of the Virgin Mary." She chuckled. "And you both were dragged out by a nun while struggling to get your clothes back on."

"Jesus Christ, that's not what happened."

"Yeah, well, better than everyone thinking you were diddling yourself."

Penny was going to voice disagreement but then realized Olivia was probably right. In fact, Olivia *was* right.

"So," Olivia said. "Nothing to worry about."

"Yeah," Penny said with a forced laugh.

"Seriously. You're going to be a legend now. Sex in the chapel, and you've managed not to be expelled. That's, like, top shelf."

"And once the real story comes out?" Penny asked.

"No one will believe it. They won't want to."

Penny sighed.

"And then, on top of all that, my mom lets you move down here," Olivia said.

"More like strongly encouraged me to move down here," Penny said.

"It wasn't your idea?"

"No. Your mom is worried—" she started and stopped.

"About what?"

"Well, let's put it this way. Nicky isn't the only one who thinks I may be possessed by something."

"You've got to be kidding me."

Penny shook her head.

"All because of the Ouija board?" Olivia asked.

Penny nodded. "And because my mother apparently had something similar happen to her when they were in college."

"What?"

"It's the main reason they had a falling-out."

"Really?"

"That's what your mom said."

Olivia took a few seconds to process that, a puzzled look on her face, and then said, "I still think it's ridiculous, but hey, if that's what she wants to believe, then that's what she'll believe."

*I'm starting to believe it too...*

Rather than voice this, Penny asked, "How's Martin doing?"

Olivia sighed. "I don't know. He wasn't at school today and he hasn't been replying to any of my texts."

"After what he saw..." Penny started and then let the rest go unsaid.

Olivia didn't reply to that, her face getting a faraway look.

"You okay?" Penny asked after a few seconds.

"Yeah, it's just that, well...do you think Martin was cheating on me?"

"What? No way!"

"Then why would Jocelyn have been in that house?"

"There could be a dozen different explanations for that, none of them having anything to do with him."

"Like what?"

"Like some twisted pervert took her there because it was isolated."

"Yeah, but how would they have gotten inside?"

"Easy. They knew the key code."

"But how would they have known that?"

"I don't know. Maybe they watched his mom punch it in once while touring a house. Maybe they guessed it. Maybe Jocelyn knew it because Joey knew it from back when he was dating Leanne."

"Joey knew the code?"

"Yeah."

Olivia processed that for a few seconds and then said, "Still seems weird, especially since he won't talk to me now."

"You're overthinking things."

"Maybe."

"You are," Penny insisted. "Think about it. Not only did he find her body, but he found it in a house that you two technically broke into, one that his mom has been trying to sell for years. She's probably pissed. Not only will this make it even harder for her to sell it, she has learned that her son was using her key code to have sex with his girlfriend in the houses she's been showing."

Olivia didn't reply.

"Hell, for all you know, he is, like, grounded to the ninth degree. No phone, no internet, no nothing."

Olivia still didn't reply.

"And to top it off, there is a freaking killer out there."

"Do you think he did it?" Olivia asked.

"Martin?" Penny questioned, unable to keep the surprise from her voice. "No way."

Olivia went silent again.

"Do you?"

"I don't know," she said, voice so soft it was almost inaudible. "The police seemed to think that when they were talking to me."

"The police were fishing."

"Hmm."

"Seriously, they don't have a clue and simply were casting a huge net to see what they might catch."

"Maybe."

"Why would he have killed her?" Penny asked.

Olivia shrugged and then said, "Because he was cheating on me and she was going to reveal it."

"Okay, and when did he do this?"

A second shrug.

"Seriously, think about it. She disappeared that morning after leaving for school. You really think Martin would have had time to take her to that house, kill her, clean up, and then get to class before first bell?"

Olivia considered this.

"And," Penny added, "you said he got sick after discovering the body. I suppose they could try to say he faked that, but..." She made a gesture that conveyed how unlikely that would be.

"I guess you're probably right," Olivia said.

"WHY'S Penny in Grandpa's room?" Nicky asked while reaching for an egg roll.

Olivia looked at her mom, who looked over at Penny before saying, "Penny and I both felt like she could use her own space, and since that's the only other room in the house, we moved her stuff down there."

"But what if Grandpa wants to come back?"

"Honey, we've talked about this. He's going to stay at Sunrise because that's where all his friends are."

Nicky seemed satisfied with this answer, his focus shifting to his egg roll.

Nothing else followed for several seconds, the only sounds those of everyone munching away at their dishes.

And then...

"Is Penny really possessed by Satan?" Nicky asked.

Olivia's eyes went wide while her mother voiced, "Nicky!"

Penny herself seemed completely unfazed and went on eating.

"Where'd you hear that?" her mother asked.

"From Lonnie."

"Lonnie is just trying to scare you."

Nicky looked from their mother to Penny, his eyes darting away from her gaze once it shifted toward him.

*He really is scared of her,* Olivia noted to herself, somewhat amused.

FOLLOWING DINNER, Penny headed back down to her new room while Olivia went up into hers, the sense of emptiness odd given that she had only been sharing it with Penny for a month.

*How does she feel?*

During the course of three months, Penny had gone from living in a huge room with her own bathroom, to a hospital room, to sharing a bedroom with no bathroom, to living in a dark, somewhat creepy homemade corner room in the basement.

*But at least she once again has her own bathroom...*

It wasn't a very pleasant bathroom, but it was better than having to share one with Nicky.

A gentle knock echoed against her door.

Olivia knew it was her mother before she even stepped in.

"Are you okay?" her mother asked.

"Okay? Yeah. I'm fine."

"You sure? So much has happened these past few days."

*That's the understatement of the year,* she said to herself.

"You know, you can talk to me if you need to," her mother added. "I know that may seem awkward with what happened the other day, but please, if something is bothering you or upsetting you or if you just need to talk, I'm here."

"Okay."

Her mother stood for a few seconds, seemingly wanting more of a response, but then, when nothing else followed, she started to turn.

"Do you really think Penny is possessed?" Olivia asked.

"What do you think?" she asked, turning back.

"I don't really believe in that stuff."

"You don't?"

"Do you?"

A nod, then, "I've seen it."

"With her mother?"

Another nod and then, "Did Penny know the key code to that house?"

"What?" Olivia asked, caught off guard.

"The code to the house you and Martin were at yesterday. Was the code something she and her boyfriend would have known?"

"I don't know. I guess Joey knew it, but I'm not sure about her."

Her mother considered this.

"Why?" Olivia asked, though she had a feeling she knew.

"I'm just wondering. The police were asking about her whereabouts and I advised that she was home sick."

"They think she could have done this?"

"I don't know."

"That's crazy!"

"I know, but with the Ouija board video and her odd behaviors, and the fact that her mother was—" She halted herself.

"Her mother was what?" Olivia asked after several seconds.

More seconds came and went.

"Her mother was what?" she pressed.

"A member of the church of Satan."

Olivia's eyes went wide. "No way," she said, voice barely a whisper.

"Yes," her mother said. "I don't know if she ever really practiced, but I know she became a member."

"Why?"

"The same reason she started to star in those early porn movies. To spite our parents."

"Jesus," Olivia muttered and then quickly apologized.

A glare was aimed her way.

"Please," Olivia begged. "I can barely sit down after the other day."

"I'm not going to paddle you again."

"Ever?" she asked, hope present.

No answer.

"Please, I'm way too old to be spanked like that."

"Your school doesn't think so."

Olivia didn't reply to that.

"We'll talk about this later, once the craziness of this week has settled. In the meantime, I'm going to let you off with a warning."

"What about Penny? She uses the Lord's name in vain all the time."

"I know, and the next time I hear it, she is going to get a choice just like you did on what the punishment will be."

"It isn't fair," Olivia muttered.

"What?"

"Nothing."

"Tell me. What don't you think is fair?"

Olivia took a breath. "I dropped an f-bomb and you paddled me until I was bleeding, but Penny is caught exposing herself and masturbating in church and she isn't even in trouble."

"First, you were not bleeding, so—"

"I was!"

"Second," her mother continued, voice raised a bit, "you're right. It isn't really fair. But at the moment it's just something you're going to have to accept. I know it stinks. But that's life sometimes. I used to get away with things that your aunt got punished for and vice versa."

"Did you ever get away with exposing yourself in church?"

"I once got drunk on stolen communion wine in church, but your aunt was the one that got paddled."

"Why?"

"Because she knew my friends and I had stolen the wine and didn't make us give it back or stop us from drinking it down in the catacombs."

"How old were you?"

"I was fifteen and she was sixteen."

Olivia took a moment to process that. "Why didn't you get paddled?"

"I don't know. I certainly wasn't a stranger to it. But they decided she was to blame, and believe me, what she got was far worse than what you experienced the other day. She couldn't sit for weeks."

"You didn't get in trouble at all?" Olivia couldn't accept that. It made no sense.

"Nope. I guess they thought my humiliation of puking all over myself in front of everyone was punishment enough. Plus, there was the hangover."

"Good point."

Her mother raised an eyebrow.

*Fuck!*

"That morning you came back sick from Liz's house?" her mother questioned.

Olivia gave a slight nod.

"I had a feeling."

"You did?"

"I'm not as aloof to what goes on in your life as you might think."

Olivia fought back a grin.

She failed.

"Did I miss something?" Her mother crossed her arms.

"No," Olivia said. "I'm just...you caught me off guard."

"I see." Suspicion was present but didn't go anywhere, thanks to Nicky calling out for their mom from the hallway.

"What?" she asked.

"I need help with these charts."

"Okay, I'll be there in a second." She let out a sigh. "By the time he gets this merit badge, I'm going to be fluent in Morse code myself."

Olivia didn't reply to that.

"Anyway," she said, "all I wanted was to let you know you can talk to me."

"I know."

"And I want you to tell me if you notice anything going on with Penny. If she starts acting odd, you tell me."

"I think she's already crossed that line," Olivia said with a smirk.

"Just be aware, okay?"

"If you want me to keep an eye on her, maybe I should stay home tomorrow too."

A smile crossed her mother's face. "Nice try."

A second later, she left the room and headed into Nicky's to help him with the code charts.

Olivia sighed and then checked her phone.

Still nothing from Martin.

She then checked Facebook and Instagram.

Nothing.

Despair returned.

*He's done with me.*

# EIGHTEEN

Penny didn't like the cellar room; its old stone walls, unfinished ceiling, and narrow, blurred windows that couldn't open made it seem like a cell in the bowels of some castle dungeon. It was also cold and had a damp feel to the air.

*Is it really necessary?* she asked herself.

*Yes,* another voice said.

After what had happened in the chapel, there was no telling what might unfold. And if she did end up getting atop her cousin in the night like her mother had done to her sister...

*No!*

She shivered with disgust.

*Am I really possessed?*

A few weeks ago, she would have laughed at the idea, but now...

She turned toward the mirror that stood atop the dresser, her exhausted-looking face staring back at her.

"I don't want you in me," she said to whatever might be lurking behind her eyes.

No answer followed.

But something was in there.

Something had to be.

Nothing else made sense.

SLEEP WOULD NOT COME EASILY that night, so Penny tried to soothe her thoughts by listening to a *Sounds of Nature* collection she had downloaded while in the hospital following the car accident.

It took a while, but eventually the various sounds helped her mind drift away.

*NO!*

Penny opened her eyes upon a horror that she could barely process, one that had the body of a woman, the genitalia of a man, and the red-eyed face of a monster. It was atop her. Thrusting itself into her, her arms and legs unable to move due to bindings that held her in place, her mouth unable to scream because something foul gagged it.

*Pain.*

Between her legs, the thickness too much as it ruined her virginity, the smoky air and the odd flashing that filled the room making it impossible for her to grasp anything beyond the monster and what it was doing to her.

On and on this went, for how long she could not know, her thrashings against the bindings, the tears that streamed down her face, and the screams against the gag only seeming to encourage it.

And then a muffled grunt echoed from the creature as it finished.

. . .

*PENNY!*

*PENNY!*

*"Penny!"*

She fought against the restraints that held her, her leg seemingly breaking free and hitting flesh, a cry echoing.

Horror arrived, though this time it wasn't because of a monster that was atop her, but because she saw her aunt clutching herself where she had been kicked.

Penny sat up, panic fading, all while a horrible pain between her legs made itself known.

Gagging from the blow, her aunt curled into a fetal position on the cold concrete floor.

"Aunt Susan," Penny said, voice ragged. "I'm so sorry."

"You were...shrieking," Aunt Susan said, voice struggling between gasps. "I heard you through the vent."

"Something was on me," Penny said, a faint smell present in the room. She couldn't place it, nor could she see a source.

Her aunt shifted into a sitting position, staggered to her feet, and then cautiously eased herself onto the edge of the bed, one hand still clutching her gut. "A nightmare?" she asked.

Penny shook her head. "It seemed real. It was...it was..." *fucking me.*

"It was what, honey?"

Rather than reply, Penny lifted the bedsheets to peer between her legs. "Oh no," she said.

"What?"

Penny raised the bedsheet higher so her aunt could see.

A gasp echoed.

Blood was present, as was a crucifix that had previously been up on the wall.

"No, no," her aunt muttered while picking up and then dropping the crucifix. She stared at the blood on her fingers.

*Just like* The Exorcist, Penny thought.

"Did you..." her aunt started and then failed to finish.

Penny looked up at her.

"Did you ruin your own virtue?"

"My virtue?" And then it clicked. *Virginity.* "I didn't do this to myself. Not with this. Something was on me, fucking me."

Eyes wide, her aunt pulled back a bit.

Penny looked at her wrists and then thrust them toward her aunt. "See. It had me tied to the bedposts." She twisted to see if the ropes were still there. They weren't.

"But, no..." She started shaking her head.

"What?" Penny pleaded.

"If what you say is true, then this is more than you being possessed."

Penny stared at her.

"You've summoned something."

PENNY'S AUNT stayed with her the rest of the night.

Neither slept, her aunt simply sitting in the chair, crucifix in hand, staring, while Penny stayed curled in bed facing the stone wall, body atop the comforter so as not to mingle any further with the bloody parts within the sheets.

Her mind was a mess, her thoughts constantly shifting between utter disbelief of what her aunt had suggested, to acceptance and horror.

At one point she even said a prayer, though it wasn't to God, but her mom. She didn't ask for anything. It was more of a one-sided conversation where she constantly apologized about the accident even though she knew it hadn't been her fault. Not directly.

*I wish you were here. I wish...*

A thought arrived.

If what her aunt said was true, if she had somehow summoned a demon into this world, could she also summon her mom back into it?

If one, why not the other?

But how had she summoned the demon?

All she had done during the party was place her fingers on the planchet and then bam, all hell had broken loose. She hadn't called anything, or anyone. She hadn't spoken the name of any of hell's inhabitants. No one had. The two girls who had gone before her had simply asked for the names of those who would ask them to homecoming.

It didn't make any sense.

And even if she had spoken a name, it couldn't be that easy.

The world would be overrun with demons if it were.

And yet she had not imagined what had happened. Of this she was certain. The marks on her wrists and ankles were proof of this, as was the blood that had leaked out.

Something had tied her to the bedposts.

Something had fucked her.

Something with the body of a woman and the penis of man.

# PART TWO

# NINETEEN

"A crucifix?" Conrad Collins questioned while lighting a cigarette. "You mean like in *The Exorcist*?"

"Yes, exactly," Susan said.

"That's pretty fucked up."

"I know." She took the cigarette from his fingers. "That's why I want you to talk to her."

"As if I'm a priest," he confirmed, unease present.

"Yes."

"I still don't understand."

Susan sighed and took another drag before handing the cigarette back and saying, "I'm pretty sure she is making all this up just to fuck with me. She hates me, the church, and the school, and resents the fact that she is now stuck here rather than being out in sunny California."

"Okay, so call her out on it. Let her know you won't put up with this bullshit."

"That's exactly what I was going to do, but then I realized that it might be better to go along with everything. Make her think I'm a total believer in this possession bullshit."

"Why?"

"To control it. And to get her so tangled up in her lies that she has no choice but to admit that she was making it all up."

"Okay, so take her to a real priest. Let them look into it."

"I can't do that."

"Why not?" He rubbed at himself beneath the motel sheets, fingers finding a glob of goo on his shrinking penis.

"Because the school is this close"—she held up her thumb and index finger—"to expelling her. In fact, it was only after I reminded them of all the money my mother donated to them over the years that I was able to get them to back down."

"And you think what, that if she talks to a real priest, word will get back to the school?"

"Exactly."

He shook his head and rubbed away another glob of goo from between his legs, fingers smearing it onto the bedsheets. "I don't know. Pretending to be a priest." He shook his head again. "I could get in some serious trouble for that."

"You've done it before," she noted.

He didn't reply to that.

"And honestly, between that time and this, I'd be more worried about getting in trouble for *that* than for helping me out with Penny."

Once again, he didn't reply, her implication clear.

"But of course, no one ever has to know about that. Or this." Her hand slithered between his legs and started toying with him. "Oh my, what's going on down here?"

He pushed her hand away, but it quickly returned.

"Daddy, it's getting hard again," she said, voice taking on a child-like tone.

His heart skipped a beat, his mind wanting to go one way while his body went another.

"I DON'T THINK I should wear the priest costume," Conrad said twenty minutes later.

"Why not?" Susan asked, her back now to him as she sat on the edge of the bed, arms holding her knees to her chest. It was a familiar position, one she always assumed after he fucked her in the ass.

"Because that really will be over the top."

She let out a heavy sigh.

"Seriously, during their off hours priests walk around in normal clothing. I think that will be more realistic."

"Whatever."

"Susan."

Nothing.

"Susan, look at me," he said, voice stern.

She turned.

"I'm not backing out. I'm just making a suggestion. Okay?"

She continued to stare at him, seconds stretching, her silence a way of tormenting him. And then she smiled and said, "Daddy, are you sure I won't make a baby in my tummy now?"

"What have I told you, sweetheart?" he asked, playing along even though he wanted to be serious right now.

"That butts and mouths can't get pregnant."

"That's right, sweetheart."

SUSAN CHECKED her phone while Conrad was in the shower, his concern having caused her own to spike, though hers was not focused on Penny but on Olivia. Her daughter had turned into a wild card, what with her having skipped school the other day.

*I shouldn't have paddled her.*

The goal had been to get her hands on Olivia's phone, a recent password change on Facebook having made it so Susan couldn't view Olivia's profile and messages from her desktop while her daughter was at school. Getting control of the phone would have fixed that issue because she could have simply clicked the Facebook icon, which would have had the new password saved. It always did. Plus, she had wanted to see what Olivia and her "secret" boyfriend were up to.

She hadn't counted on Olivia being so stubborn.

And then for her to choose the paddling over giving up her phone?

That had really caught her off guard.

Pissed her off too, especially after she had given Olivia several chances to change her mind.

That was why she had hit her as hard as she could. She had been angry and had wanted to make sure Olivia would choose giving up the phone the next day when she caught her in some other act that required discipline.

"YOU GOT JIZZ all over Olivia's skirt," Susan said as Conrad emerged from the steamy bathroom.

"Me?" he questioned. "You're the one that couldn't keep it in your mouth."

"Sorry, Daddy, next time I'll be sure to swallow it all like a good girl." She pretended to pout.

"Be sure you do," he said. Then, shifting gears, "Are you really sure about this?"

She let out another sigh of annoyance. "How many times are you going to ask that?"

"It's just that we're about to cross the point of no return here," he said. "And if she figures out I'm not really a priest..." He let that hang in the air.

"I swear to God, if you try to back out of this, I'll— "

"Whoa, whoa," he said, holding up his hands. "I'm not going to back out. I'm just making sure this is what you think is best—that you've thought it through."

The glare she produced was intense.

"Come on, don't look at Daddy that way," he said.

She didn't sink back into their fantasy roles, which was never a good sign, given that it meant she was pissed.

"Be there in an hour," she instructed.

"I will," he replied.

"And put on the fucking priest costume like we agreed."

"Okay."

With that, she packed up her things, her daughter's extra school uniform back in the bag along with a few other items she had brought, and headed for the motel room door, her body once again attired in the office wear she always donned for these visits, even though she hadn't been to the office in weeks.

SUSAN TOOK a deep breath after leaving the motel room. It did little to calm her, but that was okay. Stress was to be expected after everything that had happened these last few days. Plus, Conrad had fucked her in the ass, which always put her on edge. She hadn't planned on that for today and hadn't properly prepared, even though the possibility of it happening when they got together was always present—especially if she was wearing one of Olivia's uniforms. And deep down she knew she had wanted—no, needed—the pain and humiliation of just such a fucking. In fact, it hadn't been enough, the guilt of what she had done the night before to Penny still present.

*I shouldn't have enjoyed it.*

Enjoy it she had though, so much that she had actually orgasmed while thrusting her sister's large strap-on penis deep into Penny's pussy.

It was the horror on Penny's face that had done it, as well as the pain she knew she was causing the girl.

Such a reaction from her own body had not been anticipated.

The fact that she wanted to do it again only made things worse.

# TWENTY

Aunt Susan had made her a fresh pot of coffee before taking Nicky and Olivia to school, a promise of being back by noon leaving her lips before the three headed off.

The priest would be there around one.

Penny had no idea what to expect.

Would he be skeptical of what she was experiencing, or familiar with such situations? If familiar, would he know what to do to make it stop?

In horror movies, homeowners would often bring priests into their homes to try to rid the place of spirits. Sometimes it worked, sometimes it didn't. Sometimes it seemed to work but then rebounded, the second time around worse than the first.

*This can't get any worse.*

*Or could it?*

A thought arrived, one that caused the coffee she was sipping to turn bitter against her lips.

She hurried down into her room and grabbed her iPad, fingers pulling up Google as she headed back up into the living room.

Hesitation hit.

She took another sip of her coffee, the newfound bitterness making her grimace.

*Demons sleeping with women* she typed into the search bar.

Over seventeen million results were returned, the first one titled *Sex With Demons Was Totally Chill Until the Church Ruined It.*

The next result proposed that since demons slept with women in the early parts of the Bible, it was safe to assume they still did in modern times.

The third result was titled *Incubus* and had a partial description that read: *a demon in male form that lies with sleeping women...*

She clicked that result.

A Wikipedia page appeared.

Quite a bit of information was presented on the history of demons sleeping with men and women, but what caught her attention was a sentence that read: *some sources indicate that it may be identified by its unnaturally large or cold penis.*

Chilled, she thought about the encounter, and while she couldn't say for certain that the penis had been cold, she did know it had been unnaturally large, the pain from its insertion still present.

Another part of the page talked about how a demon could take on characteristics of both men and women, which explained the large breasts.

After that was a paragraph that talked about the five ways to rid yourself of a demon, but then those were contradicted by a statement that read: *incubi do not obey exorcists, have no dread of exorcisms, show no reverence for holy things, at the approach of which they are not in the least overawed.*

However, it was a sentence farther down that stopped her in her tracks.

*A child fathered by a demon is called a cambion.*

Penny pushed away from the dining room table and then, after a few seconds, ran into the bathroom, the coffee she had consumed coming back up with a force that brought tears to her eyes.

Afterward, she leaned against the wall near the radiator, her body wishing it was on so that she could absorb some of its warmth.

She had questioned if things could get worse and the answer was yes. She could now be pregnant with a demon baby.

THE PRIEST WAS FAR YOUNGER than Penny had expected, her mind having visualized an older, slightly wrinkled man. Instead, he was a nice-looking middle-aged individual who had no wrinkles.

"Penny," Aunt Susan said, "this is Father Collins."

"Hi," Penny said, forcing a smile.

"Hello," Father Collins replied, holding out a hand.

Penny hesitated for a second and then shook it.

Nothing happened.

Relieved, she released the hand and then turned to her aunt, who suggested they head into the family room.

"Can I get you anything?" Aunt Susan asked once the two were seated. "Coffee, tea, soda?"

"No, nothing at the moment," he said and then looked at Penny.

She shook her head.

"Well then..." Her aunt wavered with indecision "Should I stay or do you want to talk with Penny one on one?"

Father Collins gave Penny an inquiring look, almost as if he wanted her to decide, but then said, "I think maybe it would be best if Penny and I spoke one on one."

"Okay. I'll be in the other room if you need me." With that, her aunt stepped from the family room, hands pulling shut the French doors so that they would have some privacy.

Penny watched her go and then turned to Father Collins.

He gave her a nervous smile and said, "Susan told me you're worried you might be possessed by a demon."

Penny nodded.

"And she said something about an encounter last night?"

Penny nodded again, fighting back tears.

"Tell me what happened."

TEARS FLOWED down the teen's face as she described the events that had unfolded during the night, Conrad struggling to accept that this was all an act. She was too good for this to be fake. Too distraught. Too emotional.

But then that would mean...

*No!* he said to himself, pushing the idea away.

Demons weren't real, and thus being fucked by one wasn't possible.

She was acting.

Plain and simple.

And as far as the tears were concerned, she was likely

thinking about her mother and the car accident to help produce them.

"...might now be pregnant with a demon baby," Penny concluded.

He handed her a tissue and then asked, "You were a virgin until last night?"

"Yes," she said with a nod.

"Then I think it is highly unlikely that it impregnated you this time around," he advised.

"Really?" she asked, some hope present.

He nodded and put a hand out to comfort her.

"But what if it comes to me again tonight?"

"If it does, and if it successfully penetrates you again, there are steps we can take that can rid you of its seed."

"Online I read that incubi are not frightened away by priests or exorcism."

"Where online did it say that?" he asked.

"Wikipedia."

He raised an eyebrow.

"I did some research today," she added.

"Well, it is true that some demons are harder to get rid of than others, but that is the demon themselves. Ridding yourself of the demon seed is a different matter all together, one that I'm guessing they didn't really talk about on the web page."

"I don't think they did," she admitted. "Or I might have missed it. I was upset while reading it."

"Understandably so."

A few seconds of silence followed and then Penny asked, "How did this happen?"

"Your aunt says you were fooling around with a Ouija board."

"Yeah, but I only touched it. I didn't even ask a question."

"Sometimes that's all it takes, which is why we are so adamant about urging young people—or anyone really—to avoid messing around with them. Olivia should have known better than to let you fool around with one."

Penny gave him a puzzled look and for a moment he thought she was going to ask a question, but then nothing followed.

"Plus, Susan mentioned your mother was a Satanist?"

"I guess."

"You didn't know?"

Penny shook her head.

"Well, if she really was and she kept it a secret, then there is no telling what types of activities and ceremonies she took part in over the years. It's entirely possible that something had already latched on to her and then bounced over to you during the accident."

"Bounced over?"

He nodded. "Demons are tricky, and once they are in our world, the last thing they want to do is go back to hell. This one likely stayed with you, hovering, waiting. The Ouija board was the invitation it needed to complete the transfer."

Penny gave this some thought, her face once again taking on that puzzled look while she processed what he had said.

*She's probably startled by how ready I am to believe all this, given how ridiculous it all sounds.*

In movies, the priests were always a bit skeptical, trying to point toward rational explanations before leaning toward the supernatural one.

*Should I have gone that route?*

*Will she grow suspicious of my readiness to believe?*

*Does she know I'm bullshitting her while she is bullshitting me?*

No.

A priest wouldn't do something like that.

"If I'm possessed, how did it also come to me last night?" she asked.

"That's a bit more difficult to explain. Demons are not of our world, so they have abilities that are way beyond our comprehension." He paused for effect and then added, "What troubles me about your situation is that for a demon to manifest the way it did so that it could actually be seen in physical form and penetrate you speaks of a power that I've not yet encountered before. Whichever demon this is, it is not a minor figure. And the fact that it wants to reproduce is even more troubling."

"So what do we do?" she asked.

"First things first, we need to figure out which demon this was, and if he was a major or minor figure within the ranks of hell."

"How do we that?"

"Let's start with a description. Every demon has peculiarities and personalities, and though this was only the first time it manifested itself to you, there might be things you witnessed that can help in identifying it."

# TWENTY-ONE

*Did you tell your mom about the party?*

Olivia stared at the text for several seconds and then typed: *No, why?*

*A priest she is having me talk to knows about it.*

*WTF?*

*Yeah.*

*How?*

*That's what I'm trying to figure out.*

*Are you at the church?*

*No. He came to the house.*

*Really?*

Nothing else followed.

"What's wrong?" Martin asked, crumpling up the brown paper bag that had held his lunch, the confiscation of his car keys by his parents having made it so they now had to eat at school.

"Penny says my mom is making her talk to a priest and that the priest knew about the party with the Ouija board."

"Whoa, really?" He tossed the crumpled-up lunch bag toward a garbage can. It missed.

"Yeah. Did you tell your parents about it?"

"No," he said, getting up to get the bag. "Of course not."

"What about the police?"

He shook his head. "But that doesn't mean someone else didn't mention it. They've been talking to everyone."

"But why would the party even come up? It was weeks ago."

He shrugged. "I have no idea, but with the video having gone viral and them asking about the occult, it seems likely that someone mentioned it."

Olivia thought about this but then said, "But if that is the case, why haven't they talked to Penny or spoken to your parents? And how would this priest know about it?"

Martin didn't have an answer for that.

"It doesn't make sense," Olivia voiced.

"Word spreads," Martin said. "Or maybe your mom knew about the party all along and just didn't say anything."

"So she'll paddle me for saying 'fuck' but not for going to a party and then lying about it?"

"I don't know," he said.

"I'm telling you, something is off about this. And her."

Martin motioned for her plate, which had a half-eaten hamburger and some soggy fries on it, all from the cafeteria.

She handed it to him.

He dropped it into the garbage can.

"Why is your mom having her talk to a priest?" he asked, returning to her side at the outdoor table.

"She thinks she's possessed."

"What? For real?"

"Yeah."

"Yikes."

"Tell me about it. She even made her move into the basement room."

"The one your grandpa used to live in?"

"Yeah."

"Jeez." Then, after a few seconds, "Didn't you want that room?"

"Eh..." She made a *so-so* motion "For a while. I thought it would be perfect for sneaking in and out."

"Ah, for illicit midnight encounters with yours truly?"

"Something like that," she said with a grin. "But then your mom started showing houses and you got the key code..." Her voice faded, thoughts of what they had discovered returning.

Martin seemed to experience the same somberness that hit her.

"Did they really fire her?" she asked.

"Yeah," he said.

"That is such bullshit."

"Tell me about it."

Nothing else followed, Olivia unsure of what to say.

Then, "You know, my mom asked if Penny knew the key code."

"Really?"

"Yeah."

"Does she think Penny might have killed Jocelyn?"

"I have no idea."

"But she doesn't even have a car. And she was in the hospital. Wasn't she?"

"No. She came home on Sunday."

"Oh."

"But like you said, she doesn't drive. She wouldn't even have had access to a car."

"Unless Joey picked her up and they are in cahoots."

Olivia shook her head. "That's not funny."

Martin didn't reply.

"Plus, he was here that day. Remember? He was totally panicked about his phone dying after he promised to call her during lunch."

"Oh yeah." Martin chuckled. "I've never seen him freak out like that."

"He really likes her."

"So much so that they had sex in church."

Olivia smacked him.

"Ow." He rubbed his arm. "Seriously though, what the hell happened to her? Joey won't talk about it. And you know what everyone is saying."

"I honestly don't know," Olivia said. "She doesn't either. One moment they were chilling in the chapel, and the next she had ripped open her shirt and was fingering herself."

"That's really fucked up."

"Yeah."

"Maybe your mom is right. Maybe she is possessed."

"Oh please!"

"Seriously, think about it. That moment with the Ouija board was really chilling, and then whatever happened to her in the chapel was totally fucked up."

"You don't even believe in this stuff," Olivia noted.

"True, but that doesn't mean I don't think there could be forces at work here. Things we don't understand."

"Aliens," she said, her hands motioning as if she were the guy on the History Channel show.

"Maybe..." he said and then hummed a really poor rendition of the *X-Files* theme. "Come on, we better get back."

"What time is"—she started while looking at her phone —"oh shit."

She had ten minutes before her PE class started, which meant she had to be changed and ready to go before the bell or else Ms. Carver would make her run laps.

GYM CLASS DID NOT GO WELL.

Olivia wasn't late, but she still had to run laps.

Everyone did.

Four laps around the school property, which equaled a cross-country mile.

Making it worse, the guys' gym class was playing flag football in the upper field, many of them turning to watch while the girls ran by.

Some even cheered.

It was humiliating, especially for those who had shirts that didn't fully accommodate the extra growth that puberty had given them.

Olivia was one, and like most of the girls in her class, she hadn't changed into a sports bra for PE—didn't even have one in her locker—and simply relied on the support of her standard underwear, which did little to prevent the bounces that her running produced.

Four passes, and each time Olivia felt like she was on a catwalk or an auction block.

It was ridiculous.

Running a cross-country mile itself was stupid, but to have to do it right by the guys' class was downright sadistic. And the fact that the guys weren't reprimanded for their cheers all while the girls could get in trouble if they folded in the waistbands of their skirts to shorten the length was unacceptable.

In fact, if she said anything about the cheers she would probably get sent to the office for being a distraction to the guys, her lack of a sports bra used as evidence that she somehow wanted to have her breasts bouncing around for their amusement.

"Boys will be boys" was the typical response to such things.

Girls, however, couldn't be girls.

It pissed her off.

And then she tripped, her frustration with the fourth round of cheering having clouded her awareness.

"*Cushioned landing!*" someone shouted.

"*Watch out!*" someone warned.

"*Olivia is down!*" someone laughed.

No one offered to help her up, the girls in her class simply sidestepping her as if she were an obstacle, all while the boys continued to hoot and holler.

"You okay?" a voice finally asked as she pushed herself back onto her feet.

Olivia twisted a bit and saw that it was the guys' PE instructor.

"Fine," she snapped, dusting herself off.

"Ground's uneven over here. You have to watch your step."

Olivia bit back a response, the newfound frustration and anger she felt over the fact that he had been present during the cheering and hadn't put a stop to it almost too much for her to contain.

She continued her run, her own PE instructor chiding her on her time as she passed by.

Olivia wanted to tell her to fuck off, but once again managed to bite back the response.

Not long after that, she was in the locker room pulling her PE shirt off, arms crisscrossed over her head, when she was shoved from behind, her elbows smashing into the metal edge of the open door.

Laughter echoed from several different girls as two held her against the locker, her arms stuck in her shirt, which nullified her ability to fight back. She also couldn't see, the fabric blocking her view.

Hands grabbed her gym shorts and pulled them down, along with her underwear, comments on the bruising from the paddling being made while someone wrote something on her with a marker, her struggles useless against all the hands that kept her pressed into the corner, her cries muffled.

"Do her shirt too!" someone said.

"Totally!" someone else agreed.

The sound of a picture being taken followed.

And then it was over, the girls fleeing before Olivia could get her shirt off to see who it had been.

Stunned faces of her classmates turned away as she looked toward them.

And then she saw her blouse sitting on the bench, a giant pentagram having been drawn on the back in red marker along with the words *Satan's Whore* and *Bitch* and *Cocksucker*.

OLIVIA KNEW one of the girls involved in the incident was Leanne, but she couldn't prove it, and since none of her classmates would admit that they had seen what had happened, Ms. Carver and the dean decided they couldn't do anything about it.

Making things worse, they wouldn't let her go home because her mother didn't answer the phone when they called, so she had to finish up the day wearing her school sweater over her blouse to hide the writing, the heat far too much for the extra layer, which made her sweat like crazy.

It was either that or wear one of the loaner blouses the school had on hand, but she didn't want to do that, the only one that wasn't too small being far too big for her.

"IT'S MY FAULT," Joey said as they walked home.

Martin and Olivia both looked at him, Martin asking, "Why?" while Olivia said, "What?"

"She cornered me at lunch," he said. "Thinks we're still together even though we clearly aren't, and then started talking homecoming." He shook his head. "And then she got royally pissed off when I told her I was going with Penny."

"So why the fuck did they jump me?" Olivia demanded, even though she already knew the answer to that. She was there and Penny wasn't, so she had been the next best thing. "And why the fuck does she think you two are still together?"

"You know how she is," Joey said, voice weary.

"Denial, baby," Martin said. "Not just a river in Egypt."

Olivia gave him a look followed by a headshake and then turned back to Joey.

"She feels we were just going through a tiff—her word," Joey said. "And that after being together for a year we just needed a few weeks apart so that we could reaffirm our love or something."

"What a loon," Martin said.

"And she promised to start putting out once we're together again."

"Oh, well in that case—" He dodged a swing from Olivia.

"She thinks you two had sex in the chapel," Olivia said and then sent a second jab at Martin as he rejoined them, this one catching him in the upper arm.

"Jeez," Martin said. "So violent. Is it that time of the—"

Olivia sent a glare his way that halted him in his tracks, the words freezing in his throat.

Joey waited a second and then said, "You really think that's it?"

"I know it is," Olivia confirmed. "And she has probably convinced herself that the only reason you're with Penny is because of it."

Joey didn't reply.

"So you two never..." she started and just let it hang in the air.

"No, well, not *it*. Other stuff."

"Didn't you make her ralph all over herself behind the bleachers?" Martin said.

"Jesus," Olivia said.

Joey didn't reply. Didn't need to. They already knew it was true. And they weren't the only ones. Almost everyone in their class was aware of it, the ridicule and scorn Leanne had suffered in the weeks that followed one of the worst things Olivia had ever seen.

She grinned.

Maybe it was time for a resurgence of that event, a reminder of the humiliation she had endured.

# TWENTY-TWO

Conrad listened but didn't really hear what Juliet Howard was saying as she spoke to the crumpled tissue clutched within her hands, knuckles white, cheeks streaked with salt where the tears had fallen, his mind too focused on Penny and the description she had given him of the demon to process whatever new bit of "evidence" Juliet had imagined that proved her husband didn't love her anymore.

"Dr. Collins?" Juliet asked.

He didn't reply, not at first, but then after she asked if he was okay he said, "I'm fine, I'm just trying to wrap my mind around why you think this proves he doesn't love you anymore."

"Isn't it obvious?"

"No, I'm sorry."

"But his email clearly stated that we're just staying together for the sake of the kids and once they're in college —" She burst into tears again, the sobs sounding like the shrieks of a dying animal.

*Shit.*

*Email?*

*To whom?*

The one time she actually did have legit evidence of her fears and he hadn't been paying attention.

"Have you spoken to him about this email?" he asked.

Juliet shook her head.

"Why not?"

"He'll get upset that I read it."

"Yes, but that will just be his attempt at deflecting."

Juliet contemplated this, lips tight as she once again began to stare at the tissues she clutched.

He waited, his focus shifting toward Susan once again.

"Maybe I should talk to his mother," Juliet said, words wet.

"You've tried that before."

A nod.

"She'll find a way of using your words to manipulate her son."

Another nod and then, "But this time I have evidence that she is doing this."

"How so?"

"The email."

Conrad frowned. "What email?"

Her eyes went wide. "The one Bradly sent her."

"Yes, but how is that evidence that she is being manipulative?"

"Because she was telling him not to wait and that if he isn't happy now he needs to end it, and that he shouldn't worry about losing half of everything in a divorce because of the new evidence she has of my affair."

Had Conrad been sipping a beverage he would have spit it out. "What affair?"

"I'm not having one, but she clearly wants him to think

that I am so that he then leaves me." More tears. "I don't know what to do."

Conrad waited several seconds and then said, "You need to talk to him. Explain that you're not having an affair. Nip that in the bud before it grows."

Juliet shook her head. "I almost wish she hadn't replied to me by mistake."

"Replied to you?"

"Have you been listening to anything I've been saying today?" she demanded, her anger catching him off guard.

"Of course I have, but sometimes it's hard to understand what you're saying when your words are mangled by tears."

"Oh, well then I'll try not to be so emotional when baring my soul to you."

"Juliet. Are we going to have to bring out the pillow again?" he asked.

She stared at him for several seconds, struggling to maintain a look of anger.

He waited.

The anger fell away and she shook her head. "No."

"Okay. Now explain what you mean by she replied to you."

"The email I read. I only saw it because she replied to me by mistake rather than to Bradly."

"Are you sure it was a mistake?" he asked.

"She clearly was talking to him in her reply," Juliet said.

"Yes, but maybe she wanted you to see this and think it was sent to you in error so that you and he would have another argument. Think about it. When you reply to a message, all you do is click Reply. You don't have to type anything up in the Send To bar. So the chance that she would send this to you by mistake seems far-fetched."

Juliet started nodding.

"And given how manipulative she is, this does seem like something she would do in an attempt to sow discord."

More nodding and then, "But what about his message, the one talking about how we are going to stay together until the kids are in college?"

"Were there any other back-and-forth conversations between them below the message she replied to?"

"No."

"Then maybe he didn't even write it."

"What?"

"What if she created an email address that looks like his and sent it to herself so that she could then 'accidentally' reply to you?"

Juliet considered that and then gave another nod.

"You've said before, she is pretty tech savvy and that you've caught her a few times spying on you with sock puppet accounts on Facebook."

Another nod and then, "Do you think that maybe I shouldn't say anything to him at all? Simply ignore the email?"

"That is certainly an option. Especially if you do discover the email address is a fake."

A smile appeared, one that temporarily brightened his day as their session concluded.

*"It had breasts and a giant penis that it wagged at me several times,"* Penny had said.

*"Wagged?"* Conrad had asked. *"What do you mean?"*

*"Grabbed it in its hand and flopped it up and down at me."*

His smile faded.

Her tears had seemed so real.

*Too real.*

*And the marks on her wrists from the ropes were so deep.*

Memories of Susan wagging the giant strap-on at him while laughing echoed in his mind.

*No, she wouldn't.*

*Would she?*

*Why?*

"Dr. Collins?" a voice asked.

Conrad blinked and looked toward the office door.

Terry, his temporary receptionist, was standing in the doorway, concern present on her face.

"Yes?" he asked.

"No one else is on the schedule for this evening," she said.

"I know, and I'm sorry, I should have let you know that I would be staying a bit late, but that you could close up."

"Okay, thanks."

She didn't leave the doorway.

"Something else?" he pressed.

"No...well...I was wanting to ask you, have you given any more thought on my becoming full-time?"

"Sorry, not yet. But I will."

"Okay. It's just that, like I said, I've had another offer and they're waiting for a reply and it really doesn't seem like Susan is coming back, so I was hoping—"

"If you have another offer, I think you should take it," he said.

"I...oh..."

"Anything else?"

"Um...no, I guess not." She turned and left.

Conrad took a deep breath.

Terry was good at her job, and having her full time would have been ideal, but that would have meant he would need to let Susan go, which would not have been ideal.

Susan was crazy.

He had known this for quite some time now, but had always overlooked it given how much he enjoyed their time together outside of the office.

*And sometimes while in the office...*

*"Look what was in my sister's things,"* Susan had said that day, wagging the giant strap-on, which had been hidden beneath her skirt all morning while she sat behind the desk, signing in patients and taking calls. *"Want to bend over and give it a try?"*

The answer had been a solid no, and following that, he had never seen the strap-on penis again, the item having disappeared from his thoughts until that morning.

*"It had breasts and a giant penis that it wagged at me several times."*

No.

Susan wouldn't have done that to her.

She couldn't have.

Penny would have known it was her.

Wouldn't she?

He dwelled upon this for another hour, his mind unable to reach a conclusion. One thing he did know, if Penny was telling the truth—if she really had been fucked by someone that night—then this was no longer a simple matter of him pretending to be a priest to help out Susan. No. If that penis had actually been that strap-on, and if Susan had been the one wearing it, then she had crossed a line that could not be excused, one that she was secretly dragging him across as well.

SUSAN STARED at Olivia's ruined blouse for a long time, anger building with each passing second.

*Leanne Duncan.*

Though she hadn't seen her attackers, Olivia was confident it had been Leanne and her clique who had carried it out.

The fact that Leanne was best friends with Jocelyn and had helped publicize the video of Penny having a seizure while playing with the Ouija board helped cement this theory.

*"She's upset because she thinks Penny stole Joey,"* Olivia had needlessly explained.

Susan had nodded during this even though she had already known it, the messages that Olivia and Martin had shared on the topic having been previously read prior to Olivia changing her Facebook password.

*Leanne Duncan.*

She pulled up the girl's profile on Facebook and almost laughed with pity when she saw that the profile picture had recently been updated to one of her and Joey, their cheeks pressed together while they took the selfie.

*Poor pining fool.*

The pity was short-lived.

It had been one thing for Leanne to torment Penny, since that had helped push her toward the point of believing she was possessed by a demon, but for her to go after Olivia...that was another thing altogether.

*And the school won't do anything about it.*

She thought about Jocelyn and the muffled noises she had made as the blade opened her flesh.

Would Leanne squeal like that too?

# TWENTY-THREE

Nothing happened during the night, but the next morning drama unfolded. Fortunately, it didn't involve Penny. Instead, Olivia was throwing a fit about her mom's insistence that she go to school.

It lasted for nearly thirty minutes, Olivia refusing to put on her uniform while her mom demanded that she get dressed or else she would drag her to school as is and let her get a uniform infraction.

Had bets been taken, Penny would have put money on Aunt Susan winning this one, her mind expecting her aunt to eventually bring out the paddling threat.

She would have lost.

It was surreal.

So much so that even Olivia said, "I didn't think she would give in like that."

"Me either," Penny said.

Several seconds came and went, the two simply staring into their coffee mugs.

Penny's phone buzzed.

It was from Aunt Susan.

It read: *Father Collins is going to call you in a little while to discuss some things.*

*Okay,* Penny replied.

"Who's that?" Olivia asked.

"Your mom," Penny said. "Just wanted to let me know that Father Collins is going to call me soon."

"Do you have another meeting with him today?"

"I don't think so."

"Does he really think you're possessed?"

Penny hesitated. "I think so."

"Jesus."

"And he's not the only one."

"I know. My mom is totally fruit loops about this shit too."

Penny didn't reply to this.

Olivia stared at her for several seconds and then said, "Oh my God, you don't think so too, do you?"

"I didn't, but then..." Her voice faded as the memory of the other night came into focus.

"What?" Olivia pressed.

Penny burst into tears.

OLIVIA LISTENED while Penny described what had unfolded, her mind wanting to call bullshit on the entire thing but unable to, given how devastated Penny obviously was.

"Was it like before?" Olivia asked.

Penny wiped at her eyes. "Before?"

"In the chapel. When you were...you know." She made a masturbatory gesture.

Penny shook her head. "I don't know. This seemed different."

"What do you mean?"

Another slight shake of the head. "It's like—I don't know—it was more real."

"More real?"

Penny nodded. "I think it crossed over this time."

"Crossed over?"

Another nod.

"What does that mean exactly?"

"Father Collins says that these things can take a bit of time. Like the demon has to work its way into this world. That's why the first few times I just heard it calling my name, and then in the chapel actually saw it, and then the other night it finally made it through and...and..." Her lip quivered.

Olivia put a hand out onto Penny's and said, "It's okay."

Penny pulled her hand back. "It's not okay."

Startled, Olivia didn't know what to say.

"It fucking raped me," Penny said.

Olivia didn't reply.

"And there was nothing I could do to stop it," Penny added.

"You just woke up to it being there?" Olivia asked, needing something to say.

Penny nodded. "One moment I was asleep, and the next I was tied to the bed and it was on top of me."

"It took the time to tie you down?"

Another nod while she presented her wrists, marks visible where the skin had been sheared away.

"And you woke up like that?"

"Yeah." She pulled back her wrists, left hand rubbing the right one.

Olivia frowned.

"What?" Penny asked.

"It seems weird, doesn't it?"

Penny blinked.

"I mean, the entire thing is weird and horrible, but it tied you down, all without you even knowing it." She paused for a second. "I don't know why, but that just seems odd to me. Like why would a demon need to tie you down? Wouldn't it be strong enough to simply keep you still?"

"Father Collins said that being tied like that is pretty common once one enters into the physical world," Penny noted.

"Oh." She considered that and then said, "Wait a second. Is being raped by a demon so prevalent that there are actually elements that can be considered common?"

"I guess."

"Huh."

"I'm not making this up," Penny said, bitterness present.

"No, no, I'm not suggesting that," Olivia said. "I'm just surprised is all."

"Surprised," Penny muttered.

"I'm sorry. I can't even begin to imagine how horrible this was." She reached out again in an effort to cup Penny's hands, but Penny didn't allow it.

Hesitation followed.

Olivia eyed her coffee, which was getting cold.

Penny hadn't even touched her own.

"Do you think moving back into my room will help?" Olivia asked.

"I don't think your mom would like that," Penny said.

"But what if the only reason it finally crossed over was because you were alone?"

"And what if it wasn't? What if it crosses over again and fucks us both?"

Olivia hadn't really considered that, mostly because she

still hadn't fully accepted the idea that a demon had crossed over into their world and raped her cousin. It just didn't seem possible.

"We could sleep in shifts," she suggested. "Like in that movie. The one with the guy that killed the kids in their dreams."

Penny gave her a puzzled look.

"Fuck, what was"—it clicked—"Freddy Krueger. *Nightmare on Elm Street.* They would sleep in shifts so they could wake each other if they started having nightmares."

"But this wasn't a nightmare," Penny said.

"Yeah, but still, do you think this demon thing will come if someone is watching?"

"It hasn't stopped it before."

"Those other times no one else saw it, just you. So maybe it's the same with what is happening now."

"You think so?"

"I have no idea, but I do know you said my mom shook you awake, so it seems that works."

"Huh, yeah, maybe."

"Did my mom untie you?"

Penny thought about that for a second and shook her head. "I don't think so."

"You simply woke up to my mom shaking you and then found the crucifix and the blood?"

"Yeah."

"I wonder then..." She didn't know what she wondered, but something was tickling the back of her mind.

Penny didn't press her. Instead, she asked, "Do you think Martin would let us use his Ouija board again?"

"What? Why?"

"I was thinking. If I was able to call up a demon with

barely even touching the thing, maybe I can call up something that could help when I actually put effort into it."

Olivia shook her head while saying, "I don't know if that is such a good idea."

"Why?"

"What if you just end up summoning something even worse?" she asked.

"How could this get any worse?"

"I don't know."

Penny eyed her for several seconds and then sighed. "You don't believe any of this anyway, so what do you care?"

"Come on, don't be like that," Olivia said.

"So you do believe it?"

Olivia didn't reply.

"See," Penny snapped.

"Okay. I'm not a hundred percent on it being a demon that crossed over and fucked you, but I do know something horrible happened to you."

"If not a demon, then what?"

"I don't know."

"You think I fucked myself with that crucifix?"

*Yes.* "I don't know."

"And what about my wrists? How would I fuck myself while tied up like that?"

"I don't know."

Penny pushed herself up from the table but then didn't make a move to leave. Instead, she just stood there.

Olivia waited.

"If not a demon, then who?" she asked, voice a bit calmer.

"Like I said, I don't know what—"

"No, never mind all that," Penny said with a wave of her hand. "Something fucked me. Of that, I have no doubt. It slammed itself into me with a cock that was so big that I thought my insides were being ripped apart."

Olivia grimaced.

"And it had breasts. Big ones that bounced while it was fucking me. So. If not a demon, then who? Who was in the house that night and went into my room that has red eyes, a twisted-up face, giant breasts, and a huge horse cock?"

Had the situation been any different, Olivia would have burst out laughing, but the desperation in Penny's face kept that in check.

Penny waited.

"I have no idea," Olivia admitted.

"Exactly."

Her phone rang.

"FATHER COLLINS," Penny said.

"Penny, how are you?" Father Collins asked.

"Okay."

"How was last night? Any incidents?"

"No," Penny said, shaking her head even though he couldn't see her.

Olivia watched from her seat at the table, the look on her face one of intrigue.

"That's good."

"It is?" Penny asked, hope present.

"Well, good that nothing happened," he said. "But I don't want you to think this means it's over. Things like this, a few days can come and go between incidents."

"So you think it will happen again."

"Unfortunately, yes. I'm certain of it."

Penny felt a sinking sensation in her chest.

"And the second time it will probably be worse," he added.

"Worse?"

"Demons like to cause pain. Human suffering is their drug of choice. I don't mean to sound crass, but now that it has deflowered you, it will likely want to cause trauma to other parts of your body."

"Other parts?" The sinking feeling grew. "You don't mean..." She couldn't say it.

"Anally," he said, voice somber.

"My God," Penny muttered.

"But there may be something we can do to prevent it," he said. "Or at least make it realize it isn't worth the effort once the pain starts."

"How?"

"It isn't pleasant, especially if you're carrying a demon taint with you, but it will certainly be better than the alternative. If it works."

"What is it?" she asked.

He told her.

# TWENTY-FOUR

Conrad stared at the phone for a long time before slipping it back into his pocket, disgust worming its way through his system.

"So?" Susan asked.

"She said maybe," he said.

"Maybe?"

"Yeah, she wants to think about it."

"Think about it?"

"Yeah."

Susan shook her head in frustration.

"Maybe this is for the best," he voiced.

"What do you mean?" Susan asked.

"It could make her really sick."

"No, it wouldn't."

"It might, and then she'd end up in the hospital again."

"Nah, it would just burn like hell for a few hours and make her rethink this entire ruse."

"How do you know?"

She gave him a coy smile, one that actually sent a chill

through his body, and then said, "Daddy, are you going to punish me for being so mean to poor Penny?"

"DADDY, PLEASE, YOU'RE HURTING ME!" Susan cried, the pain real as Conrad forced his dry cock into her butt while she was bent over the arm of his patient sofa, her voice echoing throughout the empty office.

Conrad didn't reply as he went on pressing himself into her, his average-sized manhood somehow feeling like a bowling pin as it stretched her.

*It'll be worse for Penny,* she thought and grinned before biting into her own arm as her bowels spasmed against the intruder.

Several thrusts followed before he pulled out, hands spinning her around by her pigtails, a demand that she finish him with her mouth being made.

She did and then spit it up all over herself as if she couldn't swallow the disgusting load.

"I'm sorry, Daddy." She pouted as she twisted against his hold and looked down at herself. "Oh no, I ruined my blouse."

"It's okay," he said while pulling his pants back up from around his ankles. "You just need more practice."

"Yes, Daddy," she said and then, looking up at him with her big brown eyes, asked, "Can I go wash up?"

"You may."

Susan pushed up from the floor and headed into the bathroom, her hands carefully removing the semen-stained blouse and putting it into a plastic bag. Following that, she washed out her mouth with some Scope and then sat on the toilet for ten minutes to see if any blood came out. A bit did, but nothing she needed to worry about. It wasn't like when she was in college and missed class for three days.

A shudder at the memory arrived.

And then anger.

She took a deep breath and then finished up in the bathroom.

Conrad was waiting, a desire to ask her if she was okay being suppressed.

*Poor guy,* she thought to herself with amusement.

He totally loved what he did to her, but then felt guilty afterward. It was great.

"Seven o'clock," she said while grabbing her things.

He nodded and then asked, "What about your kids?"

"I'm setting Nicky up with a sleepover at Kyle's house."

"And Olivia?"

"Not sure yet. I'll figure something out." *I'm going to drug her ice tea.*

Nothing else was said, which was good because she needed to get moving, her fingers pulling out a pre-paid phone she had bought earlier and thumbing a text while walking to her car.

SHE LEFT WEARING *the pleated uniform skirt,* Conrad realized as he sat in his office chair, eyes staring at the empty patient couch, disappointment with himself for not bringing up his thoughts on the strap-on dominating his mind.

*The blouse too.*

*Not the same one though?*

*No.*

She wouldn't have done that, not with his cum all over it.

But why stay in the skirt and leave looking like a schoolgirl?

Normally she would have put her slacks or dark skirt back on after one of their sessions, thereby making it look like she had truly been at work when she went home to her kids. Today she wouldn't. Today she would look like a student.

Had it slipped her mind?

Did she forget that Penny was home and might see her walk in?

No other explanation seemed to fit.

*Warn her.*

*Before she gets home.*

He shifted in the chair to pull his phone free from his pocket, his eyes startled to see he had missed a call from Penny.

Why had she called him?

Had something happened?

No message had been left.

He hit the call button and put the phone to his ear as it rang on the other end.

"WHO ARE YOU?" Leanne demanded as Susan approached through the overgrown area beneath the football bleachers.

"I'm Suzi," Susan said, overemphasizing the "zi" part of the name. "We had biology together last year."

Leanne eyed her for several seconds, suspicion present.

Susan pulled a pack of cigarettes from the waistband of her pleated skirt, her mind suddenly wondering if teens still did that with their smokes. "Want one?"

Leanne nodded and reached for the offered cigarette

while saying, "You said you have video of Penny sucking off some guy?"

"I do," Susan said, stepping close with a lighter in her left hand while her right went into her coat pocket where she had five rolls of quarters knotted into the bottom of a sock.

Leanne put the cigarette between her lips and leaned in toward the waiting flame.

Susan swung the sock, the quarters catching Leanne right behind the left ear, her body crumpling to the ground like a sack of potatoes.

THE AREA beneath the bleachers on the far side of the football field was overgrown and isolated, but not to the point where being stumbled upon wasn't a possibility, so she worked quickly, her gloved hands ripping free the blouse Leanne wore so that she could get her into the semen-stained one she had secured in the plastic bag.

Once that was done, she pulled Leanne's underwear off and wiped some of the semen between her legs, and then worked a glob up into her with her fingers, all while looking around to make sure no one was heading their way.

No one was.

Hesitation hit.

She wanted the girl to suffer. Needed her to. Simply killing her now wouldn't be satisfying, not after what she had done to Olivia.

Indecision gripped her.

She looked around a second time.

A few students were in the parking lot, having likely returned from an off-campus lunch. They were of no concern given that they were a good two hundred yards away and headed toward the school entrance rather than the football field.

No one else was present.

It was secure enough for now, and unless someone came out to do some maintenance on the field itself, which seemed unlikely at this point in the day, it would probably stay that way until school let out at three.

Leanne began to stir, an odd squeak leaving her lips.

Susan considered hitting her again but then decided against it for fear that a second blow might send her off into a prolonged unconsciousness. Instead, she hurried over to her backpack and retrieved the roll of duct tape she had slipped inside.

# TWENTY-FIVE

"Oh shit, that's him," Penny said as her phone buzzed.

"Answer it," Olivia said.

"What do I say?"

"Ask him if he was watching porn."

"I can't ask that," Penny said. "It's too...I don't know!"

"You're gonna miss the call," Olivia warned. "Again!"

"Hello," Penny said.

"Hi, Penny," Father Collins said. "I saw I missed your call. Is everything okay?"

"Yeah, fine. I just saw that you called me and tried to call you back, but then figured you were busy since you didn't answer." An image popped into her mind at the word *busy*, one that sent a wave of disgust through her.

"I didn't call you," Father Collins voiced.

"You did, but I think maybe it was a butt dial."

Olivia giggled.

Penny waved at her to shut up.

"*Sorry, Daddy*," Olivia whispered.

Penny waved again and glared.

Olivia put a hand over her mouth to stop her own laughter.

"You ended up leaving me a voice message," Penny added.

"I did?"

"Yeah. Um..."

*Daddy, not in my butt!*

*Daddy, you're hurting me!*

*Daddy...*

"But if you didn't mean to, I guess it wasn't really important and I'll just delete it."

"Okay, yeah, sorry about that. Phones today, they're—" He stopped suddenly. "What time did this happen?"

"Just a little while ago, shortly after we got off the phone."

"I see," he said, voice changing.

"Father, I'm sorry, but I have to ask. Were you watching porn?"

Olivia burst out laughing.

Penny tried to cover the mouthpiece, even though she knew it was pointless.

"I gotta go," he said.

The call ended.

"He just hung up on me," Penny announced.

"Busted!" Olivia shouted, more laughter following.

"I can't believe it."

"Guys will be guys."

"But that daddy stuff. Jesus. That's, like, even worse than regular porn."

"It is pretty sick," Olivia agreed. "Let's listen to it again."

"Ugh! Why?"

"Because. It's not every day you get to hear a priest whacking off to kinky shit."

"That's a good thing," Penny said. "Once was enough." She shook her head and grimaced.

"You know, what if it wasn't porn?" Olivia asked.

"What? You mean, what if he had an actual—" She couldn't even finish the thought.

"Exactly," Olivia said, not needing to hear the rest of Penny's sentence. "And right after he called you to explain about putting holy water up your butt, which is creepy in itself."

"No, there has to be an explanation," Penny said. "I can't see him calling me with someone there and then fucking them. Or even watching porn right after. It just—I don't know."

"Let me hear the message again."

"No, come on," Penny said.

"I want to see if it sounds like a video or a live performance."

"You can't tell that from a voicemail."

"We might be able to. Especially now that we know what we're going to be hearing."

"Okay, fine." She thumbed in her password and then pulled up the voicemail once again.

"*Daddy! Please! Not in the butt!*" echoed.

Penny crossed her arms, disgusted.

"*Daddy! It's too big. Daddy, you're hurting me!*"

The voicemail ended.

Neither said anything for several seconds.

"I hate to say it," Olivia said. "I'm pretty sure that's him fucking someone in the ass."

Penny didn't reply.

"And now he wants to put stuff up your butt," Olivia added.

Penny still didn't reply, her mind too jumbled up to voice anything.

"And he's friends with my mom. Go figure."

"Oh shit," Penny said, suddenly remembering all the weird ebook titles she had seen on Aunt Susan's Kindle.

"What?" Olivia asked.

"Nothing," she said. "I just...never mind."

"No, no, no," Olivia said. "You can't do that. What happened?"

"I found something the other day. While snooping through your mom's room."

"Snooping through my mom's room?" Olivia questioned, eyes wide.

"Yeah," Penny confirmed, a bit of guilt present.

"Whatever possessed you to do that?" Olivia seemed amused.

"Boredom, I guess." She waved a hand. "Anyway, I bumped your mom's Kindle and saw a bunch of crazy porn books on there."

"Porn books? My mom?"

Penny nodded. "And a drawer full of sex toys."

"Oh my God," Olivia said, hand going to her mouth. "This I gotta see."

"FUCK ME," Olivia said while looking in the nightstand drawer. "Do you think she'll notice if I steal one?"

"Ugh, that's sick," Penny said.

"Seriously though, I can't believe this. I mean, I know she's single and all, and hasn't been on a date in, like, forever, but still, why does she need so many different—*holy hell, is that a butt plug?*"

"I think so," Penny said.

"Jesus!" Olivia said and then shoved the drawer shut in disgust.

A buzzing began to echo.

"Oh for the love of God," Olivia cried.

"That's why you never leave batteries in your toys," Penny said. "They have a habit of turning themselves on."

"How do you know that?" Olivia asked.

"Because my mom's work bag started vibrating once after she set it down when I was a kid, and I looked inside to see what it was. She had been in a hurry to get to the bathroom and then was horrified when she came out and saw me holding a vibrating dildo."

Penny felt a wave of sadness arrive.

She had been eleven years old at the time, and while certainly too young for a full-on detailed explanation of her mother's career, she had been old enough to get a watered-down explanation of what it was her mom did for a living.

From that point on, there had been no secrets about her career. If Penny had questions, her mother answered them.

"Why did she bring her stuff home?" Olivia asked.

"Oh, um, back then when she was with that particular studio she was very leery of their thoroughness when cleaning things and always brought everything home to do it herself."

"Probably a good idea."

"Yeah." Then, opening the drawer once again, "We should turn this off so your mom doesn't know we were snooping."

"I'm not touching that," Olivia said.

"A second ago you wanted to steal one."

"And I was totally joking."

"Fine, I'll do it." She reached over for a tissue only to discover the box was empty.

Olivia saw this and said, "I'll get some toilet paper."

"Thanks."

Olivia headed into the master bathroom.

"Oh my fucking God!" she cried.

"What?" Penny asked, startled.

"I take back what I said about my mom not seeing someone."

"What do you mean?"

"Stay there for a second."

Penny did, confused.

Several seconds came and went, the buzzing in the drawer continuing as the vibrator jiggled all over the place.

Olivia peeked around the bathroom doorframe.

"You ready for this?" she asked.

"Ready for what?" Penny asked.

"All those toys in there are obviously for self gratification," Olivia said, still only peeking her face around the doorframe.

"Yeah..."

"Well, this toy certainly isn't," she said and sprang into the doorway, a giant strap-on penis flopping back and forth as she twerked her hips.

Penny's jaw about hit the floor.

"Not only is my mom obviously seeing someone, they're kinky as fuck!"

Penny was speechless, her eyes unable to look away from the giant flesh-colored monstrosity.

Olivia pumped her hips, thrusting. "You know, I've always wondered what having a penis would be like," she said, laughing.

Penny felt herself waver a bit, a hand going to her head as a memory from the other night unfolded, one where the demon thrust its hips back and forth, the giant penis flopping up and down.

"You okay?" Olivia asked.

"What?" Penny asked. Then, lying, "Yeah, fine. Just got dizzy for a moment."

Olivia eyed her for several seconds and then walked over to the floor-length mirror that stood in the opposite corner.

*It had breasts and a giant penis.*

*But had the penis been real?*

*What if...*

*"Your mother would have me tie her down at night so that she didn't climb on top of me again,"* Aunt Susan had said the other day, her worry being that Penny would do something to Olivia or Nicky.

But what if the opposite had happened?

What if something had possessed Olivia, who had then climbed on top of her?

No.

But the face.

It had been hideous.

The face of a demon.

Or...

*A mask?*

"Hey, what are you going to be for Halloween?"

"Halloween?" Olivia asked, twisting back around, penis swinging.

"Yeah."

"No idea. Maybe a nun with a giant strap-on!" She laughed. "You?"

"Don't know. I want to do something freaky. Do you have any creepy masks?"

"Creepy masks?" She shook her head. "No." She grabbed the penis and jiggled it. "I so want to sneak this with me one night and put it on while Martin isn't looking. Can you imagine the horror on his face once he saw it?"

"Can you imagine the horror on yours if he was totally into it?" Penny countered.

Olivia laughed and then pulled out her phone.

"What are you doing?" Penny asked.

"I'm going to send him a picture."

Penny shook her head.

# TWENTY-SIX

"You butt dialed her while fucking me!" Susan cried.

"The phone was in my pocket when you undid my pants and let them fall to the floor," Conrad said.

"You're blaming me?"

"No, no, of course not. Just explaining."

"Christ!" Susan shouted. Then, more subdued, "Did she know it was me?"

"No. They think I was watching porn."

"They?"

"I could hear Olivia in the background laughing."

"I can't believe this," Susan said.

One minute she had been on a high after having brutalized Leanne beneath the bleachers, the next she had seen a dozen missed calls from Conrad.

"I think we need to call tonight off now," Conrad said.

"No," Susan said. "We need to keep going."

"She's not going to trust me now, not after hearing that."

"Just shut up for a second and let me think," Susan snapped.

Conrad went silent.

Susan pulled up to a stop sign, her mind a total blank.

In her ear she could hear Conrad breathing.

"You know what, I'm going to call you back. If Penny calls you again, just ignore it until I call you."

"Okay."

She disconnected the call and threw the phone onto the passenger seat.

Less than a minute later she was pulling into a gas station, one hand on the wheel while her other called Conrad back, an idea having arrived, one that was perfect.

"ARE you sure she made videos with stuff like that?" Conrad asked, pacing his empty office.

"I don't know," Susan said. "You really think I watched her stuff?"

"I know you did."

Susan was quiet for several seconds

Conrad stopped pacing and waited.

"Okay, yeah, I might have watched a few out of curiosity."

"And did she do any daddy-themed ones?"

"I don't remember any, but she made hundreds, maybe even thousands of videos. I'm sure at some point she made something that had a daddy-daughter theme to it."

"But what if she didn't?" he asked. "And what if Penny calls me out on it?"

"You think Penny has watched her stuff?"

"I don't know."

"Why the fuck would Penny want to watch her mom getting fucked?" Susan snapped.

"I'm just saying, we should think about the possibility

that she might call foul. That's the problem with lying. Sometimes it can blow up in your face."

"I suppose we could just tell her the truth, then. That you like to be called Daddy while fucking schoolgirls in the ass."

Conrad shook his head.

"And while we're at it, tell her that the holy water suggestion wasn't even going to be holy water and that you just want to pump ginger extract up her butt so that it burns like—"

He hung up.

SUSAN STARED at the phone in disbelief, the Call Ended note flashing a few times before the screen went dark.

Anger arrived.

She called him back.

"Yes," he answered.

"You just fucking hung up on—"

Call Ended.

*Son of a bitch!*

She hit the Call icon again.

The other end rang and rang before going to voicemail.

She tossed the phone onto the passenger seat and shifted the car back into drive, her eyes catching sight of an SUV at one of the gas pumps, the passenger within smoking and flicking his ashes out the window while the driver pumped gas.

*Are you fucking kidding me?*

Her phone beeped.

She picked it back up and looked at it.

*Call me back once you've calmed down,* was all it said.

Anger erupted.

It was everything she could do not to reply with a threat of sending the videos to his wife.

*Deep breath.*

Across the way, the driver of the SUV was getting back into the vehicle to leave, all while his passenger continued to smoke. And then, as if that wasn't enough, the passenger pushed the smoldering butt through the gap in the window so that it rolled out onto the ground in the area between the pumps.

*What if that causes a fire?*

Investigators would likely review the station security footage to see how it happened and might spot her car in the lot, and while they wouldn't automatically be like "you were near the school, you killed Leanne!" any little connection could prove to be a toehold that could eventually lead them her way.

*Am I on camera?*

If she got out and walked across the pavement to where the smoldering butt was, she would be for sure.

*I'm overthinking things.*

No one would connect her to Leanne, not when they discovered all the semen on her clothes and inside her. And by the time they matched it to Conrad, and then saw the videos on his hard drive, he would be in no condition to reveal the truth.

*If everything works...*

*It will.*

It had to. If it didn't...

Susan pushed the thought from her mind.

CONRAD WAS glad that he had canceled all his patients

for the day—Susan's idea—because he didn't think he would have been able to focus on a single thing any of them said. Plus, it gave him time to watch some videos of Penny's mom before heading over there this evening, Pornhub providing him quite a selection from the days when she had been in front of the camera rather than behind it.

Only he couldn't find any daddy-daughter stuff.

The closest he came were some videos where she was wearing a school uniform, but nothing within the clips, which were just snippets taken from longer videos, had any role-play context to them. Instead, they were just scenes of her giving blowjobs and having sex while in the uniform.

*Was it a limit?*

*Was that a role she simply would not take, given the abuse she had suffered as a teen?*

*Had she even suffered abuse?*

Susan was a compulsive liar. He had come to realize this during their time together, so the stories she told of the abuse she and her sister had suffered at the hands of a local priest and her father could have simply been lies she crafted and used to create the segue into the tales of her own abuse.

*Lies she actually has come to believe?*

No answer followed.

One never did.

*Did she fuck her niece with that strap-on?*

*Penny would have known it was her.*

He shifted his focus back to Susan's sister, his fingers opening a new window so that he could use Google to try to find a list of videos she was credited with.

No list appeared in any of his searches, but he did find quite a few articles about her, the most recent being about the car accident that had taken her life.

*Former Porn Star Killed While Teaching Teenage Daughter How to Drive.*

*Porn star.*

Every article about the accident found a way to reference her career, even though there was nothing about being a porn star that had any bearing on the accident.

Even the articles that talked about Penny did this.

*Daughter of Porn Star in Coma.*

*Daughter of Porn Star Awakens From Coma.*

And then there was a headline that managed to double up the use of the word with *Porn Community Mourns the Loss of Porn Star Turned Producer*.

Several pictures were present within the article, though only one of them actually showed the funeral, which, given its somber nature and lack of shock value, had been put near the bottom of the text. The others were older photos that had been taken on the porn sets themselves during interviews, Penny's mom always in a suggestive pose and a state of near undress.

DROPPING NICKY OFF at Kyle's house turned out to be a test of patience, Kyle's mom cornering her with questions about Penny.

"Gwen says she was having sex in the chapel," Rebecca said, voice nothing more than a whisper as Kyle and Nicky headed off toward Kyle's room. "There's even a picture of her with her shirt open. And videos of her talking in tongues while playing with a Ouija board."

"The school is looking into what happened," Susan advised. "I'd be careful about accepting things that Gwen says since the students are all coming up with their own—"

"My daughter would not lie to me."

"I'm not suggesting she is. I just think we need to be careful, given that students are prone to exaggeration."

"What exaggeration? There's videos of her with the Ouija board and pictures of her with her shirt open."

"Yes, and we're trying to get to the bottom of everything. She's seeing a therapist now, and she has a doctor who is looking into her head injury from the accident."

"I'm still surprised you let her stay with you."

Susan blinked. "She's my niece."

"Still. With a mother like that..."

"She's family."

"Just be aware, we're all keeping an eye on this, and several of us have let the school know we have concerns with her being around our children."

Susan didn't reply.

"You understand, a line has to be drawn. Gwen goes to that school so she can have a good Catholic education. If I wanted her exposed to the sinful filth of the world, she would go to the local high school."

Susan wanted to say something in reply, but instead simply nodded.

"We'll be praying for you and your family," Rebecca added.

"Thank you," Susan said.

# TWENTY-SEVEN

"I think he's pretty embarrassed," Aunt Susan said.

"I still don't understand why he would be watching those old videos," Penny said, her mind trying to blank out the thought of her mom bent over and taking it up the butt.

"That's part of his embarrassment. He was simply doing research on your mom, trying to figure out if he could find evidence of possession, and I guess one thing led to another..." She shrugged. "You know how guys are. Even a man of the cloth can get sucked into watching such things."

"I know, it's just..." She couldn't find the words to express what she was feeling.

"It's hard. I know. You're proud of your mother and her accomplishments, yet at the same time you want to distance yourself from the visual imagery that goes with it."

"Yes, exactly," Penny said. Then, "Olivia doesn't think it was a video. She thinks he was with someone."

"Do you think Olivia has enough experience at listening to things like this to be able to tell the difference?" Aunt Susan asked.

"I don't know," Penny admitted.

"What do you think? Is Father Collins lying? Did he have someone there with him? Or was he simply watching videos of your mom?"

"I really can't say."

"Me either," Aunt Susan said. "But I trust Father Collins, so if he says he was watching videos, then I believe him. I think you should too."

Penny nodded. "Okay."

*Ask her about the strap-on.*

*And then what? Suggest that either she or Olivia had been the one to fuck me?*

Her aunt would not take kindly to such an implication.

She needed evidence first.

"Now, about his suggestion how to protect yourself," Aunt Susan said.

Penny grimaced while shaking her head. "I really don't want to do that."

"Honey, I know it seems gross, but don't you think it might be better to endure that than waking up with that thing on top of you again?"

Penny didn't reply to that, her eyes simply shifting downward.

Susan touched her hand. "Just think about it, okay?"

"Okay."

Aunt Susan made as if to stand, but then halted and said, "I know you're scared and that everything that has happened these last few days has been very overwhelming, but we'll get through this."

Penny forced a smile.

"And I admire your bravery with all this."

Another smile and then, "Was Father Collins involved in trying to help my mom back when you two were in college?"

Aunt Susan seemed startled by the question, but then quickly composed herself and said, "No, he wasn't around for that."

"But there was a priest involved?"

Aunt Susan hesitated, her eyes shifting toward the ceiling for a moment and then over toward the wall.

Penny waited.

"I think now might not be the best time to discuss what happened, but once this is all over, I promise you and I will have a sit-down and talk about everything. Okay?"

"Okay."

OLIVIA LOVED Martin's reaction to the strap-on picture, but then grew weary of his follow-up questions, given that he now was speculating on why her mom had it and who she was seeing.

*Could she be with another woman?* Martin had asked at one point, catching her off guard.

*Maybe,* was her reply.

Internal questions on if that was the reason her dad had left followed. She had always thought it was simply due to PTSD, but maybe her mom had been having an affair with another woman while he was deployed and he found out about it.

*Maybe this Father Collins knows?*

The thought came out of nowhere, and for a moment it tried to lead her back to the voicemail he had accidentally left, the sounds of the sex echoing in her mind. But then she pushed that away and focused on the fact that her mother had mentioned that Father Collins was a friend from way back, one who had come down from Chicago to help out, so maybe there was a chance that he had known her father.

*But why have I never heard of him before?* she asked herself, her fingers suddenly pulling up Google so she could type in his name to see what came up.

This didn't bear any fruit.

The last name was too common.

She needed a first name to help narrow things down.

Her phone buzzed.

It was Martin again.

*You want to do something tonight?* he asked.

*You don't have a car,* she replied.

*Is that the only reason you're in love with me?*

*Yes.*

*LOL!!*

*What did you have in mind?* she asked.

*Beats me, though I do have it on good authority that my parents are going out tonight and will be gone for at least four hours.*

*Well then, I know exactly what you have in mind.* Then, after a few seconds, she added: *I'll bring the strap-on.*

A dozen eek-faced emojis followed.

*What time are they heading out?*

*Around six.*

*Okay, sounds good.*

*HEY,* the text from Joey said.

*Hey,* Penny replied.

*You free to talk?*

Concern appeared. They hadn't spoken since the incident in the chapel. Penny had wanted to but didn't really know what to say and instead had been hoping Joey would instigate a conversation. Now that he had, she worried that it was because he wanted to end things, realizing that being with her was too risky given what had happened.

*Yes,* she typed.

Her phone rang.

"Hey," she said, trying not to sound nervous.

"Hey," he said back. Then, "How are you?"

"I'm okay. You?"

"I'm good."

Nothing followed for several seconds.

"I'm really sorry about what happened," Penny said, heart racing.

"Oh hey, it's all cool."

"No, it really isn't. You got in trouble because of it and now I feel—"

"Hey," he said, cutting her off. "Seriously, it's okay. Nothing happened."

"Really?"

"Really."

She didn't reply.

"Anyway, the reason I wanted to talk—aside from the fact that I just like hearing your voice—was because I wanted to see if you wanted to go into the city tonight and try the sushi place."

"Oh. Um..." *Would Aunt Susan be okay with that?*

"If you're not feeling up to it after what happened, I understand."

"No, no, I...um...what time?"

"I could pick you up at six."

"Okay. Yeah. That works."

"Excellent. I'll see you at six then."

"Great," she said, beaming.

The call ended.

. . .

"I'M GOING to be hanging out with Liz tonight," Olivia said while entering the kitchen, a backpack slung over her shoulder.

Susan looked at her daughter and said, "Oh. Are you staying the night?"

"Nah, probably will be back around ten or eleven."

"Okay."

A moment later, Penny appeared, clad in a dark skirt and sweater.

"You too?" Susan asked.

"What?"

"Going to Liz's house?"

"No," she said, confused, eyes shifting over to where Olivia was putting on her shoes. "I have a date tonight with Joey."

Susan blinked. She had figured they were through after the incident in the chapel.

"Where're you two going?" Olivia asked from the hallway.

"We're getting sushi," Penny said, excitement present.

"Ugh, epic barf!"

"You should try it. You might be surprised."

"Not a chance!" She opened the front door. "Speaking of Joey, he's here."

Penny ran a hand through her hair and then grabbed her shoes.

"Hold it," Susan said. "I'd like to meet him."

"Oh, we have reservations," Penny voiced.

"It'll be quick."

"Okay."

"SORRY ABOUT THAT," Penny said once she was in the passenger seat, hands securing her seatbelt.

"It's all good. She's not what I expected at all after everything Olivia has said." He shifted into reverse.

"Oh, well, her nun habit is at the cleaners."

Joey chuckled.

"She really mellowed out all of a sudden," Penny added. "It's weird."

"Any idea why?" he asked.

"Honestly, I think it was the paddling she gave Olivia."

"Really?"

"Yeah. It, like, flipped a switch or something. I don't know."

"That's good, I guess."

Penny agreed. "You know what's funny though? Olivia still lied about where she was going tonight."

"She hanging out with Liz?" Joey asked with a laugh.

"Yep."

"Nice."

"You want to know what the crazy thing is?"

"What?"

"I think my aunt knows it's total BS but just isn't saying anything."

"Why do you think that?"

"Well, okay, so she now knows that Olivia has been seeing Martin for quite some time, so she has to know that all those Friday and Saturday nights that she spent at Liz's house had to be a cover."

"Good point."

"Best of all, it appears that my aunt may have been fibbing herself when it comes to being in a relationship. I'm pretty sure all those evenings when she was going to church group, she was actually seeing someone."

"Martin thinks it's another woman," Joey said, surprising her.

"What? Why?"

"Olivia sent him a picture of your aunt's strap-on, which led him to say, and I quote, 'Olivia's mom is totally the man when she has sex.'"

"He showed you the picture?"

"We were in the hallway when it arrived. I about spit out the Coke I was drinking when he showed it to me."

"You know, it might not be another woman," Penny said.

Joey shifted his gaze toward her for a second while merging onto I-44. "You don't think..."

"You never know."

Joey gave an exaggerated shudder.

# TWENTY-EIGHT

Leanne's body was discovered around seven that evening.

Susan was sitting on the couch with her laptop, typing up a nasty email to Penny from one of her fake Gmail accounts, when the story broke on the TV.

Heart racing, Susan set the laptop aside and turned up the volume.

Few details were given, and due to the overgrowth and all the law enforcement personnel moving about, nothing could really be gleaned from the camera view, yet even so, Susan watched intently, her mind filling in all the details that weren't visible.

Questions followed.

*What do the police think?*

*Have they connected it to Jocelyn yet?*

*Do they feel there is a sadistic serial killer on the prowl?*

Memories of Leanne's screams against the duct tape pushed the questions away.

She grinned, her own reflection visible in the upper corner of the large TV.

It startled her.

She shouldn't have enjoyed what she did to the girl, yet she had. It was bizarre. When killing Jocelyn in the basement of that empty house a few days earlier, she hadn't gotten any sort of satisfaction beyond the fact that it was a step toward riches she couldn't even imagine possessing. With Leanne, an orgasm had blossomed. She had been on her knees at the time, shoving a tree branch up inside the squirming girl, tearing things that would have led to a bleed out if she hadn't eventually strangled the sobbing creature.

Never before had she experienced one of such intensity.

The closest any prior orgasms had come was when she had been fucking Penny with the strap-on, though that had had physical elements to it given the way the base had been rubbing against her clit. With Leanne, it had been purely mental.

*Revenge based?*

*Or am I simply a sadist?*

She hoped it was the former but feared that the latter might be more accurate, given that she had always had a bit of a mean streak.

Still, if she was a sadist, why hadn't she gotten off when she had been torturing Jocelyn? Also, why did she get off on being humiliated by Conrad?

The questions lingered in her mind for quite some time, but no answer ever arrived, her focus eventually shifting to her plans for that night.

She was going to fuck Penny again, and since the girl was being stubborn about doing the holy water enema, there would be no reason for her to pull out as if the demon were being burned.

*Poor Penny.*

The spoiled brat had no idea how horrible it was going

to be, the girth of her sister's strap-on something that she didn't even think she could take without some serious preparation.

*But that's what one gets for not listening to Father Collins and Aunt Susan.*

Live and learn.

On-screen, the female reporter was now confirming that the body was that of a student who attended St. Katherine's.

*Still no name...*

*Soon.*

"*Unconfirmed reports indicate that the student was sexually assaulted,*" the reporter said, voice taking on the necessary solemnness for conveying such information.

*By a pervert named Conrad Collins,* Susan said to herself.

Had that been the right move?

When she killed Jocelyn, she had wanted it to eventually seem like Penny had done it, as if the demon inside of her was making sacrifices of those who had taken part in the Ouija board event, Penny eventually "killing herself" once she realized what she had done. But then she had realized that had too many implausibilities, the biggest being Penny's reluctance to get behind the wheel and drive. Next, she had figured the killer was a religious nut, one who had tracked Jocelyn down to find out who the girl in the video was, torturing her for information so that he could eventually find and kill Penny.

Now she was simply framing Conrad.

It was simpler this way.

Or was it?

She really didn't know.

Two birds, one stone.

At some point in the near future she would make it

seem like he had killed Penny, her own hand killing him in the process while trying, but failing, to save her niece. It wasn't perfect, but with the DNA evidence on Leanne, it would be accepted.

In fact, some might speculate that he had been obsessed with her porn star mother, given all the videos he had been watching.

*And that's why he was fucking me.*

*Blackmail.*

*Because he had learned the truth about the videos?*

No.

Too complicated.

She would only go that route if absolutely necessary.

For now, she just needed to get Penny into a situation where it would look like Conrad had killed her.

After tonight, she hoped that situation would present itself.

She had to get them in the house together.

Once that happened...

CONRAD WATCHED the video a dozen times, his face nearly touching the screen as he tried to get beyond the graininess of the poorly uploaded file so he could truly see the young woman that was leaning over the edge of a bed, cheek pressed into the bedspread while a man took her from behind, the skirt of her uniform carelessly thrown up onto her hips while her panties were around her thighs.

*Susan.*

Nothing within the grainy video could be pointed at to prove this, yet somehow he knew. It was her. She had posed as her sister for a film. And given how similar the two had looked back in those days, chances were good no one had questioned it.

But why?

And when?

Based on some of the articles he had read and interviews that had been conducted, Susan's sister had started starring in low-budget porn films during her junior year of college, shortly before turning twenty. A year later, she was starring in high-budget porn films, ones that earned her awards within the industry as well as an income that most people her age couldn't even imagine.

And yet, based on the grainy footage he had just watched, she hadn't really been the star of those early low-budget films. Susan had.

*CHECK YOUR EMAIL,* the text from Conrad instructed.

*Why?* Susan asked.

*Because I think we have a problem.*

Startled, Susan did as instructed, her fingers closing out of the fake Gmail account she had been in and opening her regular one.

A forwarded email from Conrad was waiting.

In the email was a message that said: *Your secretary used to be a porn star.* A Pornhub link followed.

Susan clicked on it.

The video was grainy to the point of being almost unwatchable, yet even so, she recognized herself.

*That's my sister,* she texted.

*That's you,* Conrad replied.

A second later the phone rang.

She answered.

"I can tell it is you," Conrad said.

Susan didn't reply.

"Well?" Conrad pressed.

"Okay, so it's me," Susan said. "So what?"

"So what?" Conrad questioned. "Why would my wife be digging into your past like this if she didn't suspect something was going on between us?"

"Your wife?"

"Yeah, didn't you see who the email was from?"

Susan hadn't really paid any attention to that, but now that she looked, she saw his wife's name within the email address of the original sender.

"Hang on a second, she just sent me another email."

Susan waited.

"Jesus," he said.

"What?"

"She was watching the office today and wants to know why you were leaving dressed like a schoolgirl. Shit, you didn't change, did you?"

"Of course I changed," she said. "I had your cum all over my shirt."

"Yeah, you changed that, but not your skirt."

"Didn't I?" she asked, even though she knew she hadn't, not when she had wanted Leanne to think she was a fellow student when approaching her beneath the bleachers.

"You didn't!" he said, voice raised.

"Calm down," she snapped.

"Calm down? Really? Did you know she has been spending odd amounts of money on something that she refused to talk about when I questioned her the other day?"

"So?"

"So? I bet she hired a PI to watch us, one who did some digging and realized it was you and not your sister who was in those early porn videos."

Susan felt her stomach drop.

It was one thing if his wife had suspicions, it was another if she had a private investigator following them.

Would they have followed her?

To the school?

No. If they had, she would be in jail right now.

No one had seen what had happened between her and Leanne.

Still, this was bad.

Especially if it was documented that Conrad had been at his office all day.

"We're going to have to call things off for a while," Conrad said. "Wait until this blows over."

"We can't!"

"We have to. If I'm being followed by a PI, they can't see me going to your place dressed like a priest. Especially not after you were seen leaving the office in a school uniform."

"Okay, okay, let me think on this for a while. I'll figure something out."

"What should I tell her?" he asked, desperation present.

"I don't know. Make something up."

"What about this video? Why were you in those early films?"

"It's a long story."

"I need to know why."

*Fuck it.* "She stole my boyfriend."

"What?"

"My sister. She stole my boyfriend, so I did some porn videos under her name to get back at her."

"Jesus."

"Now go straighten things out with your wife. And find out if she really has a PI watching us."

"Okay."

The call ended.

SATISFACTION OOZED through Conrad as he set the phone down and got ready to head home for the evening. He had finally gotten one over on Susan with the fake email.

Unfortunately, it was just a temporary reprieve, one that did absolutely nothing to absolve him from the part he had already played in whatever it was that Susan was up to.

Did she really fuck her own niece?

If so, how in the world would Penny not know it was her?

He was missing something.

He sighed and called home.

His wife answered after two rings.

"Hey, honey, sorry I'm running so late tonight. Want me to pick up something on the way home?"

"Oh sure, that would be great."

# TWENTY-NINE

"Holy shit!" Martin cried. "It's huge."

"That's what she said," Olivia said, chuckling. "Now bend over."

"No fucking way!"

"Aw, you scared?"

"Terrified," he said and then leaned in to kiss her.

Olivia poked him in the balls with the strap-on.

"Hey, watch it with that thing," he joked while stepping back.

"Oops, sorry," she said and then swung it so she could hit him in the thigh.

"Ow."

She swung again.

He dodged it and then started to open his pants.

"Whoa, what are you doing?" she asked, not actually wanting to fuck him in the ass.

"I need my own sword," he said, unsheathing himself. A lightsaber noise followed, along with a dramatic, "Luke, I am your father."

"Okay, this just got way too weird," Olivia said, unbuckling the harness.

"You're the one that brought it," he said.

"I'm regretting it already."

"You do not know the power of the dark side."

"Keep that up and I'll put my hair into cinnamon rolls and destroy your ass with this thing," she said, holding up the strap-on.

"You wouldn't do that to Daddy, would you?" he asked.

Olivia didn't reply.

"You know, Leia and Darth Vader," he explained, panic appearing.

She waved a hand, dismissing that, and asked, "Do you still have the videos of Penny's mom?"

"What?" he asked, the question obviously catching him off guard.

"The porn videos of her mom. Do you still have them?"

"It was just a clip that had been emailed to me."

"Was there any daddy-daughter stuff in it?"

"Any what?"

"You know, daddy-daughter stuff. Like her calling the guy Daddy while he fucks her in the ass."

"Ugh, no."

"Can you show me?"

"Why?"

"Just because."

"Seriously? You want to watch them?"

"Yes."

"Why?"

"Curiosity."

"Okay," he said. "Come on."

They headed to his bedroom.

. . .

"HOW IS IT?" Joey asked.

Penny finished chewing a piece of the shrimp tempura roll and said, "I'm a bit disappointed."

"Oh..."

She chuckled at his panic and said, "Disappointed that it's so far away. I'd eat here every day if I could."

Relief spread across his face.

She pointed to the flying fish roe she had suggested from the nigiri part of the menu. "Don't forget. You promised to try it."

"I know, I know, I'm just psyching up. I've never had fish eggs before."

"Never?"

"Nope."

"What about eel?"

He shook his head.

"Surf clams?"

"I normally just stick to the rolls."

She once again pointed to the flying fish roe. "Today will be the first step into a world of tastes you did not even know existed."

"Okay, here we go," he said, chopsticks taking hold of the seaweed base that held everything together.

Penny watched as he popped it into his mouth and began to chew, his face going from one of curiosity to disgust.

"Oh God," he said after swallowing, his hand grabbing his cup of tea. "It's so salty."

"Like getting a mouthful of seawater," Penny said, grinning.

"Do you really like those?" he asked, chopsticks struggling with a piece of ginger that he was going to eat raw.

"Not at all."

"What?"

She laughed.

"I'm totally going to get you back for that," he said.

"I'll make it up to you."

"You better." He popped the raw ginger into his mouth.

Penny grimaced and then said, "The eel won't be bad."

He eyed her.

She raised a hand and said, "Scout's honor."

His look of suspicion remained as he picked up the piece of eel that sat atop some rice.

She waited.

He put it into his mouth and started chewing.

"See," she said.

"Okay, yeah, that is really good. Kind of sweet."

She nodded. "That's what I thought the first time too. It really surprised me."

"You still owe me though. I'm going to find something gross for you to swallow."

She raised an eyebrow.

"I mean..." he stammered. "Not that."

"Not what?" she teased.

"You know."

"A sour lollipop?"

He shook his head while looking down at his plate.

"Oh, oh, I know. A candy apple that is really an onion on a stick."

He laughed.

She smiled for a second and then felt it fade away.

"What's wrong?" he asked.

"Ah, nothing," she said, waving a hand and then reaching for but not actually picking up one of the surf clams.

"Something I said?"

"No. Not at all." She hesitated. "Did Olivia mention why I've been staying home from school?"

He shook his head.

"That day in the chapel..." she started and then stopped.

He waited.

She poked at the surf clam for a few seconds and then set her chopsticks down. "I saw something that day," she said.

"Saw something?" he asked.

"I've actually experienced quite a few odd things since that night with the Ouija board. Sounds mostly. In class, in the mall...it was always a voice calling my name. But then in the chapel I actually saw something." She paused. "One second everything was fine, we were joking around, the next I watched as Jesus came down from the cross and started walking toward me."

"Seriously?" he asked, amusement briefly visible on his face before he pushed it away.

She ignored that and said, "He tried to fuck me."

Joey's eyes went wide. "Jesus did?"

"I know it sounds crazy, but that's what I saw, and then that night..." She felt her lip start to quiver as the horror of that night returned to her.

Startled, Joey looked around.

Penny tried to halt the emotion that was arriving, but couldn't keep it back.

Tears began to fall.

"Hey, it's okay," he said.

She wiped at her eyes. "I'm sorry," she muttered.

"Don't be. Nothing to be sorry for."

She took a sip of tea and then reached for the pot they

had ordered, but stopped as Joey took hold of it and poured her some more.

"Thanks," she said, once again wiping at her eyes.

Joey handed her some more napkins.

She used them and then said, "God, I'm a mess."

"You've been through a lot," Joey said.

"Yeah," she muttered and dabbed at her eyes again. "I'll be right back. I'm going to go compose myself."

"You want me to come with?"

"In the bathroom?" she asked with a weak laugh.

"No, just...walk you back there?"

"I think I'm okay to do that, but thanks."

She stood, half expecting the room to fill with smoke and the demon to appear. It didn't. Even while in the bathroom, it mercifully left her alone.

"YOU HAVE an entire folder dedicated to her mom?" Olivia said, astonished.

"I was—" Martin started.

"And what the fuck is this? Bowsette?" She double-clicked the icon.

A video player loaded.

"Cartoon porn!" she gasped. "You watch cartoon porn?"

"I don't know," he stammered. "Some of it is hot."

"You think this is hot?" She pointed.

"Don't you?"

She had no words and simply shook her head.

Martin reached for the mouse.

"No you don't," she said, snatching it away. "I want to see what kind of stuff you're into." She ended the video and started scrolling through the various folders.

He hovered behind her, obviously agitated.

Eyes wide, she went from one bizarre video icon to another, her finger resisting the urge to double-click on each one simply because she wanted to get a good overview first rather than being sucked into each offering. She was also a bit scared. Not in a horror way, but a "don't know if I really want to delve any deeper" way.

"I haven't even watched most of these," he muttered. "Sometimes you just download hundreds of them at a time for future viewings."

"*Hundreds*. Why?" she asked.

"I don't know," he said, defeat present in his voice.

"You really dig the Asian chicks," she noted.

"Oh, most of those are game shows."

"What?"

"In Japan they have some of the craziest shit you'll ever see." He leaned in and pointed. "Here's one where a woman has to guess which glory-hole penis is her boyfriend's. She then sucks it off. Afterward she finds out if she was right or if it was just some random dude's dick."

"That's horrible!" she said, jaw about hitting the floor as she turned to look at him.

"I know, yet they seem to love stuff like this. And believe it or not, that's one of the tamer ones."

Olivia didn't know how to reply to that.

"You know what the craziest thing of all is?" he continued.

"What?" she asked.

"They actually blur out the pubic regions in their porn over there."

"Who? The Japanese?"

"Yeah."

"Why?"

"I don't know. You'll see the most outrageous stuff going

on. Things that might make you sick to your stomach even. But during it all, the genitals will be blurred out. It's so weird."

"And you jerk off to this sick shit?" she asked, failing to mask her disgust.

"No way. Like I said, most of this stuff I haven't even watched. It's just like you go through a download craze. Once I do start to watch something, if it's really sick, I delete it."

Olivia doubted that. Most likely he emailed the file to his buddies so they could see it. Just like they had all done with the videos of Penny's mom.

*Speaking of which...*

She exited out of the folder she was in and went back to the one she had originally wanted to look at before getting sidetracked, a comment on how grainy the video was leaving her lips.

"I think someone uploaded this one from an old VHS," Martin noted.

Olivia didn't reply to that, her eyes simply watching as the two figures on-screen went about having sex. How anyone could get off on watching it given how dull it was, she didn't know, though maybe the fact that her aunt was in a school uniform provided the trigger for some perverts.

"There are like six or seven pieces from this particular film, though I've only found five of them," Martin said.

"What do you mean?"

"Whoever uploaded it split it into pieces, each one being ten minutes."

"Oh."

"You want to see her interview?"

"Interview?"

"Yeah, they did, like, a casting-couch thing with her before filming."

"Okay."

Martin took control of the mouse and shifted it to the right of the folder, his finger double-clicking. "Pretty sure this is it."

The video player came back up, a scene that simply had a camera pointed at a young woman sitting in a motel room chair filling the screen. She was wearing the school uniform, hair in pigtails, a nervous look dominating her face.

"Why is this one clearer than the others?" Olivia asked as the young woman on-screen introduced herself.

"Probably something to do with the lighting and where the camera is sitting. It's a pretty low-budget film."

"And yet guys paid money for this back in the day and she eventually became a star."

"Yep."

Olivia shook her head and then watched as a man off-screen asked questions. Some were general questions about her life and what she did for a living: *student*. Others were about her sexual preferences and what she had and had not done before, the man getting excited when he learned that she had never given a blowjob before or tasted semen.

"*I like your outfit*," the man said. "*This is your actual uniform from when you were in school?*"

"*Yes*," she said.

"*And now you're a student at St. Mary's University?*"

"*Yes.*"

"*What year?*"

"*Sophomore.*"

"Did you catch that?" Martin asked.

"Catch what?"

"She told them she was a sophomore even though she was actually a junior."

"Huh."

"In later interviews it was always noted that she began her career as a junior. Everyone always seemed to get a kick out of how she was expelled from school because of this but then went on to make a fortune. In one interview a few years back she actually joked about how getting kicked out for this video was the best thing that ever happened to her because there was no way she would have become a multi-millionaire from being an accountant."

"She was studying to be an accountant?"

"I guess."

"Huh."

"What?"

"Nothing, that's just what my mom studied and got a degree in."

"Oh."

"Can you send me this video?" she asked.

"Why?"

"I want to show it to Penny."

"Do you think that's a good idea?"

"I don't know. Something feels off about this and I can't put my finger on it, but maybe she can."

"Okay."

"And the other interviews too. Links. Videos. Everything you've found during your searches."

"*Nancy Drew and the Mystery of the Porn Star Aunt.*"

She smacked him and then said, "If I'm Nancy Drew, then that makes you my pudgy friend Bess."

"Do the two ever get it on during their cases?"

"No, but they eat a lot of ice cream."

"Works for me."

He leaned in and kissed the side of her mouth.

She started to pull away, but then felt like she had tortured him enough this evening and shifted herself so their mouths could line up, her tongue quickly darting between his lips while her hands reached for his belt.

# THIRTY

"Another girl was killed," his wife said as Conrad walked in with a bag of Chinese food, her finger pointing toward the TV screen.

"What? When?" he asked, setting the bags down.

"This afternoon. They haven't released a name yet, but they say she was raped and murdered within sight of the high school."

Conrad stared at the screen but couldn't tell anything from the display. "Which high school?"

"St. Katherine's."

"That's where Susan's kids go."

"Susan?"

"My receptionist. Her kids—well, her daughter and niece—go there."

"Is she the one whose sister was killed in that accident?"

He nodded. "She was teaching her daughter how to drive and someone ran a red light."

"Jesus."

"Yeah."

Silence settled as the two briefly contemplated human

mortality before shifting their attention to the Chinese food, Conrad having picked up a standard assortment of Americanized delicacies: egg rolls, sweet and sour pork, BBQ spare ribs, fried rice, and a handful of fortune cookies.

SUSAN WATCHED the video of herself being fucked, the link that Conrad had forwarded her having spurred her onto a quest of trying to locate all the clips from the videos she had done during the winter of her sophomore year in college.

*Five hundred bucks per shoot.*

It had seemed like a fortune to her at the time, one that was initially sweetened by the fact that it was sprinkled with revenge.

*Five videos.*

*Twenty-five hundred dollars.*

Her sister had made twice that during her first video shoot, the publicity of being expelled from a conservative Catholic university for doing porn videos in her old Catholic school uniform having piqued the interest of agents and studios, all of whom offered her deals that would have made the most devout church figure reconsider their celibacy.

*Thanks Suzi.*

The unsigned note had been attached to a flower assortment that had been sent to her apartment shortly before she graduated. It was the only acknowledgment her sister ever made toward what Susan had done to her, the silly act of revenge having backfired spectacularly as it springboarded the young woman into a life of riches and fame that Susan couldn't even contemplate.

*It should have been mine.*

If she had simply admitted to what she had done, she would have been the one expelled and then offered obscene amounts of money to get fucked on camera. But no, she had kept her mouth shut as the school expelled her sister, who had remained equally silent. Not once had her sister pointed toward Susan, even though she obviously had known what had happened once the videos had started to circulate.

It wasn't fair.

Nothing ever was when it came to her life.

Adding insult to injury, she had eventually tried to get a piece of what her sister had, first by querying her sister to see if she could help her get some good-paying film roles, and then, when her sister didn't even bother to reply, answering an ad she found online to appear in an amateur porn video that a local guy was filming. The result: she had been paid a couple hundred bucks to be gangbanged in a dingy basement, and unexpectedly left with a baby growing in her belly since one of the guys had either failed to use a condom or used one that broke.

Fortunately, the jarhead she was seeing at the time thought it was his and, being a good Catholic, agreed to get married before his deployment to Iraq. He had then deposited his own seed into her while home after a second deployment. That was the last she ever saw of him. He never came home from his third deployment. He wasn't one of the fallen; he simply disappeared after that tour somewhere between the airport and their home. Even the military couldn't find him.

Just one more way for the world to screw her.

Had he been killed, she would have gotten benefits to help keep the three of them afloat, but with him simply vanishing...nothing, the three of them eventually having to move in with her parents.

On-screen, she watched as the guy fucked her, her virginity vanishing with a few simple thrusts while her hands fisted the bedspread.

*Five hundred bucks.*

*Twenty-five hundred total.*

Compared to the empire her sister had built.

She was owed.

Without her, her sister never would have achieved any of this, and yet it was a spoiled teenage brat who was set to inherit everything.

Her sister hadn't willed her a penny, unless one counted the niece named Penny she now had to care for.

It was infuriating.

The teen had done nothing to earn any of what her mother had achieved, whereas Susan had lost her fucking virginity for it.

CONRAD WANTED to learn more about the girl who was killed and what the circumstances surrounding the horrific slaying were, but his wife and he had established a routine of watching *Seinfeld* reruns after dinner and he didn't want to disrupt that, not while she was snuggled against him.

*They probably don't have more details yet anyway,* he told himself.

*But what if they do?*

He did check his phone at one point, the device sitting within reach on the arm of the sofa.

As expected, nothing new.

"What is it?" his wife asked, sensing his shift.

"Nothing," he said. "Thought I had a message."

"Oh."

Nothing else followed, though halfway through their third episode of *Seinfeld* she did mention that his heart was racing. She could feel it through his chest where her head was resting.

"Probably the MSG," he said, even though he knew it was bullshit.

"You didn't ask for it without?" she questioned, startled.

"I forgot."

She pushed herself off him and said, "I should probably go take a pill then. Get ahead of it."

"Oh, yeah, sorry," he said. She was prone to headaches, ones that she attributed to all kinds of things that weren't scientifically sound.

"It's okay."

She left the room.

He checked his phone again, but still no updates beyond what he already knew.

On-screen, George was worrying about getting married to Susan, the name once again causing his heart to race.

*Had the email from the fake account under his wife's name been a good idea?*

*What if she found out it wasn't real?*

His wife returned, pill taken, her tiny body once again snuggling up against him.

He put his arm around her, fear that this might be one of the last times he got to sit with her like this worming its way into his system.

SUSAN GREW restless in the empty house, eventually heading downstairs into Penny's room to stand and contemplate how the events of that evening would unfold.

As before, she would wait until 3:00 a.m. before creeping into the room, given that most horror movies featuring demon possession used that infamous hour as a plot device.

Once in, she would quietly light the apple-cinnamon candles, Penny's sensitivity to scents a seemingly surefire way of triggering a seizure.

After that, it was easy.

Ropes would be tied while the creepy demon mask was in place, the giant strap-on penis protruding from her naked body, all while a cheap strobe light flickered, its flashes providing the perfect disorienting effect as the groggy girl came to following her spasms.

And then...

Memories of taking the giant dick up her butt for the first time during her video shoot returned to her, her tear-streaked face pressing into the dirty bedspread so that she didn't alert other motel guests with her cries of pain.

It had been one of the most horrific moments of her life, one that had made the sharp discomfort of losing her virginity several minutes earlier seem trivial.

She grinned.

Tonight Penny would learn the true cost of her inheritance.

# THIRTY-ONE

"Uh-oh, what's this?" Joey said as they came to a complete stop within sight of the on-ramp to I-44, brake lights stretching as far as the eye could see.

"Whatever it is, it doesn't look good," Penny replied, leaning forward in her seat.

"No, it does not," Joey agreed.

Up ahead, the green light of the intersection where they needed to turn went to yellow and then red, the backed-up turn lane to get onto the ramp having made it so only a few people who were heading beyond the intersection had made it through. Joey and Penny were one of the cars helping to block those that wanted to go straight.

Several minutes came and went, the light ahead changing to green once again.

Behind them, people that wanted to go straight began honking.

The light cycled back to red.

"We didn't move at all," Penny said.

"I noticed that," Joey replied.

More honking, and then shouting as one person uselessly screamed at another person to move.

"Feel like going on a roundabout adventure through the city in hopes that we can find a way around all this?" Joey asked.

"Is there a chance we might get hopelessly lost and then find ourselves across the river in a dangerous and inhospitable land?"

"Worse," he warned. "We might end up in Illinois."

"Eek! Let's go for it."

Joey twisted a bit to make sure no one was trying to get around them at that particular moment, and then edged them around the car ahead so they could proceed forward into the wide-open area of the intersection that would take them beyond the ramp and into the northern parts of the city.

"ARE WE HOPELESSLY LOST YET?" Penny asked about fifteen minutes later.

"Eh, almost," Joey said. "Though this time we actually know your address, so it's better than last time we got lost."

"Last time?" she asked. Then, remembering the day they tried to walk home from Martin's house, said, "Oh yeah, ha. Why does that seem like so long ago?"

"A lot has happened since that day," he said.

"It's only been, like, a week!"

"Makes you wonder what the next few days will—" His voice faded as he took a deep breath.

"You okay?" she asked.

"Yeah, I'm fine."

She could tell that was a lie but didn't press.

Up ahead a light turned red.

Joey eased them to a stop and then reached down to his waist to pull at his seatbelt, almost as if he were loosening it a bit.

Penny frowned.

"Can you look up how to get to the Galleria from here?" he asked, a slight bit of panic in his voice.

"The mall?" she asked, puzzled.

"Yeah, it should be west of here, but I'm not exactly—" His face scrunched up.

"Jesus, what is it?"

"It's okay. I just—" He grimaced again.

"UH JEEZ," Olivia said, looking at her phone. "Penny and Joey are stuck at a gas station."

"What do you mean?"

"You know how Joey is always eating shit he shouldn't and then we have to find him the nearest bathroom?"

"Yeah."

"Well...Penny just got to experience that for the first time."

Martin laughed. "Oh, Joey."

Another text came in.

"Oh God, it gets worse."

"How?"

"Apparently the gas station they are at is full of hookers trying to score dates."

"What? Where the hell are they?"

"No idea. Guess they tried to get around an accident while leaving the city."

Martin shook his head.

"Ha, she says all the hookers are hanging around an old gutted payphone and that Joey parked like five feet away from it before running inside to use the bathroom."

"That sounds like Joey."

"And she says they're all glaring at her."

"She should totally go hang with them, see if anyone tries to buy an hour of her time."

"Are you crazy?"

"I'm not saying she should accept if someone does, just that she should see what is offered for her—"

"You should really just stop talking," Olivia said, cutting him off.

"You're probably right."

"Okay, she says Joey is coming back."

"Let's hope he doesn't suddenly turn around and run back inside."

"Or worse yet, get pulled over down the road because some cop thinks Penny is a hooker he picked up."

"That would be hilarious."

She elbowed him.

"SORRY ABOUT THAT," Joey said.

"It's okay," Penny replied. "Can happen to anyone."

"Yeah," he muttered.

"I still have the directions to the mall pulled up if you want to go hang out there."

"You want to?"

"Sure. Unless you just want to head home in case of..."

"Let's play it by ear."

"I think you mean *play it by rear*."

He turned and gave her a look.

"Sorry," she said, face going red. "That sounded way funnier in my head."

"It actually wasn't too bad—"

*Thunk! Thunk!*

Penny yelped and then rolled down her window.

"You two want a third?" a scabbed-up middle-aged woman who had apparently bathed in perfume asked.

Penny felt her eyes starting to water at the scent.

Panic followed.

"A third?" Joey asked, confused.

*Something is coming.*

*No.*

*It's here!*

*In the car!*

"ME, honey. Together the three of us can—"

Penny didn't hear the rest as she tried to get away.

"*WHAT'D YOU GIVE HER?*" a voice asked.

"*Nothing,*" another replied.

*"She be tweaking."*

*"She's not tweaking."*

*"Hey, man, it's all cool."*

*"Penny?"*

Penny blinked.

Joey was leaning over her as she lay on the pavement while several of the women who were working the parking lot stood behind him.

"You okay?" Joey asked.

"What happened?" she asked.

Joey didn't seem to understand.

"I'm telling you, she be tweaking."

"He gave her something."

"Roofied for sure."

"Hey, girl, this guy bothering you?"

She looked at Joey, blinking several times to clear her mind.

Red lights began to flash.

*Whoop! Whoop!*

"Cops!" someone shouted.

"Go!" another cried.

The sounds of heels scattering across the pavement echoed.

"ARE you sure you don't want to go to the hospital?" Joey asked once the police had finally left and they were back in his car, the two having somehow convinced the officers that Penny had simply started to feel nauseated and stumbled while getting out of the car to run to the bathroom. The fact that they had just eaten sushi and had a receipt to prove it helped with the convincing, both officers grimacing.

"What? It's just a scrape," she said, holding up her hand.

"No, I mean because of the panic attack, or whatever that was. Shouldn't you be documenting things like this for your neurologist?"

"My neurologist?" she asked.

"Because of your head injury?"

"It was just a mild concussion."

"You were in a coma for nearly a month."

"Oh! I thought you meant when I hit my head at the mall." She frowned. "I don't think I have a neurologist."

"What? Seriously?"

She shook her head.

"What about after you woke up from the coma? Didn't they run tests and stuff?"

"Well, yeah. Of course. I was stuck in the hospital for like three weeks after that. It sucked."

"And then what?"

"I came here."

"But didn't they, like, give you a list of things to keep an eye out for, or refer you to someone out here to see for checkups or anything?"

"I don't know. They suggested tons of things, but everything was a bit crazy and I wasn't the most pleasant person to be around at the time, given that I felt like I had killed my mom and learned that I was going to go live with my crazy aunt."

"Pleasant or not, they should have referred you to someone to keep an eye on things and monitor any oddities."

"Maybe they did. I just wasn't paying attention or it got lost in all the paperwork they gave my aunt." She sighed and looked out the passenger window, thoughts on all the shouting and posturing that had occurred in the hospital room flooding through her mind.

At one point she had tried to run away, a ridiculous decision to go stay at their ski cabin being made. Why she had thought that would work, she didn't know. She just knew she couldn't move out here with her aunt and cousins.

"I think you should look into it," he said. "Having panic attacks and hallucinations isn't normal, and after major head trauma, it could be a sign of something serious."

She didn't reply.

They drove in silence for a while.

"I apologize if I'm overstepping myself," he said in reply to her silence.

She turned and looked at him, tears once again in her eyes. "It's not that," she said. "I appreciate the concern. I really do. But it isn't just panic attacks and hallucinations."

"What do you mean?"

She hesitated and then said, "Can we stop somewhere? For, like, coffee or something."

"Coffee?" he asked. "Um...okay."

"Or just somewhere with some privacy so we can talk."

"I know a spot. It's not a diner or anything, just a bluff overlooking the river, so there wouldn't be any coffee, but we could sit on the edge overlooking the water. It's nice. Unless you actually want some coffee. Then we could go—"

"The bluff sounds perfect. Cozy even. Let's do that."

"You sure?"

"Yeah."

*EVERYTHING OKAY?* Olivia typed after discovering that Penny wasn't home yet.

A knock echoed.

"Yeah?" she asked as her mother stepped in.

"You and Liz have a good time?"

"Yeah. We pretty much binged *Gilmore Girls* while eating pizza and ice cream."

"Ah, fun."

"Yeah."

Her mother hesitated.

*She knows I'm bullshitting her,* Olivia realized. *Yet she isn't calling me on it.*

*Why?*

*Because she doesn't care, or because she's busy hiding something herself?*

*Her own boyfriend?*

*Or girlfriend?*

*Or...*

Her phone buzzed.

She looked at it and then said, "Penny," to her mother.

"Ah, I was going to ask if you had heard from her."

"Joey had some stomach issues, so they got stuck at a gas station," Olivia said.

"She have any idea when she'll be back?"

Olivia looked at the message.

*We stopped off at the river bluffs,* the message read.

"Looks like they stopped off at another gas station," she lied. "Joey must really be sick."

"Oh, that's too bad." She paused. "Well, I'm going to call it a night."

"Okay."

"I made a pitcher of ice tea earlier if you want some. Turned out pretty good. It's in the fridge."

Olivia gave her a quizzical look.

"I got bored," her mom said with a shrug and then disappeared from the doorway.

Olivia shifted her attention back to her phone, an image of Penny and Joey hanging out at the bluffs entering into her mind.

*Are they going to do it?*

*Even after his stomach issues?*

If that were her, there was no way she'd want to go to a local lovers' lane to have sex. Then again, Joey was a guy, so he'd probably be okay with having sex even when he felt like his stomach was going to flush itself.

Another text arrived, this one from Martin.

*Turn on the news,* it said.

*Why?*

*Just do it.*

Olivia did.

"SOME HALLUCINATION, HUH?" Penny said after telling Joey about the demon that had fucked her in the middle of the night. She left out the part about her newfound concern that the demon had actually been Olivia in some sort of possessed state.

Joey didn't reply, his eyes simply staring out beyond the bluff toward the dark river.

Penny waited.

"I-I—" He shook his head.

"It's hard to wrap your mind around, isn't it?" she said.

"That's putting it mildly."

Several seconds came and went.

"This priest you're seeing, he has experience with things like this?" Joey asked.

"That's what my aunt says."

"And he isn't, like, a publicity hound or anything like those Conjuring people, right?"

"Conjuring people?"

"You know those horror movies. *The Conjuring*. I think there are like three or four of them now with the spinoffs. They're about these ghost-hunting demonologists back in the seventies who either faked a lot of what they saw or embellished it in order to get book and movie deals."

"Okay, I know who you're talking about but can't think of their names. Didn't they get famous because of the movie about the house that has the windows that look like eyes? What was that one called?"

"Let's see," Joey said and pulled out his phone. "I bet if I type *haunted house movies* it will be one of the first—"

"What?" she asked after a few seconds, concern brewing.

Rather than reply, Joey simply turned his phone toward her so she could see the text he had gotten from Martin. It read: *Leanne's dead.*

# THIRTY-TWO

The house was empty once again, a frantic knock on her bedroom door followed by a "Can I use the car?" plea from Olivia having alerted Susan to the fact that Leanne's name had finally been released to the media and word was spreading quickly through the student body.

"Where're you going?"

"To help comfort Joey. Penny says he's a wreck."

"Didn't they break up?"

"Yeah, but they were together for nearly a year."

"Okay, yes, go. Keys are in the dish by the door."

"Thanks."

Twenty minutes later Susan realized she should have appeared more hesitant about letting Olivia head out, what with there being a killer on the loose that was targeting teen girls.

She feigned worry with a call, but Olivia didn't answer.

Next she sent a text.

*It's okay,* Olivia replied. *We're at Martin's house.*

A few seconds came and went, then another message arrived.

*His parents are home.*

Susan wasn't sure why, but that text made her smile. It was like Olivia had felt the need to point that out as a way of assuring her that nothing unseemly was going on.

*Could I lure Penny away from the group, and then—*

*No.*

First, she had no idea where Martin lived, and while uncovering that info wouldn't be all that difficult, getting into the house unseen and then luring Penny out would be next to impossible.

Second, she needed Conrad to be present.

Third, and most important, she still had no idea if they were being watched by some grubby PI that Conrad's wife had hired.

She needed to figure that situation out before doing anything else that involved him.

*But how?*

She couldn't simply ask his wife if she had hired someone.

Or could she?

Torture her for information on the PI and then kill her?

If she did that, the police would be all over Conrad, and while that was part of her end goal, she needed it to happen after he was dead and thus could not implicate her in anything.

THE GIRLS CAME BACK HOME AROUND ELEVEN, Susan throwing on her bathrobe at the sound of the garage door opening and then heading downstairs, a question on how Joey was doing leaving her lips as the two entered the kitchen.

"He's a mess," Olivia said.

"Yeah," Penny added.

"What about you two?" she asked. "You okay?"

"I'm okay," Penny confirmed.

Olivia simply shrugged.

Nothing else followed, the silence stretching until Penny finally said, "I'm going to call it a night."

"Me too," Olivia said.

"Okay. Well. If either of you need anything or want to talk..." She simply left it at that.

Both girls nodded.

Susan followed Olivia up the stairs while Penny headed down into the basement.

After that, time ticked slowly by as Susan waited for the 3:00 a.m. hour, her eyes struggling to stay open as she sat up in bed watching a near-muted TV, her inability to use an alarm clock to wake herself during the early morning hour for fear that it might also wake up Olivia making it so she couldn't fall asleep.

THOUGH EXHAUSTED, Penny couldn't sleep, and after nearly an hour of tossing and turning, she headed out to the old battered couch on the opposite side of the basement with her iPad, the statements Joey had made about the accident and seeing a neurologist spurring her into doing a search about head trauma and what the possible side effects might be.

Tons of information was available, the most popular search results talking about soldiers and how much damage their brains suffered during an IED blast due to the organ bouncing within the skull. Apparently, football players suffered a similar type of injury from being tackled over and over again. Car accidents were another common cause.

As interesting as this was, she didn't feel it spoke to what her experience had been, given that her skull had actually depressed inward during the accident and pressed into her brain. It had been so serious that a surgeon had to go in and relieve the pressure. How they did this, she didn't know, but the large scar above her left ear was evidence of how serious it had been.

BY TWO THIRTY in the morning, Susan was wired on caffeine from the three Cokes and an energy drink she had consumed, her inability to sit still obvious as she paced the bedroom waiting for the 3:00 a.m. hour to arrive.

At 2:40 she couldn't take it any longer and started to get herself ready, pulling out the demon mask from a box in the closet before going to the nightstand drawer to grab the giant strap-on penis.

It wasn't there.

Startled, she thought back to the other night, mind trying to recall what had happened after she had fucked Penny, a memory of tucking the strap-on and demon mask away in a box outside the bedroom door and then donning her robe so she could console the horrified teen appearing.

After that...

She had brought the box back up to her bedroom and...

*Bathroom.*

The penis part of the strap-on had been streaked with blood from Penny's ruined virginity, so she had cleaned it in the sink and hung it up to dry.

And then forgot about it.

Stupid.

She headed into the bathroom.

. . .

SOMEONE WAS IN HER ROOM!

Olivia could sense it as she lay with her back to the door, a rustling noise having awakened her from a troubled sleep.

The floor creaked.

*Oh my God!*

Olivia held her breath, fearful of making a sound, thoughts on what Penny had said about the demon having raped her dominating her mind.

Silence.

She waited, her heart beating faster than it had ever beaten before.

The sound of a zipper being quietly opened reached her ears.

*What?*

Confusion joined her terror.

Several seconds came and went.

Another creak.

Olivia stifled a growing scream and slowly twisted, eyes going wide as she saw her mother leaning over her desk chair.

SUSAN SMELLED the rubber before she saw the strap-on, her earlier concern that Olivia had snatched the item from the bathroom confirmed.

But why?

No answers followed as she pulled the harness free from the backpack that sat on the chair.

"Mom?"

Susan shrieked with surprise and spun around, the strap-on falling to the floor with a heavy *thump*.

"What are you"—the bedside light came on—"doing?"

. . .

OLIVIA STARED AT THE STRAP-ON, horror-laced embarrassment rising.

Her mother seemed in a similar state.

Neither spoke for several seconds.

Then, “Why did you take this?” her mother asked while bending down to grab it.

Olivia couldn’t find her voice.

“Did you use it with Martin?”

Still nothing.

“*Did you use it?*” she repeated, giant penis wobbling as she thrust it toward her.

“No,” Olivia whispered.

“Then why did you take it?”

Olivia shook her head. “I don’t know.”

“Olivia.”

“I wanted to show him.”

“Why?”

She shrugged.

“Why were you even in my room?”

“I don’t know.”

“You don’t know?”

Olivia didn’t reply.

“Well, until you do know, consider yourself under house arrest. Penny too.”

“But—” she started and then stopped when she saw the glare.

“But?”

Olivia shook her head.

SUSAN SAT on her bed for a long time after that, eyes

staring at but not really seeing the strap-on that she held in her lap. Instead, she was envisioning the girls in her room, going through her things, gasping and giggling as they pulled out various items from her toy drawer.

*Had they seen the mask?*

*If so, had Penny recognized it?*

*No.*

If she had, this evening would have been a lot different. Penny would have—

A knock echoed.

Susan hesitated.

"Mom?" Olivia asked.

Susan sighed while tucking the mask beneath the bedsheets, and then got up to open the door.

Olivia stood in the doorway.

Susan crossed her arms and waited.

"I'm sorry," Olivia eventually said. "We shouldn't have been going through your things."

"You're right, you shouldn't have," Susan said.

Olivia seemed surprised by the reply.

Susan waited.

"Are you seeing someone?" Olivia asked.

Susan blinked, the question catching her off guard. "What?"

"It's just...well...that"—she nodded toward the strap-on —"it's not something you use by yourself."

Susan stared at her daughter for several seconds and then quickly said, "Go to bed."

"Mom, come on. You can talk to me."

"Go to bed," she repeated and started to close the door.

"Is it a woman?" Olivia questioned.

This gave Susan pause, her hand halting the door.

"If it is, it's totally okay. I mean, I know the church would have a fit, but come on, it's the twenty-first—"

"Olivia," Susan said, cutting her off. "I don't want to talk about this at three thirty in the morning. Go to bed."

Olivia looked as if she were going to protest but then simply nodded and turned to head back to her room.

Susan closed the door.

PENNY CAME AWAKE WITH A START, terror slithering through her bloodstream as she looked around for a demon that wasn't there. And then she heard a creak up above as someone moved about on the ground floor, someone who seemed to be heading into the kitchen at...?

She reached for her phone to check the time, eyes instantly seeing she had a Facebook message from Joey.

It had arrived two hours earlier.

*I couldn't sleep and started doing some research and found this.* A link followed, one that directed her to a Wikipedia page titled Temporal Lobe Epilepsy.

# PART THREE

# THIRTY-THREE

Susan was exhausted, the two hours of sleep she had managed after shooing Olivia from her bedroom and then staring at the ceiling for an hour having done little to rejuvenate her weary body. In fact, it seemed to have made things worse, almost as if her mind were protesting the tease of sleep she had shown it.

*Coffee.*

It didn't remove her exhaustion but did help in distracting from it, an extra scoop of grounds having made it bitter to the point of being nearly undrinkable yet a great delivery method for caffeine.

She was on her third cup when Penny came up, an unenthusiastic "good morning" being voiced as the teen headed for the coffee pot.

Susan returned the good morning and then warned, "I made it extra strong."

"Oh good. I need it after last night."

"Did something happen?" Susan asked.

Penny gave a dismissive wave. "Nothing serious. Just

couldn't sleep." She poured some coffee and then grimaced at the bitterness.

"How come?" Susan pressed.

"Not sure," she said and then took another sip, this grimace less expressive but still noticeable. "Joey said something yesterday that got me curious." Another sip. "Am I supposed to be seeing a neurologist?"

Susan nearly choked. "A neurologist?" she questioned, stalling.

"Yeah. Joey was surprised that I don't see one given my head injury."

"I see."

"Do you remember them saying anything about that?"

"No," she lied. "They just mentioned the pills that could be prescribed if you had moments of vertigo. Oh, and the warnings about the antibiotics and sunlight."

Penny nodded, her tired face seemingly deep in thought.

Susan waited, concern turning the coffee to acid in her gut.

"Do you think everything that is happening could be from the accident?"

"I suppose the possibility exists that this could all be in your head, but do you really think that the demon you saw the other night—the one that you felt forcing itself into you—was just a hallucination?"

Penny hesitated before giving a slight shake of her head.

"Me either."

"DO YOU STILL FIND ME ATTRACTIVE?" his wife asked.

"What?" Conrad stammered, caught off guard.

She waited, obviously knowing he had heard the question.

"Honey," he said. "Last night...it wasn't you. I've just had a lot on my mind."

"You always have a lot on your mind, but I used to be able to distract you from that. Now"—she lifted her hands —"after a month of nothing, I couldn't even get you interested."

He shook his head.

"Something's bothering you," she said. "Has been for quite some time."

He didn't reply.

She took his hand. "What are you always telling me about your patients and their issues?"

"What?" he asked, the question genuine. He had no idea what she was trying to direct him toward.

"You've said time and time again that most of their problems could be solved if they would just communicate with their spouse rather than bottling everything up."

*Shit.*

"So," she continued. "Don't bottle it up. Talk to me. What's up?"

He stared at her hands as they held his.

"What has you so tangled up that I can't even distract you with my feminine ways?"

His eyes shifted up to her eyes, a plea hovering within as she stared at him.

Words nearly followed but then were halted, both by a sudden vibration in his pocket and his own knowledge that his actions did not fall into the "if they would just talk to each other" category.

. . .

SUSAN CHECKED her phone for the tenth time, her frustration with Conrad reaching a level she had never before experienced.

*Check your texts!* she silently screamed.

It remained unread.

Penny was so close to realizing the truth.

Too close.

She needed to finish this.

*Calm down,* she urged herself.

Easier said than done.

*"Should I be seeing a neurologist?"*

Penny's question echoed through her brain.

She couldn't focus on anything else.

The answer to the question was yes. Penny's surgeon had recommended it. In fact, she had given Susan a list of neurologists in the area. Susan had even planned on setting something up with one, but then got sidetracked by the ordeal of getting Penny enrolled at St. Katherine's, the school officials having been very uneasy with the idea of allowing the daughter of a porn star within their sacred hallways.

In the end, they had agreed, reluctantly.

And then the Ouija board incident had occurred.

After everything Susan had done to get Penny into the school and she went and did something like that.

It had almost been a breaking point, but then two things had happened. First, she realized the school officials didn't seem to be aware of the video; second, she had remembered the doctors talking to her about the potential for seizures given the damage to her temporal lobe, ones that could be triggered by things like stress, smell, lights, or a variety of other stimuli.

Scented candles.

And incense.

Both were visible in the brief video of the Ouija board incident, an idea quickly forming within her mind.

"Mom?"

Susan blinked herself back into the moment and said, "Yeah?"

"You okay?" Olivia asked.

"Yeah," Susan said, rubbing at her eyes. "Just drifted off for a moment." She looked at her coffee, which had gone cold, and then over at the pot, which was nearly empty. "I was thinking of getting us some donuts. How's that sound?"

"Donuts?" Olivia questioned.

"Yeah. I have a sweet tooth this morning."

"Cool."

"What kind do you want?"

"Where you getting them from?"

"Donut Café."

"Mmm, chocolate then."

"Okay. Can you find out what Penny wants while I go get my purse?"

"Sure."

With that, Olivia headed downstairs while Susan headed upstairs to throw some clothes on and grab her purse, her only goal in heading out of town to the Donut Café being to see if a PI was following her.

# THIRTY-FOUR

"You actually took it?" Penny gasped.

"I did," Olivia said.

"Why?"

"I don't know. I wanted to see his reaction."

"The picture wasn't enough?"

Olivia shrugged.

"How did she know you took it?" Penny asked.

"I have no idea," Olivia said. "I simply woke up and she was in my room pulling it out of my bag."

"Jesus Christ."

"Yeah."

"Did she say anything?"

"Not really. She just seemed upset that I had it. And that we had gone through her things."

"You told her?"

"She knew."

"How?" Penny asked. "Does she have, like, a nanny cam or something in there?"

"I doubt it."

"But then how did she know you took it and that it was

in your bag? Why was she even looking for it in the middle of the night?"

"I think I figured that last part out."

"Oh."

"I bet she was sexting with her girlfriend and went to get the strap-on or something and realized it wasn't there."

"Why would she need a strap-on if they were just sexting?"

Olivia shrugged.

"Unless...ohhh wait a second," Penny said.

"What?"

"Your mom has a webcam on her computer."

"Everyone does."

"True, but maybe she was using hers and that's why she needed the strap-on."

Olivia was momentarily puzzled, but then her eyes went wide with understanding. "You think they were camming with each other rather than just sexting?"

"Maybe," Penny said. "Or she might be..." Her voice faded.

"Might be what?" Olivia asked.

"Nah, nothing," she said, waving a hand.

"Come on, what?"

"I was just thinking. All those sex toys in her drawer. What if she has been using her webcam to make some extra money?"

"How?"

"You know. Using the toys on herself while guys pay her to watch."

"What! My mom? No way!"

"You never know."

"Oh, I know."

"Do you?"

Olivia didn't reply.

"You never expected to see all those toys in the drawer, or that strap-on hanging from the door."

Still nothing.

"And given all the money my mom used to make, she might have gotten curious."

"Did she webcam?"

"In the early days. And then, once she started her own studio, she had an entire web page set up just for webcam girls."

"Really?"

"Yeah. It's amazing how much money guys will pay just to watch someone following their instructions on camera."

"Men," Olivia muttered.

"Yeah," Penny said with a chuckle.

"Seriously, Martin showed me his porn folder yesterday. The amount of time guys spend downloading and watching this shit is insane."

"Why in the world would he show you that?" Penny asked.

"Oh...we sort of just stumbled upon it while looking at his computer."

"Gag!" Penny said.

"Big time. You should have seen it. He had cartoon porn and hundreds of videos of these twisted Japanese game shows that involve twisted sex acts and stuff." She crossed her arms and shivered. "It was sick."

"What about my mom?" Penny asked.

"Huh? What about her?"

"Does he have videos of her?"

Olivia didn't reply.

"Did you watch them?" Penny asked, taking the silence to be a yes.

"I told him to stop watching them."

"Eh," Penny said, waving her hand. "Millions of people watch them."

"Still, he shouldn't be watching those. It's just...I don't know."

"Really, it's fine." Then, as if needing to add more, "It doesn't bother me."

Olivia eyed her for several seconds and then said, "You know, I think he has one of her early videos. In fact, based on the interview they did at the beginning, I think it might have been her first."

"Are you serious?"

"Yeah."

"She always hated those videos. Never wanted them on her sites and would send copyright notices to the free sharing sites if she found them on them, even though she didn't really own the copyrights herself."

"Seriously? Why?"

"I think they embarrassed her. She was so young and inexperienced."

"Pssh. Like guys care. Look at the acting that happens in those videos. It's a joke."

"Yeah, but even so, they still bothered her."

"She did seem pretty nervous during the interview. And so young. Not much older than us, actually. It's surreal."

Penny went quiet.

Olivia sipped her coffee.

"Do you think Martin would let me see it?" Penny finally asked.

"What?"

"Not the sex parts, just the interview."

"Why?"

"I'm just curious," she said after some hesitation. "There's so much from her life I don't know or understand."

"I totally get that," Olivia said.

Penny pursed her lips.

"I actually have the interview if you want to watch it."

"You do?"

"Yeah. I had Martin email it to me."

"Why?"

"I don't really know. Something about it felt off, but I couldn't put my finger on what exactly. I figured I'd watch it again, but then the news of Leanne came and"—she waved a hand—"it slipped my mind until just now."

SUSAN DIDN'T spot anyone following her as she headed to the Donut Café, but then realized this would have been a really odd time for a PI to be watching her. In fact, it was more likely that the PI was watching Conrad since he was the one whose indiscretions were being documented.

A newspaper dispenser was present next to the entrance of the Donut Café, *Second Student Murdered* splashed across the top of the display paper.

Seeing this, an idea began to form, though it wasn't one that she fully recognized until she was heading back to the house, donuts secured.

"THAT'S NOT MY MOM," Penny said after watching the short interview.

"What?" Olivia questioned, the denial catching her off guard, given that her mom gave her name at the very beginning of the video. "Of course it is."

"No," Penny insisted, shaking her head. "It isn't."

"Then who?" Olivia asked, her own denial starting to build, even though Penny didn't voice what she herself suddenly knew. "No, it can't be."

"It is."

Olivia hit replay on the video and watched it again.

And then again.

Penny waited.

After the third viewing, Olivia turned toward her, eyes wide.

"It's her," Penny said. "She pretended to be my mom for the video."

"But..." Nothing followed for several seconds. "Why?"

"I don't know."

Several seconds came and went.

"Your mom got kicked out of school for this," Olivia said.

"Yeah."

"Why didn't she say anything? Tell people it wasn't really her?"

Penny simply shrugged.

"Fuck."

SUSAN TOOK a scenic route home from the Donut Café, one which allowed her to drive by Conrad's house.

No one was watching it—that she could see.

But then why would they be?

If a PI had been hired, they wouldn't need to be watching Conrad while he was at home with his wife. Instead, they would only be interested in those moments when he was on his own, moments when he was supposed to be seeing patients at the office but instead was at a motel.

*Had the PI observed any of those motel moments?*

*Had they snapped pictures of us two leaving the room?*

No.

If pictures had been taken, then Conrad would not be inside with his wife right now, but instead would be at one of those motels. Or on the couch in his office. The fact that he was home with his wife meant that no evidence had been presented yet.

*He doesn't even know if a PI has been hired.*

*Could he be mistaken?*

The only evidence he had was that she had withdrawn some money that couldn't be explained. And the only reason he suspected a PI was due to the Pornhub video links that his wife had sent to him.

*How did she even know it was me?*

The two had never met before, and the only other person who had ever known about her impersonating her sister for those films was her sister, and she had never revealed it.

*Conrad knows.*

How exactly she didn't know, given that she no longer looked anything like she did back in college, though she guessed it must have had something to do with them having been together in bed. Somehow he had recognized something. The same could not be possible of his wife or her PI. There would have been no way for them to come to such a conclusion. The best they could do was speculate, but even that seemed far-fetched.

"WHAT SHOULD WE DO?" Olivia asked.

"What do you mean?" Penny questioned.

"About this," she said, motioning toward the video.

"Nothing."

"Nothing! She paddled my ass for saying fuck, yet she starred in porn videos and lied about it for years."

"And what, you want to confront her about it? Throw it in her face?"

"Don't you?"

"No."

"Your mom got kicked out of school for this!"

"And used it to her advantage," Penny noted. "She always said getting kicked out was the best thing that ever happened to her."

Olivia contemplated that and then nodded. "True."

"Actually, if I was your mom, I would be kicking myself for not having done those videos under my own name.'

Olivia frowned at first, but then nodded with understanding. A grin followed. "Karma's a bitch, isn't it?"

"Big time."

A buzz echoed.

Penny pulled out her phone.

"Joey," she said.

"How's he doing?" Olivia asked.

"Eh, hard to say," Penny said while reading the message. "Aw, he's actually apologizing for texting me so late last night."

"Ah."

"Poor guy. He couldn't sleep and then started doing research into head trauma and seizures."

"That's random."

"Oh, it was because I had another incident last night while we were together."

"What? When?"

"After his stomach issues, while we were in the parking lot with the prostitutes."

Olivia blinked and raised her hands in a "what the fuck?" gesture and said, "Why didn't you tell me?"

"We found out about Leanne right after and it just...I don't know...got pushed into the background." She waved a hand. "Anyway, he thinks all these incidents are actually temporal lobe seizures caused by the accident."

"Really?"

"Yeah, and he was kind of irked that I wasn't seeing a neurologist."

"A neurologist?"

"Yeah, because of my head injury and being in a coma for a month."

"Oh shit, he has a good point."

"He does."

"Did you mention it to my mom?"

"Yeah."

"And?"

"She's split. On the one hand, she does realize that I should probably be seeing a neurologist and that one was probably recommended but then lost in all the drama of the funeral and me moving out here."

"And on the other hand?"

"My being fucked the other night was no hallucination. Something was in the room with me."

Olivia felt a chill. "What does Father Collins think?"

"Oh wow, I didn't even think to mention it to him."

"Well...no time like the present."

Penny sent him a text.

# THIRTY-FIVE

Though the donuts were a hit, Penny and Olivia packing away the empty calories without a care in the world, something seemed off. Susan couldn't put her finger on what it was, but something odd was certainly in the air.

And then she caught Olivia staring at her.

"What?" she finally asked.

"Nothing," Olivia said and quickly stuffed her mouth with some surgery goodness.

Susan eyed her for several seconds and then shifted toward Penny, who pretended to focus on choosing another donut.

*What did they do?*

*My room again?*

She was about to press them when a phone buzzed.

*Olivia's.*

Susan waited.

"They're having a vigil for Leanne tonight," Olivia said while looking at her phone, fingers carefully touching the screen so as not to get chocolate on it.

"Oh?" Susan said. "Where?"

"At the school. By the football field."

"What time?"

"Looks like it starts at eight."

Susan considered this. The vigil could provide good cover for meeting up with Conrad. In fact, it could provide good cover for quite a few activities, one of them being to lure Penny away from the group and into the church catacombs to finish things. After all, if a serial killer was targeting teenage girls, the vigil would be like an all-you-can-eat buffet.

Then again, the police would probably be out in force.

But they wouldn't be focused on a mother like her.

"It's kind of odd," Penny said, her voice bringing Susan back to the moment.

"What is?" Olivia asked.

"A vigil for Leanne, but they didn't do one for Jocelyn."

"Well, they had that assembly."

"True, but still..."

"Plus, I think this is kind of a 'we will not be afraid' sort of thing, especially since she was killed at school."

"You think they're trying to save face?"

"Totally."

"Hmm."

"Mom, what do you think?"

"About what?" Susan asked.

"The school. Are they trying to save face?"

Susan considered this for a few seconds and then nodded. "That's probably part of it." Quite a few parents were likely freaking out and now questioning whether the school could provide adequate safety for their children. "But they might also want to give everyone the chance to come together and reflect upon the young lady's life."

"I wonder if they'll have a microphone set up so people can share stories about her," Penny said.

"If they do, we could enlighten everyone about who she really was."

"No, no," Susan warned, all while deep down inside she grinned.

*If only they could really do that.*

*It would be quite the spectacle.*

"You two will be respectable," Susan continued. "Both in appearance and conduct."

"Appearance?" Olivia questioned.

"Yes."

"It's not a funeral."

"It's a somber event that most of the community will attend. I will not have you dressing like it's a kegger."

"Mommmm," Olivia groaned.

"Oliviaaaa," Susan groaned back.

"Fine. Whatever."

Susan waited, but nothing else followed, the two going back to their donut binge.

"DID SHE SEEM WEIRD TO YOU?" Olivia asked.

"A bit," Penny said and then looked at her phone.

"Joey?"

"Yeah," Penny confirmed while thumbing a reply. "We're trying to figure out what to do today, but..." She shrugged. "Any ideas?"

Olivia shook her head. "Nada. Whatever you do end up doing though, don't get dirty. We have to look *nice* for the vigil."

"She kind of has a point about that. It's not a party."

"Oh, I know. But the fact that she felt she had to say

something kind of irked me. As if I would think this was a kegger that I could strut my stuff at."

"I'm still planning to strut my stuff. Funeral attire is very sexy and gets one in the mood."

Olivia laughed.

Penny's phone buzzed.

She eyed it.

"What is it?" Olivia asked.

Penny turned the phone toward her.

*Your mother sucks cocks in hell.*

"Holy shit," Olivia said. "Who sent that?"

"Unknown," Penny said.

"Does it show the number though?"

"Yeah." Penny read it off to her.

"That's a local number."

Penny didn't reply, her thumbs typing a reply.

"What are you doing?"

"Telling them to go fuck themselves."

"Nice."

A few seconds came and went.

"Anything?" Olivia asked.

"They've read it but aren't replying."

"They probably weren't expecting you to clap back."

"It wasn't much of a clapback."

"What? No. *Fuck you* is the ultimate clapback."

Penny's phone buzzed.

"Oh shit, now what?" Olivia asked.

"It's just Joey."

"Ah."

Penny read the message. "He says that Martin says we can all chill at his place if we want."

"Works for me."

Penny thumbed a reply.

. . .

SUSAN LOOKED AT THE "FUCK YOU" reply that Penny had sent to the "your mother sucks cocks in hell" quote and grinned.

*What next?*

*A picture?*

Several were present. Some of Penny. Some of her mother having sex and with dicks in her mouth. One of Susan herself from the early porn videos that Leanne had probably thought was Penny's mother.

Hesitation arrived.

She pulled out her regular phone.

Still nothing from Conrad.

*How did they know it was me?* she asked herself again.

*Could a PI have dug that up somehow?*

The answer was no.

It just wasn't possible.

Everything about the videos had pointed to her sister. Even the paychecks had been in her name, ones that Susan had had no trouble cashing given how closely she resembled the photo on her sister's driver's license.

*Does Penny know?*

*Would her mother have told her?*

Susan didn't think so.

The story of how her mother had entered into the porn industry had become legendary. So much so that her sister had used it to her advantage every chance she got, the effect twofold because it not only had gotten her high-paying roles and notoriety, but also was a great way of sticking it to Susan.

*What else does his wife know?*

She had to find out. Today. Before the vigil. If she

didn't, she might finish things only to learn that the PI had seen something that might ruin the narrative she had concocted.

*Does Conrad have any appointments today?*

If so, the PI would probably be watching the office just to make sure he didn't visit someone afterward.

That would leave his wife all alone in their home.

Susan would pay her a visit.

"YOU ALL WANT to know something creepy?" Martin said. "The other day, we"—he motioned toward Olivia—"were eating lunch right by where Leanne was killed."

"No..." Olivia started, but then stopped, eyes going wide. "Shit, you're right."

"Makes you wonder if the killer was watching us. Waiting. Hoping for one of us to venture out alone."

"More like waiting for me," Olivia said. "No offense, but I don't think you're his type, considering the two chicks he's offed."

"Guys," Penny said.

Martin looked over at Penny and Joey, a muttered apology leaving his lips.

An awkward silence settled.

"So, you two going to the vigil tonight?" Martin asked.

"Yeah," Penny said.

"And we have to dress appropriately," Olivia muttered.

"Appropriately?" Martin asked with a slight chuckle.

"Her mom insisted on reminding her that this isn't a kegger," Penny said.

"She wants us to be respectable in conduct and appearance," Olivia added.

"You gonna wear a dress?" Martin asked.

"Are you?" she countered.

"Yep. Got one all laid out on my bed."

"In that case, I'll wear some pants and bring the strap-on so that we can go off into the brush and—"

"Olivia," Penny said, voice stern.

"What?" she demanded, eyes going from Penny to Joey.

Penny just shook her head.

A few seconds came and went.

"I vote no on the strap-on," Martin said.

"ARE YOU OKAY?" Penny asked a few minutes later, the two having stepped out into Martin's backyard.

"Yeah," Joey said. "I'm fine."

"You sure?" she pressed.

He nodded.

"I really can't believe those two. I mean, I know Olivia and Leanne had their differences, but still, they shouldn't be—"

"Honestly, it's not bothering me."

Penny went quiet, suppressing an urge to insist that it was bothering him and that it was okay to express his feelings on it.

"You know what does have me concerned?" he said.

"Hmm?"

"Jocelyn is the one that taped you and then posted the video of you during the Ouija board incident, and then Leanne is the one that kept sharing it and making comments about it and the other incidents."

Penny waited, but when nothing else followed asked, "And what, you think I'm taking revenge on them?"

"*No, no,*" he said, startled. "Not at all. I'm wondering if some nut is targeting those who were involved, like some religious freak that's worried a demon has entered our world."

"Why not just go after me then?" she asked, trying to mask her own concern. "You know, since I'm the one that was apparently possessed by the demon and all."

"Because they didn't know who you were. It was never mentioned in the video. That's why Jocelyn was tortured. And then Leanne. They're trying to track you down."

Penny considered this for several seconds. "I can buy that Jocelyn was tortured for information, what with her being in the basement of that house in the middle of nowhere. But Leanne was killed beneath the bleachers. Her screams would have been heard if she were being tortured for information."

"True," he said with a nod. "But then maybe she gave you up right away and then the killer still—"

"Is that a tree house?" Penny asked, nudging him and then pointing.

"Huh?" Joey questioned and then followed her gaze to the structure that stood several feet off the ground in a tree that bordered the rear of Martin's property line. "Oh yeah, we built that in grade school."

"*You built that?*" she said, impressed.

"Well...we watched our dads build it. But we helped by handing them stuff they needed and fetching beers when requested." He shook his head. "I can't believe it's still standing."

"When was the last time you were in it?"

"At least five years ago."

They walked up to the area beneath the structure.

"How do we get up there?" she asked.

"We used to have a rope ladder that could be pulled up and down, though back then most of us could simply climb up the tree." He circled the trunk, studying it. "Actually, I might still be able to." He turned toward her. "How are you at climbing?"

"I've climbed a fair share of trees in my day, but..." She looked up. "I'd prefer a ladder for this one."

"Hmm, okay. Let me see what I can find."

He hurried over to the shed and disappeared inside.

Penny waited, eyes going from the shed back to the tree house and then the tangled mess beyond it that had grown up around a drainage area that separated this row of houses from the ones behind them.

A chill appeared.

What if Joey was right and some twisted religious freak was stalking her?

What if they were somewhere within the tangled mess right now?

No.

Though dense, the tangled mess could be crossed in seconds—unless one got tangled—and even if someone were dragged into it, there would be no privacy whatsoever for whatever horrible task they felt the need to complete, nor could they get a victim to an area that was more private without venturing out into one of the backyards of the McMansions that made up this subdivision.

She was safe—

A rope dropped across her line of vision and snugged itself beneath her breasts as it was pulled taut, her body connecting with another.

"Gotcha!" Joey announced.

"Jesus," she snapped. "I about pissed myself."

"Sorry," he said, though his grin made the apology somewhat suspect.

She replied to his grin with a playful scowl and then nodded toward the rope. "We going up on that?" she asked.

"Depends. If I climb up the tree and tie this to the branch by the entrance, do you think you can climb up this?"

"Maybe," she said, fondling the rope a bit to see how thick it was. "Only one way to find out."

# THIRTY-SIX

Susan whittled away the midday hours by studying some of the financial documents that detailed her sister's holdings, her eyes once again going wide as she silently counted the digits that came before the decimal point. It was surreal. Just the house alone, which was considered modest in the community where it stood, was worth seven figures. And then there were the CDs, mutual funds, and stocks, her sister's interest in financial markets and trading having proven profitable once she had gotten a couple decent-sized paychecks.

It was ridiculous.

In fact, had Susan not known any better, she would have said that a higher power had been directly involved in generating all this success simply as a way of punishing her for trying to ruin her sister's life.

But alas, that wasn't the case. It couldn't be. If it were, that would mean that she shouldn't even bother with securing this inheritance herself because her actions would never bear fruit. The higher power would intervene. At the last moment, just as the money was in sight, it would be yanked away.

*Maybe that's what's happening?*

She envisioned the private investigator while thinking about this, the image her mind produced one that managed to check all the boxes of what a hard-boiled private investigator looked like. He was even wearing a fedora, one that stayed atop his head as he came to Penny's rescue and foiled everything.

Susan checked her phone.

Still nothing from Conrad.

Frustrated, she pulled out the other phone and sent a new text to Penny, this one far more grotesque than anything she had sent previously.

MARTIN'S DAD COCK-BLOCKED JOEY.

The two were up in the tree house, making out, his hands having worked themselves up her sweatshirt, fingers toying with her nipples in a way that she had never experienced before, her own hand having slipped beneath his waistband to toy with his manhood, when down below the lawnmower started up.

Startled, Joey broke off their kiss and twisted toward the small window, eyes peering out as if spying on the scene below.

Penny wiped her hand off on the floor while he did this, some of his pre-juices having clung to her fingers.

"Do you think he knows we're up here?" she asked when he turned back to look at her, horror-laced surprise etched into his face.

"I don't think so," he whispered.

She grinned.

He returned it.

"So, back when you built this thing, did you ever imagine you'd one day be up here with a girl making out?" she asked.

"At twelve? Pretty much every hour of every day."

"Perv."

"I am as God made me."

She shook her head and then crawled over to join him at the window, eyes peeking out and watching as Martin's dad followed the lawnmower on a journey toward the front yard.

"Now's our chance to make a break for it," Joey said and started to shift toward the doorway.

"Not so fast," Penny replied, hand reaching for and resting on his thigh. "If he doesn't know we're up here..."

Joey seemed lost for words.

She gently pushed him backward and crawled on top of him. "Is this how you imagined it when you were twelve?"

"No," he said. "My imagination never pictured someone so beautiful."

She gave a slight shake of her head and then pressed her lips into his, tongue eventually poking through and dancing with his.

"YOU DON'T THINK they're in the old tree house, do you?" Olivia asked while scanning the backyard, her text to Penny asking if they wanted to go get some food having gone unanswered.

"You know, if it were anyone else, I'd say no, but with those two, that feels like something they'd do," Martin replied, joining her at the window.

"I wonder if your dad knows they're up there."

"Probably not."

Several seconds came and went, the two simply staring at the structure.

"Okay, yep, they're in there," Olivia said.

"You see them?" he asked.

"No, but the leaves on the branches around it are moving."

"You don't think..." he started.

"Yep," she said. "In a tree house."

"And here I thought we had won the prize for craziest location."

She twisted. "What crazy location?"

"The confessional."

"That doesn't count."

"What! Yes it does."

"You were in and out so fast I thought it was just the wind."

"Someone was coming," he said.

"Yeah, and it wasn't either of us."

He laughed.

"Speaking of...how sturdy is that thing?"

"Why, you want to try it when they're done?"

"No, fucktard. I'm wondering what the chances are that they'll bring it down just as your dad is passing alongside it."

"Hmm, I'd say just this side of average."

"This side of average? What does that even mean?"

"Fifty-five percent chance they'll bring it down."

She turned back toward the window, eyes once again focused on the leaves.

Martin joined her.

"Whoa, those leaves be really moving now," he noted.

"I can't believe they're actually doing it," she said.

"Why not?"

"I don't know," Olivia said. It was the truth. She didn't know why her mind leaned toward disbelief, yet it did. It just didn't seem like Penny. Or Joey. But then again, they each had been through quite a bit in the last few days.

NEITHER SPOKE ONCE they were finished, Penny resting with her cheek on his chest while Joey used his pants as a pillow to cushion his head, his right arm wrapped around her, hand cupping her right breast through her T-shirt, which had stayed on as she rode him to completion.

It was a perfect moment, one that had followed a perfect act.

In a tree house.

A giggle rose up but then was suppressed before it echoed from her lips.

She did not want to shatter this.

Not yet.

It wouldn't be long before they had to get up and go back down, but until then she simply wanted to bask in the warm glow that encased her body, one that was enhanced by Joey's embrace.

"WE CAN'T LEAVE them up there," Olivia said.

"They'll be fine and I'm starving," Martin replied.

"I think you'll live."

"They probably won't even want any food."

"What? After they almost shook all the leaves off the tree? They'll be starving."

"Fine. We'll wait. But just so you know, it could be a while. I doubt they'll come down while he's cutting the back."

"How long does that take?"

"At least an hour."

"Really?" she asked, a frown developing, given that she was hungry too.

"Yeah."

"Hmm." She looked out the window once again.

"You know, we could just go poke our heads into the tree house."

"Are you serious. They could be naked and gooey."

"Gooey?" he asked with a laugh.

"Yeah. Plus, you said they probably won't come down until he's finished. What will he think if you go up and then suddenly they follow you down?"

"Given his focus, he might not realize it was just me going up. Plus, if we time it just right, his view will be blocked by the shed while they both come down."

"You know what, I'll just call them." She pulled out her phone again. "That way no one has to risk seeing them all gooey."

He laughed again. "You know, I'm going to be thinking 'gooey' the next time we do it, and it'll totally ruin the moment."

She shook her head while putting her phone to her ear.

"I BET that's Olivia wondering where we went," Penny said as her phone began to ring.

"You should probably answer it before they launch a search party," Joey said, shifting himself a bit.

"Yeah," Penny muttered and pushed herself up so she could crawl over to her crumpled pants, suddenly recalling Father Collins's butt dial the other day.

Could that have been the result of his pants dropping to the floor?

While jerking off to videos of her mom?

Or videos of Aunt Susan?

Or had he actually been with someone?

She shook the imagery away and pulled the phone free just as the ringing stopped.

*Missed call.*

It wasn't the only message that was displayed on the screen.

"What's wrong?" Joey asked, sitting up.

Penny didn't reply right away, her thumb opening the first of several texts from the unknown number.

CONRAD WAS AT THE OFFICE, his old turquoise Saturn obvious in the near-empty parking lot of the professional building. A travel agency, financial planning, and a dentist office were also within the building, and though all were open, none seemed to be generating much traffic.

*Where's the PI?*

*Would he even be in this lot?*

No answers followed.

And none would.

Susan drove away.

Spotting the private investigator had not been her goal during this little visit. Confirming Conrad was at the office and not at home had been.

His wife was all alone.

"ARE YOU SURE?" Olivia asked.

"Yeah," Joey said. He pulled out his own phone and showed her his contacts. "See."

"That's fucked up," Martin said.

No one replied to that, the silence stretching out to a minute and then two.

"We need to show this to the police," Joey said.

"Do you think they can trace it?" Olivia asked. "See who has the phone?"

"I don't know," he said. "Maybe."

"What do I do?" Penny asked. "Call the tip line?"

"Either that or bring it right to the police station."

"I think bringing it to them is the best idea," Martin said. "Who knows who is answering those tip lines. Could be some stressed-out volunteer who brushes it off or, worse yet, adds it to a pile of tips that are being looked at first come, first served."

"Could that many people be calling in with tips?" Olivia asked.

"Probably. The post they put up on their Facebook page has been shared like ten thousand times already. They're probably getting calls from every angry girlfriend who thinks her boyfriend is the killer."

"What?" Olivia questioned. "No."

"Um...yeah. Remember that Ted Bundy thing we watched on Netflix? They said that as soon as the phone number for tips went out, all these women were calling saying they thought their boyfriend or husband was the killer."

Olivia sighed.

"I think going to the station would be best," Joey said. "That way they can see what was sent and the number it was sent from."

"Do you think your mom will let you have your keys back?" Olivia asked Martin.

"Only one way to find out."

"YES?" a wary voice asked through the partially opened door.

"Mrs. Collins? My name is Susan. I work in your husband's office."

"Oh." The door opened wider. "Hi."

"Hi," Susan returned.

"Um...Conrad isn't here," Mrs. Collins said. "He had a patient this afternoon."

"Oh, I know. That's why I wanted to talk to you." Susan looked around, as if uneasy. "Do you have a moment?"

"Why?" she asked, wariness returning

"Mrs. Collins," Susan said. "I really think you'll want to sit down for this."

Mrs. Collins motioned Susan inside.

IT TOOK several minutes for the desk sergeant at the police station to understand what exactly it was that the four of them were trying to convey, but once the understanding arrived, they were quickly ushered into the deeper regions of the police station where they were instructed to wait on a bench for a detective.

That detective ended up being a young lady who didn't seem much older than them. Her name was Betty Joanne Parks.

"Why didn't you come to us after the first text?" Detective Parks asked once she had Penny alone.

"I didn't know the texts were from Leanne's phone,"

Penny said. "I just thought it was another perv who was getting their rocks off by sending me this shit."

"Another perv?" She seemed startled by this.

Penny waved that away. "A video of me went viral on Facebook and I had no idea that my phone number was listed on my profile for everyone to see."

"Ah."

"Plus, my mom used to star in adult videos, so I'm no stranger to obscene phone calls, texts, and emails."

Detective Parks blinked while considering that and then said, "Do you still have all the messages and texts and whatnot?"

"Yes."

"Okay. I want to document every message, text, and email you have gotten."

"All of them?" Penny asked, startled.

"Yes."

Penny thumbed open her phone.

# THIRTY-SEVEN

Conrad had three sessions that afternoon, the last one of the day being a couple's session involving two newlyweds whose marriage had been doomed from the start—so much so that Conrad was frequently tempted to tell them to just cut their losses and split with each other.

But he couldn't do that, not when they were adamant about making it work, their desire to prove their friends and families wrong about "how it would never last" spurring them down a road that promised years of unhappiness.

It was exhausting.

So much so that he had to stretch out on the patient sofa for a while, a hand over his eyes.

His phone buzzed.

His wife.

He opened her text.

*Goodbye.*

He stared at the word for several seconds, a hollow feeling developing within his stomach. *Goodbye? What do you mean?* he replied.

A dot bubble appeared beneath his text, one that disappeared and reappeared several times.

A message arrived.

It read: *You're a pervert that likes to fuck teenage schoolgirls in the butt while they call you daddy.*

Conrad nearly dropped the phone, his fingers fumbling a reply that got butchered by the auto-correct.

*Read at 4:17 p.m.*

No dot bubble followed.

He waited.

And waited.

And waited.

Panicked, he hit the call button.

It rang several times before going to voicemail.

*No! No! No!*

He sprang toward the door, his shin connecting with a side table, the pain a momentary distraction from the horror blossoming within his bowels.

Empty chairs greeted him in the small waiting area, his butt falling into one as all the strength ran out of his legs.

A second later he was looking at his phone, a phantom vibration against his leg having given him a moment of hope.

Nothing.

No text.

No missed call.

He dropped the phone while leaning forward, the device thumping onto the worn carpet.

*Susan.*

It was the only answer.

She had done something.

For two years he had kept her crazy at bay, their motel-room meetings after her discovery of the pictures and videos on his computer having seemed almost like the plot of an unrealistic porn video rather than real life, given that she had been blackmailing him for sex.

Many men would find such a situation appealing. They might even envy him. And honestly, he hadn't really minded it much himself—except during some of her more bizarre moments when she wanted him to really hurt and humiliate her.

Had she sent one of those videos to his wife?

*How?*

She didn't have an email address for her, the one he had used when lying about the private investigator having been fake.

But maybe that was the problem.

Maybe she had known the email was a fake because she had already gotten the real one for herself knowing she might one day have to send a video.

*Calm down,* he told himself.

Deep breath.

He reached for his phone.

Still nothing.

He tried calling again.

Voicemail.

He sent a new text that simply advised that he was on his way home.

Like the previous one, a *Read at* note appeared, but no reply followed.

*Don't...* his mind said as his thumb moved toward the Call icon once again.

He ignored his own advice.

Voicemail again.

He threw the phone, regret arriving as it smashed into the far wall.

A few seconds later, he confirmed that it still worked, though half the screen was shattered.

Frustrated with himself, he tucked the phone into his pocket and headed out to his car.

SUSAN WAS ANGRY. Conrad had lied to her about his wife hiring a private investigator, the emails he had forwarded to her having obviously been from a fake Gmail account he had set up in his wife's name.

But that was all over.

Conrad would think his wife had left him, all while the police would think that he had tried to make it look like she had left him by sending himself texts from her phone.

It was perfect.

The police would assume his wife had uncovered his perverted desires and been killed, his own body cooling in their morgue alongside his most recent victim: Penny.

Once they had that and the DNA match from Leanne, they likely wouldn't look much deeper into things.

But where to put her body?

Initially, she had thought she would leave it at the house itself, but then realized that would be a problem given that Conrad would likely find it and then become a suspect in her death while still alive, which could ruin things.

She needed him to be dead once the police turned their eye on him. That way there was no chance he could point them her way.

Only now she had a body in her trunk, one that she knew she couldn't keep for long. Not in this heat.

River?

The woods?

Dumping it would be risky due to the potential for discovery, but keeping it in the car just was not an option.

The river seemed the best bet.

It would initially sink and once it came back up, everything would be finished. She would simply be listed as another victim—a wife who wouldn't have to deal with all the shouted questions of "how did you not realize your husband was a killer?" from the media.

THE HOUSE WAS EMPTY, his wife gone.

No note was present, though he hadn't really expected one.

Hoped for, yes; expected, no.

He called her mother.

It was answered on the second ring.

"What do you mean she left?" his mother-in-law demanded. "What did you do?"

Rather than get into it, Conrad hung up and called the next contact, and then the next and then the next, his only hope being to get a reassurance that his wife was okay.

Everyone claimed she wasn't with them.

He had expected such responses but felt that with one of them he would be able to tell that they were lying, which would have been enough for him at the moment. The fact that he believed all of them was troubling.

Where had she gone?

Her car was still in the garage, so she hadn't used it.

*Uber?*

*To a motel?*

If so, she would have to use a credit card, and since they only had the joint account, he would be able to see the charges.

Well, maybe not a motel, depending on where she went, but the Uber one for sure.

A TEXT ARRIVED as Susan pulled into the driveway.

*When are you going to be picking up Nicky?* it asked.

Susan shook her head, her son having completely slipped her mind.

*On my way right now,* she texted back.

The body in the trunk would have to wait.

"AM I GOING to have to wear my uniform?" Nicky asked fifteen minutes later.

"What, honey?" Susan questioned, confused.

"To the candlelight thing tonight," he said.

"The vigil?" She smiled. "No, you don't have to wear your uniform to that."

"Lonnie said I did because it's at a school. He said I'd get in trouble if I didn't."

"Lonnie was trying to trick you. Again."

Nicky considered this.

Susan waited for the next question, experience telling her it would likely arrive within a minute.

She was correct, though the question went unanswered, the ring of her cell phone snagging her attention, her eyes going wide as she looked at the screen.

It was the police.

# THIRTY-EIGHT

"You okay?" Joey asked as Penny emerged from the interrogation room.

"Yeah," Penny said.

"You look exhausted."

"I am exhausted," she said. "We went over *everything*. Each Facebook message, email, and text." She stretched her arms until something popped. "It took forever."

"It did," he agreed, his butt having been planted on the hard wooden bench in the hallway for the better part of an hour. "So, now what?"

"She told me to wait out here for a bit while they discuss things."

His face fell.

"Sorry," she said, taking a seat on the bench.

"It's okay," he said.

He didn't join her on the bench, his butt obviously needing a break from the hard wood.

"Where'd Olivia and Martin go?"

"Bathroom."

"Together?"

"I think they were bored and just wanted to move about. Not much to do here in the hallway."

"You don't have to stay if you don't want to," she said, reading into his comment. "They want to talk to my aunt, so she'll be able to drive me home once they finish with her."

"No, no, it's all good."

"You sure?"

"Yeah."

She didn't believe him but didn't force the issue.

A second later Detective Parks returned to the hallway waiting area, a file in hand, eyes looking around for something or someone.

Penny got up and hurried over to her before she could disappear. "Do we have to wait here, or is there a place we can stretch out and chill? Maybe get something to drink?"

"We have a break room with vending machines just around the corner."

"Great, thanks."

SUSAN PULLED into the police station parking lot with Nicky in the passenger seat and a dead body in the trunk, her unease growing with each passing second.

"Was Penny arrested?" Nicky asked.

"What? No!" Susan snapped.

No other questions followed as they headed inside, Susan looking back three times at the car, which she had parked toward the rear of the lot, her hope being that if it did start to smell, it would be far enough away from everyone to go unnoticed.

The police station was busy. More so than it had been the last time when she had been there to pick up Olivia after they had discovered Jocelyn.

Reporters filled the front walkway and the lobby, waiting, ready to go on air if there were any developments before they all headed over to the school to get clips of the vigil.

Because of this, it took several minutes for Susan to get through to the front desk and then beyond, but once she did, things seemed to calm down quickly, though the noise from the front did slither into the inner working areas of the station.

Penny, Olivia, Joey, and Martin were in a break room, cans of soda in front of them.

"Mom," Olivia called, bolting up from a plastic seat.

Everyone else looked her way.

An onslaught of explanations on why they were there followed, Susan having to hold up her hands to calm them down so she could make sense of what they were saying.

A few seconds later, Detective Parks was taking her aside to explain things, Susan feigning surprise and then horror at the fact that messages from the dead girl's phone were being sent to Penny.

"Have you noticed anyone unusual?" Detective Parks asked at one point.

Susan shook her head.

"No one suspicious hanging around?"

"Not that I can say," Susan said. "Sorry."

More questions followed, some aimed at the situation involving the discovery of Jocelyn's body, others about the party the girls had been at that had led to the Ouija board incident and video.

"Do you think the video has something to do with the messages being sent to her?" Susan asked.

"It's one of the theories we're looking into," Detective Parks said.

Susan made as if she were absorbing that and then asked, "Do you think I should keep her home from tonight's vigil?"

"That's up to you."

"Hmm."

"It will be well guarded. And the media will likely be there in force, so chances of something happening are pretty slim."

Susan nodded and then asked, "Do you have any suspects yet?"

"We have a few leads we're investigating."

"That's good," Susan said, as if the non-answer had been an answer.

CONRAD'S MOTHER-IN-LAW called seven times that afternoon, leaving voicemails each time.

He didn't listen to them.

He couldn't.

Instead, he simply sat on the sofa in his home office, waiting, and when that got to be too much to bear, he started pacing the house, his feet taking him from his office on the second floor to the living room on the first, and through the dining room, kitchen, and into the family room.

Back and forth he went, his eyes looking at but not really seeing the glasses that were on the floor by the wall in the living room until the seventh or eighth pass through the room.

It stopped him in his tracks.

No!

His wife had not gone anywhere, not without those.

Something had happened to her.

Something foul.

Susan.

He grabbed his keys and hurried out to the car.

"THEY'RE GOING to take your can," Olivia said.

"What?" Martin asked.

"Joey's too," she added, pointing at his soda.

"Why?" Penny asked.

"DNA. They'll want to see if it matches what was found on Jocelyn and Leanne."

"Shit, if they want my DNA, they can just have it," Martin said.

"Same here," Joey noted.

"Good to know," Olivia said. She then looked over at her mom, who was still talking to the detective. "She's never going to let us out of the house again after this."

"You think so?" Penny asked.

"Look at her. She's ready to freak."

Penny shifted her gaze and then shook her head. "I don't know. She seems pretty calm to me."

"That's why she's going to freak. She's bottling everything up. It'll burst eventually."

Penny didn't reply to that, her head shifting back to look at Joey, who was looking at his phone.

"I wonder if they'll let us leave soon," Martin said.

"Technically, we could leave right now and they can't stop us," Olivia said.

"You think so?"

"I know so."

Martin considered this and then said, "Well, I'm not going to push it."

"Me either," Joey said.

"Slaves to the state," Olivia muttered and then turned

back to look at her mom and then over at Nicky, who was deep in conversation with a patient officer about his progress toward getting the Signs, Signals, and Codes merit badge and how they should use Morse code on their radios so that criminals with scanners might not understand what they were saying.

"IS THERE anything else you need from them?" Susan asked.

"No," Detective Parks said. "I think we're good for now."

"What about these messages? Is there any way for you to track them?"

"We're looking into that."

"Isn't there some sort of app you can put on her phone, one that will trace the calls and messages she gets so you know where they're coming from?"

Detective Parks shook her head. "Not on this side of the TV screen. The best we can do is track the phone through its GPS, though we're still waiting on the phone company to get us the data on that."

"What about cell towers and triangulation and all that?"

"We're working on it."

*Playing it close to the chest,* Susan noted.

Not that any of this would matter. The phone would be found in Conrad's pocket once his body was discovered.

And if at some point they figured out the texts were being sent from the house, she would simply advise them that Conrad had paid them a couple visits, ones that she had thought were out of concern for Penny's well-being.

*Penny thought she was possessed by a demon, so he came to talk to her,* she would explain when asked.

And if they learned about the sexual relationship she had had with Conrad...

*He was blackmailing me after he found out about the videos I made.*

She would clutch a tissue while talking about this, tears welling as she described how she would be forced to call him Daddy while wearing one of Olivia's uniforms and then take it up the butt and then in the mouth so that there was no chance of a pregnancy.

NO ONE WAS HOME.

Conrad established this by ringing the bell several times and then pounding on both the front and back door. He even started to go inside, his fingers punching in the garage code that he knew from the days when Susan's senile father was still living in the basement and they would have sex in front of him, her wearing one of Olivia's school uniforms while he was dressed like a priest.

The empty garage halted him.

His wife wasn't here.

Susan wouldn't have taken her home, not when she had two teenage girls and a preteen boy living there. No. That would just be stupid. And though she was crazy, Susan wasn't stupid. Misguided, yes. Prone to poor judgment, double yes. Stupid, no. Far from it.

*Is she even responsible?*

*Could something else have happened?*

He pondered this for a few seconds, a sudden question on whether the *Goodbye* statement had been one of finality rather than simply leaving him dominating his focus.

*Had she decided to end things?*

*Had she learned about the affair?*

But how?

Had Susan gone to confront her about the private investigator?

Was this his fault for trying to break away from her insanity?

Rather than going inside to make a pointless search, he decided to simply wait and confront Susan once she came back home.

PENNY AND OLIVIA wanted to go home with Joey and Martin, which was fine with Susan since she had the body in the trunk and didn't want them noticing a smell if one had started to seep into the passenger areas.

One hadn't, but even so, best to play things safe.

Now the question was, could she risk trying to dispose of the body while Nicky was in the car?

No.

Spontaneously going to the bluffs that overlooked the river would be notable in his mind and something he would talk about. He also would likely see her pulling out the laundry basket that she had stuffed the tiny body in and dumping it into the water.

"Mommy, who's that?" Nicky asked.

Susan shifted her attention back to the road and saw a car parked in their driveway.

*Conrad.*

What was he doing there?

"WHAT ARE YOU DOING HERE?" Susan demanded after she ordered Nicky inside.

"Where is she?" Conrad demanded back.

"Who?"

"You know who!"

"No, I don't, and you shouldn't have come here like this. Penny and Olivia might be back any—"

*"What did you do?"*

Susan stared at him for a few seconds and then shook her head. "I'm going inside now. We can talk at the vigil."

He grabbed her arm, fingers digging into the flesh through the sleeve of her shirt.

"Let me go!" she cried, trying to wrest her arm free.

"You left her glasses on the floor," he said, fingers squeezing tighter. "She wouldn't be able to leave me without those."

Susan clawed at his hand, nails digging into his flesh.

He released his grip with a grimace.

"Tonight," she hissed. "At the vigil. Meet me."

"Where is she?" he demanded, voice trying to summon up authority.

Nothing.

"I'll go to the police," he warned.

She replied with a grin that chilled him to the core and said, "I'll see you at the vigil."

# THIRTY-NINE

"We can walk there from here," Martin suggested once the four were back at his house.

"Probably easier that way," Olivia noted. "The parking lot will be a mess, what with all the reporters and police and parents."

"I don't think your mom will like it if we show up like this," Penny said, hands spreading to display her wardrobe, which currently consisted of jeans and a sweatshirt.

"I should probably change too," Joey said.

"I can swing you two by your place and then back."

"Sounds good."

"What about me?" Joey asked.

"You live three houses down," Martin said.

"I see how it is," Joey said, pretending to pout.

Martin shook his head.

CONRAD WAS WORRIED.

His statement to Susan about going to the police shouldn't have been shrugged off so easily. Not unless she knew she was safe from whatever investigation they would launch into whatever it was she had done to his wife.

*She's incriminated me somehow.*

Of this, he had no doubt.

He also knew his wife was dead.

Susan had killed her.

All because he had tried to put up some distance between them with the private investigator lie.

But why?

Penny.

She was the center of this.

Susan had fucked her with the strap-on that night and made her think it was a demon.

How exactly he didn't know, but she had used him to help cement the lie.

But why?

What was her end goal in all this?

No answers arrived.

He simply could not fathom a reason for all this.

*All because I fucked her.*

*In the office.*

*After she discovered the videos on my thumb drive.*

It had been the biggest mistake of his life, one that he had actually recognized in the moments leading up to the act yet hadn't been able to halt. Not with all the blood pumping into his manhood, the old joke about how God had given man a brain and penis but only enough blood to work one at a time echoing in his mind.

"I HAVE to run to the office for a second," Susan said. "Can you keep an eye on Nicky?"

"What? No!" Olivia said. "We just came by to change. Martin is waiting."

"I wasn't asking."

"But, Mom!"

"How about he comes with us?" Penny suggested. "I'm sure Martin and Joey won't mind."

"Perfect," Susan said.

"No!" Olivia groaned.

"Come on, it'll be fine," Penny said.

On cue, Nicky entered the kitchen area, having changed into the clothes Susan had left out for him.

"I don't want to go with them," he whined. "They'll just talk about sex stuff."

"They better not," Susan said, a warning gaze directed toward the girls.

"You don't even know what sex is!" Olivia replied.

"I do too!"

"Describe it then!"

"Enough!" Susan snapped. "Keep this up and you two will stay home while Penny and I go to the vigil."

An awkward silence descended upon the kitchen.

Susan waited several seconds, eyes gazing upon each of them, and then said, "Okay. I'm heading out and will text you when I'm there. Keep your phones handy."

"We will," Penny said when Olivia didn't reply.

Susan nodded and then headed out, her nose trying but failing to smell anything from the trunk as she climbed into the car.

"OH FOR THE LOVE OF GOD!" Olivia snapped while looking at the outfit that had been laid out on her bed, and then, despite being in the same house, texted Penny to see if something had been laid out for her as well.

*Yep,* Penny replied, a laughing emoji face following the word.

Olivia shook her head and then went to her dresser to pick out something else, hesitation getting the better of her as she pulled out a fresh hoodie and some jeans.

She looked back at the dark skirt and jacket.

*It's not a funeral.*

She then shifted her gaze back to the hoodie and jeans.

"Fuck it," she snapped.

"YOU KNOW she's going to freak," Penny said upon seeing Olivia in the hoodie and jeans.

"I don't care."

"She might paddle you again."

"Eh, not if I threaten to tell about the videos."

Penny shook her head and then looked down at herself, the outfit her aunt had set out for her being the same one she had worn to her mother's funeral.

*Did she realize that?*

*Or had she just grabbed the darkest, most somber outfit?*

"Let's go," Olivia said, moving toward the door.

"I really think you should change," Penny said.

"I'm not going to let her dress me like that," Olivia said.

"Okay, okay," Penny said, putting her hands up. "It's your ass."

SUSAN PUT Conrad's wife in the dumpster behind his office, her thinking being that the police might think he killed her before heading off to his afternoon sessions, and then, in his panic, dumped her body in hopes that it would go unnoticed and disappear into a landfill, all while his own texts to himself from her phone made it look like she had left.

It was a stupid plan given that the dumpster wouldn't be emptied for several days, but given how often killers did things like this, she figured the police would simply nod at the absurdity and believe he was just another idiot that didn't plans things out very well.

Task completed, she got back in her car and headed home, a desire to shower before dressing for the vigil going unfulfilled given the time.

CONRAD DIDN'T WANT to look in the dumpster, his eyes not needing to see what he knew they would see once he lifted the lid.

*What if I'm wrong?*

*I'm not.*

*Why else would she have driven behind the building?*

He had followed Susan from her house to the office, but not to the area behind the building complex, the isolation of the area making it so he would have been spotted. Instead, he had simply watched from the parking lot across the street, body shielded by a row of bushes, and then, once she had left the area, headed back there himself to see if he could figure out what she had been up to.

And now he stared at the dumpster, a hollow feeling in his gut.

*Call the police.*

*No.*

As he had noted to himself earlier, Susan was not dumb.

She was obviously setting him up. That much was

clear. But it couldn't simply be so that they would think he killed his own wife. No. Something bigger was at play. Something that had led to this simply because he had tried to put some distance between them with the private investigator lie.

But what?

Penny was the key.

"JESUS," Penny said as they rounded a corner and saw the school, its parking lot filled to the brim with police vehicles, news vans, and various parental SUVs—many of which had to park on the street.

"It's like the Fourth of July," Joey noted.

Up ahead, Martin and Olivia were pointing out things, though their voices couldn't be heard. Nicky was with them, his fear of Penny still too great for him to risk being near.

"I wonder where my aunt is going to park," Penny muttered.

"Nowhere close, that's for sure," Joey replied.

Nothing else followed, the only sounds those of their shoes clapping on the sidewalk.

Five minutes later, they were ushered into the football field area, almost as if arriving for a game, the bleachers on the north side looking ominous as they stood empty, crime scene tape and barriers having been set up to keep people away, all while an area in front of them had become a shrine to Leanne and Jocelyn where flowers and other items could be left.

"Now what?" Penny asked, looking at her candle, right hand now forced to stay steady so as not to spill any wax over the flimsy paper guard.

"I guess we just stand around," Joey said. "Waiting for it to get dark."

*Fun, fun,* Penny voiced to herself.

Olivia ventured over.

"Well, Nicky and Martin have hit it off," she muttered.

Penny and Joey glanced over, Penny noting that Nicky and Martin seemed to be having a serious discussion.

"Teenage Mutant Ninja Turtles," Olivia said before they could ask. "They're debating which turtle was the best."

"The best?" Joey questioned. "There is no best. Their strength is that they work as a team rather than individuals, each one bringing their own skill set that strengthens them as a whole."

Penny grinned while Olivia simply stared.

"I better go straighten this out," Joey said. "Be right back."

Olivia turned to look at Penny, a look of bewilderment on her face. "Did that seriously just happen?"

"Did what just happen?"

"That!" She waved her hand, splashing wax. "Did we just lose our men to a Ninja Turtles discussion?"

"Yep," Penny laughed. "And based on my understanding of men, this probably won't be the last time."

"Un-fucking-believable," Olivia said and then started to cross her arms before realizing the candle would make this difficult. She looked down at it with disgust and then up at the sky.

"Thirty minutes, give or take," Penny said.

"What?"

"Before it starts to get dark."

"Shit, these things will pretty much be burned down to the nubs by then."

"If that happens, we could all hold up our phones."

"Ha!"

Heads turned, Olivia's laugh earning several disapproving glares.

"Oops," Olivia said, voice low. "Almost forgot. This isn't a kegger. We have to be solemn."

Penny nodded and then said, "Speaking of which, any word from your mom?"

"Nope. She's probably looking for a parking spot."

"You know she is totally going to freak when she sees you."

"Look around. Half the people here are wearing hoodies."

"You really think that will sway her into being cool with it?" Penny asked, skeptical.

Olivia shook her head and then shrugged. "What can you do?"

"You could run home and change."

"Fuck that."

A disapproving huff echoed from someone nearby, Penny growing uneasy with the attention that Olivia was drawing upon them with her language.

CONRAD FOLLOWED Susan to the school and then watched as she struggled to find a parking spot, his own quest to secure one simple given that he had an old handicap placard from when his wife had broken her leg earlier in the year, and now used it to park in one of the restricted spots at the church.

Once there, he texted Penny, his finger hitting Send just as Susan appeared in the parking lot of the church, her feet taking her into the chapel.

*Why?*

*What is she up to?*

He decided to follow her.

"HUH," Penny voiced.

"What?" Olivia asked while relighting her candle with Penny's.

"Father Collins," Penny said. "He just texted me."

"Really?" She handed back the candle, fingers careful not to spill any wax. "What's he want?"

"He's here and says he has something important to tell me and wants to know if we can meet over at the church."

"Now?"

"Yeah."

"That's weird."

"Think so?"

"Um...yeah." Then, "Let's go."

"What? But I think they're getting ready to start." She motioned toward the area where a microphone had been set up.

"Eh, we'll be able to hear it while heading over there, and if we really want to see it, it'll be all over Facebook." She blew out her candle and then turned to Martin and Joey. "Can you two keep an eye on Nicky for a bit?"

"Where you going?"

"Secret girl stuff."

Penny shook her head and said, "Father Collins wants to meet with me over at the chapel real quick."

"I didn't think he was with the church," Joey said.

"He isn't, but I think he just wants a quiet place to talk for a bit."

"Want us to come with?"

"Nah."

"You sure?"

Penny was.

"We'll text you if we need anything," Olivia added.

"Okay."

Penny saw something in Joey's eyes. He was concerned yet wasn't voicing it.

*Should I be as well?*

The question lingered within her mind as the two broke away and headed toward the gate that encircled the football field, a bored volunteer seemingly oblivious to them as they walked through.

# FORTY

Memories flooded Susan's mind as she descended into the catacombs of the church, all while dust assaulted her sinuses.

A sneeze followed.

And then a second.

She wiped her nose and pulled out her cell phone, thumb engaging the flashlight app.

*"It used to be part of the Underground Railroad,"* her sister had said, leading her and her friends down the old steps back when they were kids.

A story had followed about how a slave family had once been caught within the catacombs after being tracked by hounds, the slave catchers taking the runaways back so they could claim their bounty while leaving the priest beaten and hanging from an old cross.

To this day, Susan didn't know if the story was true, but she did know one thing: it had terrified her as a kid. So much so that she had frequently thought she heard the ghost of the priest calling to her from the old air ducts within the Sunday school rooms.

. . .

CONRAD WANTED to follow Susan into the church, but resisted given that she would notice his presence. Instead, he waited outside to see if Penny would show up, his text having been read but not responded to.

SUSAN FOUND THE OLD CROSS, which the priest from her sister's story supposedly was hung up on. Thick railroad spikes were embedded in the arms and near where the ankles would rest, ones that made Susan think that it had actually been some sort of Easter prop back in the day rather than anything anyone had actually been nailed to before the Civil War.

It was perfect.

Tonight Penny would hang from the cross like a sacrifice, the large railroad spikes proving perfect anchor points for restraint.

CONRAD SAW Penny and another young lady approaching the side entrance to the chapel, both looking around as they sought him out.

He opened his car door and stepped out, voice calling, "Penny," before the two entered the church.

Startled, she turned toward him.

He waved.

She nodded.

He hurried over to them, joining them on the sidewalk near the steps.

"Thanks for coming over," he said and then turned to the second young lady. "Olivia?" he asked.

Olivia nodded and then, without warning, "Were you fucking someone the other day when you butt dialed us?"

"Your mom," he said.

OLIVIA BLINKED and then burst out laughing, the clapback from the priest completely unexpected. But then she saw the look on his face and realized he wasn't trying for a clapback.

Her laughter faded.

She looked from the priest to Penny, who had a startled expression, and then back to the priest.

"We've been fucking each other for two years," he said.

"But..." Olivia started, mind unable to process this. "No."

"I'm not really a priest," he added.

Olivia shook her head while taking a step back.

"Why did you—" Penny started and then stopped, hand pulling out her phone.

"No, no," Olivia muttered, her words aimless as they left her lips.

"I'm sorry," he said. "I know this is a shock, which will make this next part even worse. Your mom wanted me to pretend to be a priest so she—"

"Olivia," Penny said, cutting him off. "Have you heard from your mom at all?"

Olivia looked at her, the words taking a second to register. "What? My mom?" She checked her phone. "No."

"What is it?" the fake priest asked.

Penny didn't reply to him and instead showed Olivia her phone. "I got another text from Leanne's phone," she said.

"Oh my God," Olivia gasped.

A picture of her mom was on the phone, one of her slumped in a dark corner next to an old statue, duct tape on her mouth, ankles bound and wrists behind her back. Words were present as well, ones instructing her to go down into the church catacombs. Alone.

"What?" the fake priest asked again.

"Fuck off," Olivia snapped and then turned to Penny. "You're not going down there all by yourself."

"Down where?" the fake priest asked, voice rising.

"If I don't..." Penny said, voice fading.

"Down into the church basement?" he asked.

Olivia turned, ready to tell him to fuck off again, but paused. "How'd you know?"

"Your mother just went down there, and I suspect she wants Penny to join her."

"Why?"

"I don't know, but you shouldn't go. She is up to something." Hesitation hit. "Penny, I'm fairly certain she is the one who fucked you the other night with your mother's old strap-on."

PHOTO SENT, Susan waited, the *Read at* note confirming that it had been seen.

Now she hoped it would work.

*What if she alerts the police?*

*Would she do something like that?*

If so, Susan would simply claim someone had grabbed her from behind and brought her down here. No identity would be revealed, thus allowing for her to "seek" comfort with Conrad later that evening, his true nature eventually being revealed.

Seconds ticked by, the tape she had put over her lips for

the video of herself that she had then taken a screenshot of to send to Penny before deleting the video already growing bothersome. She also didn't like sitting on the old dirt floor, her mind conjuring up all kinds of creepy crawlers that could be slithering around.

Voices.

Out beyond the archway in the area where the old stairway was.

Penny wasn't alone.

*Olivia!*

*No!*

Rather than stay in the corner, pretending to be bound, ready to strike Penny with the quarter-weighted sock when she leaned in to help her, Susan stood up, grabbed the mask, and hurried into the alcove by the wall opening, deciding to hit Olivia in the head from behind so that she would never know what happened.

CONRAD WAS DAZED, the punch that Olivia had delivered after he mentioned her mother fucking Penny having caught him off guard. It had also split his lip and busted a tooth, her strength far greater than one would assume.

The two had hurried inside after that, Olivia saying something about knowing where the basement was.

Conrad followed, surprise at how empty the church was arriving.

It seemed everyone had gone over to the vigil, even the church staff.

Had Susan known this would be the case?

Or had she simply gotten lucky?

He pushed the thoughts away, given how pointless they were, his focus on finding the stairway that led down to the basement, a debate on whether he should call the police being made.

OLIVIA SCANNED THE DARK ROOM, looking for her mother among all the old statues, eyes somewhat thrown off by all the candles that had been lit, the scent of cinnamon strong.

A gasp echoed and then something hit her, her body momentarily useless as it crumpled to the ground.

Hands grabbed her, all while Penny shouted something that didn't fully register.

A bag went over her head, the fabric harsh.

She tried to claw it away, life returning to her limbs.

Another cry and then an *ummph*.

Olivia had no idea what was going on.

She grabbed at the bag, but something snatched her hand and before she knew it, her wrists were being bound together with tape.

*FACES! Everywhere!*

She was surrounded.

*A sound.*

*Behind her.*

Penny turned just as the demon lunged at her, its body knocking her backward into the dirt.

CONRAD EMERGED from the stairway into the musty, candlelit storage area of the church cellar just as Susan lifted a knife, her hands getting ready to plunge the blade down into Penny's chest.

"Susan!" he cried, his voice the only thing that could reach her before the blade descended.

Susan jolted, masked face shifting his way.

Penny kicked her, square in the gut, and then started to scramble across the dirt floor.

Susan slashed with the knife, the blade catching Penny in the upper thigh.

Penny shrieked.

Conrad charged toward them, his foot snagging on something in the darkness, hands going out to break his fall, the sound of his left wrist cracking reaching his ears before the pain registered.

"No! No!" Penny muttered while crawling about, twisting back and forth, almost as if she were being attacked from all sides.

Conrad pushed himself up and lunged at Susan, who was going after Penny, his body slamming into her as she raised the knife, the two crashing into an old statue of the Virgin Mary.

The knife fell.

Susan tried to reach for it but was halted as Conrad grabbed her by the throat and slammed her head into the statue.

Over and over he did this, his mind visualizing her skull crumpling beneath the demon mask, all while he screamed at her about killing his wife, his voice eventually cut off with a heavy *thunk.*

Darkness descended upon him, his body crumpling.

OLIVIA STOOD over the fake priest, the dusty brick she had grabbed after ripping the hood off her head feeling heavy in her bound hands.

Next to him, her mother was sprawled on the ground, a hideous mask covering her face.

She wasn't moving.

Olivia tried to help her up but then cried out as blood oozed out from the neckline of the mask.

She pulled it off.

Her mother's eyes were closed, face looking lifeless.

A shriek echoed.

Penny crashed into her, knife in hand, slashing.

"No!" Olivia screamed, her bound hand grabbing the knife before it could be plunged into her chest, its razor edge slicing deep into her fingers, blade growing slick with blood.

Penny continued to press down, lips mumbling something that Olivia couldn't understand.

"Stop! Stop! Stop!" Olivia shrieked.

The knife tip touched the top of her left breast, nothing but the latex mask and a thin layer of sweatshirt fabric standing between it and her flesh.

They both yielded to the blade, as did her flesh, a pain-laced scream echoing from her lips.

# FORTY-ONE

The following news clippings are from the *St. Louis Post-Dispatch*:

BLOODBATH BENEATH CHURCH During Vigil for Slain Students

WHILE PARENTS, students, and community leaders gathered together to mourn the loss of two students who were brutally murdered, a cowardly killer was preparing to slaughter two more teenage victims in the empty catacombs of St. Katherine's Cathedral. Luring the two teens into the church, the killer was thwarted by a vigilant mother, who suffered serious injury herself as she tried to protect the two teens...

MARRIAGE COUNSELOR LINKED to Four Murders

. . .

INVESTIGATORS HAVE OFFICIALLY NAMED the late Conrad Collins as the suspect in the slayings of the three St. Katherine's students, as well as his wife, whose body was found in a dumpster behind his office complex. Investigators are also looking into whether Collins can be linked to any unsolved homicides in the area. Collins was a respected marriage counselor at his own private practice in the suburbs. It is unclear what led Collins to murder the three students and his wife, though an unnamed source within the police department did confirm that quite a bit of pornography was found on his computer.

PENNY HAD KILLED OLIVIA, though at the time she had thought she was stabbing the demon in the face, the horrible eyes and lolling serpentine tongue her only focus as her hands found the large kitchen knife while coming to in the old catacombs of the church.

*Olivia.*

Guilt threatened to overwhelm her...again, as did a desire to explain to the police what had really unfolded while in the catacombs beneath the church, but she fought it back, her mind knowing that even though she had wielded the knife, it wasn't her fault.

No.

Aunt Susan was to blame.

If not for her, Olivia would not have been holding the mask.

Penny stared at the drooling woman while contemplating this, the look of fear she saw in the woman's eyes causing her to grin.

Aunt Susan was fully aware of her surroundings; she just couldn't do much with herself while in those surroundings, her brain-damaged body one that had to be strapped into a wheelchair during the day so she could be moved around the hospital, a diaper in place just in case an orderly wasn't able to get her onto the toilet in time once the frantic bathroom shrieks began.

Nicky had hopes that she would one day recover. Penny, however, knew this was unlikely to happen, the doctors she had spoken with having shaken their heads when she inquired about the possibility.

"But she can feel things and is conscious of her surroundings?" Penny had asked.

"Yes," the doctor advised, his tone suggesting this was unfortunate. "She has simply lost most of her motor functions, given the area of her brain that was damaged."

"What about pain?"

"Unfortunately, that part of her brain wasn't impacted at all. She registers a ten across the board when tested."

Penny had simply nodded at this, all while struggling to prevent a grin that threatened to dominate her face.

Aunt Susan would pay.

Once she was released from the hospital and Penny had secured her inheritance and guardianship over the woman, she would set up a special room for her to live in at the house in San Francisco and would see to it that the woman suffered.

Day in and day out, her every waking moment would be one where she would wish she had died while in the catacombs of the church.

THE FOLLOWING EXCEPT is from *In Sheep's Clothing: Serial Killers in the Heartland* by Edwin King:

. . .

OF ALL THE serial killers we've covered in this book, Conrad Collins is the most peculiar, given the lack of any display of aggression or sexual deviance in his early years that would mark a starting path toward the eventual rape and torture of the two high school students and a stabbing of a third while in the catacombs of St. Katherine's. Adding to the mystery is the 911 call he made to police alerting them to his fear that more teens were about to be killed in the basement of St. Katherine's Cathedral during the vigil for Jocelyn and Leanne.

Was this act an attempt at prevention, given the horror he felt at his own actions, or was there more going on in this situation than meets the eye? If the latter, why didn't he name who it was that would be harming these teens during his call?

Answers to these questions may not be forthcoming, given the case-closed status of the investigation. One thing is clear: if Conrad Collins was not the killer, or if he was just one half of a serial killer duo, then someone else is still out there, someone who has a taste for brutality and teenage girls...

"WE HAVE a prayer chain going and everyone has been lighting candles for you," Nicky said during his daily after-school visit. "Father Petrie also says they are going to see if they can get your name on the list for the pope to—" He stopped and stared at her.

Susan continued to blink, hoping he would understand.

"Are your eyes okay? Do you want me to get them to bring more drops?" Nicky asked, not understanding at all.

Susan squeaked, her attempt at speaking an utter failure.

"Yes?" he asked, trying to interpret the squeak.

Susan sighed with frustration and then opened her eyes as wide as they could go, waiting.

He looked at her.

Susan began to blink again, her mind screaming at him to understand.

He didn't.

Not during this visit, nor the several that followed, though one of these days he would. One day he would realize that she was trying to put all those stupid Morse code lessons they had done together for his stupid merit badge to good use. One day he would translate her blinks to say: "*Penny is a demon*" and "*kill her.*"

Lightning Source UK Ltd.
Milton Keynes UK
UKHW041915220221
379217UK00001B/153